Praise for
STILL HERE

"A powerful, atmospheric, perfectly plotted thriller.... An outstanding read."

Samantha M. Bailey, #1 bestselling
author of *Woman on the Edge*

Praise for
STILL WATER

"*Still Water* brings back the same characters in a new setting and proves that Stuart is no one-book author. . . . Even better than her debut."

The Globe and Mail

"Riveting, twisty, and full of tangled secrets. . . . A stay-up-all-night read. Impossible to put down!"

Karma Brown, bestselling author of *Recipe for a Perfect Wife*

"Complex characters with gut-wrenching backstories propel this twisty mystery toward its shocking conclusion. I was engrossed!"

Robyn Harding, bestselling author of *The Swap*

"Utterly compelling and intriguing. . . . Warn your families before you pick up this book."

Liz Nugent, bestselling author of *Lying in Wait* and *Little Cruelties*

"Her prose is rich and descriptive, building suspense and creating a moody atmosphere."

Quill & Quire

"Instantly captivating, mysterious, and relevant."

Marissa Stapley, author of *The Last Resort*

"As swift, intense, and vengeful as the river it describes, this book is a must-read."

Roz Nay, bestselling author of
Our Little Secret and *Hurry Home*

Praise for
STILL MINE

"An impressive debut, rooted in character rather than trope, in fundamental understanding rather than rote puzzle-solving."

The Globe and Mail

"Stuart is a sensitive writer who has given Clare a painful past and just enough backbone to bear it."

The New York Times

"A gripping page-turner, with a plot that takes hold of you and drags you through the story at breakneck speed. The characters are compelling, the setting chilling, and the suspense ever-present. Add to that, Stuart has an ability to tap into the dark psychology behind addiction and abuse, and to bring these complex struggles to life in a way that stays with you for days."

Toronto Star

"Haunting and compelling."

Vancouver Sun

"*Still Mine* [has hoisted] Stuart into an exciting new generation of Canadian thriller writers that includes Shari Lapena, Ausma Zehanat Khan, Iain Reid, and Elizabeth de Mariaffi."

Quill & Quire

ALSO BY AMY STUART

Still Mine

Still Water

STILL HERE

A NOVEL

AMY STUART

GALLERY BOOKS

NEW YORK   LONDON   TORONTO   SYDNEY   NEW DELHI

GALLERY
BOOKS

An Imprint of Simon & Schuster, Inc.
1230 Avenue of the Americas
New York, NY 10020

Originally published in Canada in 2020 by Simon & Schuster Canada

This Gallery Books trade paperback edition August 2020

Gallery Books and colophon are registered trademarks of Simon & Schuster, Inc.

For information about special discounts for bulk purchases, please contact Simon & Schuster Special Sales at 1-866-506-1949 or business@simonandschuster.com.

The Simon & Schuster Speakers Bureau can bring authors to your live event. For more information or to book an event, contact the Simon & Schuster Speakers Bureau at 1-866-248-3049 or visit our website at www.simonspeakers.com.

Silhouette wave design by Tony Hanyk, tonyhanyk.com
Water image by Teresa Otto, Shutterstock.com

Manufactured in the United States of America

10   9   8   7   6   5   4   3   2   1

The Library of Congress has cataloged the Gallery Books trade paperback edition as follows:

Names: Stuart, Amy, 1975– author.
Title: Still here : a novel / Amy Stuart.
Description: Gallery Books trade paperback edition. |
New York : Gallery Books, 2020.
Identifiers: LCCN 2020011262 (print) | LCCN 2020011263 (ebook) |
ISBN 9781982148256 (trade paperback) | ISBN 9781982148263 (ebook)
Classification: LCC PR9199.4.S797 S845 2020 (print) |
LCC PR9199.4.S797 (ebook) | DDC 813/.6—dc23
LC record available at https://lccn.loc.gov/2020011262
LC ebook record available at https://lccn.loc.gov/2020011263

ISBN 978-1-9821-4825-6
ISBN 978-1-9821-4826-3 (ebook)

For my sisters, Bridget Flynn and Katie Flynn,

and my sister-in-law, Beth Boyden:

I aim to write strong, resilient women,

and I draw the best parts of them from you.

SATURDAY

Clare blinks and pats at the back of her head. Warmth. She looks down at her fingertips, red with her own blood.

Strange, she thinks. I feel no pain.

The room takes shape. She sits in an empty bathtub, clothes on. The bathtub is in the center of the room. This bathroom: airy, too big, everything white, an open shower. The window over the vanity looks out to a sharp blue sky. Too bright. Clare shifts her position and cranes to check behind her. The pain comes, her skull throbbing.

Yes, Clare thinks. This place. Of course. I know where I am.

The bathroom door is closed. Clare leans back against the tub and closes her eyes to stave off the dizzy spell. She remembers. It was a strike to the head.

Voices outside the bathroom door. Clare can't decipher how many. She works to pull herself up so she is sitting on the edge of the bathtub. Two. A man and a woman. The man's voice is so acutely familiar that it brings a stabbing pain to

AMY STUART

Clare's chest. He is here. Of course he is here. Of course they are here together. A small laugh escapes her. This is what you get, Clare thinks. After everything that's happened, everything you've done, this is how it ends.

The bathroom door cracks open. Clare stands, still in the bathtub. She must steady herself. She must hold straight.

Clare, he says, pressing through the half-open door. Clare?

Clare squeezes her eyes closed, then pops them open to regain her focus. He is smiling too kindly. He holds a gun loose in one hand.

Are you hurt? he asks. I didn't mean to hurt you.

Does he look different? He's grown a beard, put on some weight. There's a deadness in his gaze. He steps forward and reaches out to take her by the arm. When Clare recoils, he frowns playfully.

Don't do that, Clare. You've got nowhere to go. This is finally over. I'm here.

It comes back to Clare now. This morning, dawn. She was alone. And then he was there.

Oh wow, he says, reaching this time for her hair. You're still bleeding.

Don't touch me, Clare says, a hiss.

Come on, he says. This doesn't have to end terribly, does it?

Who else is here? Clare asks. Who's here with you?

But she need not ask. She knows. The blood drips from her hair and travels in a stream down her spine. It takes all her effort not to sway. Clare closes her eyes again. She must find a way out.

You owe me the truth, he says. Don't I deserve the truth?

The truth? Clare doesn't answer him. She knows she is in danger. They will not let her out of here alive. She needs to

4

focus. *Focus.* But she is dizzy. Her thoughts churn too quickly. The truth. He smiles at her expectantly. Anger roils in her instead of fear. Anger that she didn't grasp the lies she was told, for trusting those she should never have trusted. Anger at herself for opening that door when she did.

TUESDAY

four days earlier

Clare is the first to descend from the bus. At once she can sense the ocean nearby, the cool saltiness in the air. She checks her phone. 7:00 p.m. The sky is already a deep pink, these early September days shorter. The bus driver tugs her bag from the undercarriage and drops it at her feet.

"Which way to the ocean?" Clare asks him.

"Way down the hill."

Lune Bay. A coastal enclave within commuting distance of two cities, this bus depot on its outskirts. On the last stretch of the drive, Clare had been struck by the inclines, the highway zigzagging, the brakes on the bus squealing with the effort to maintain its speed. The earth here feels tilted, the landscape pouring into an ocean she can't yet see. *A beautiful spot*, Detective Somers had called it, as if Clare were arriving here on vacation and not to search for a man disappeared.

The bus station is crowded with lone travelers. A fierce stench greets Clare when she opens the door to the women's bathroom. In the tight stall Clare hangs her backpack on the back of the door and straddles her duffel bag. She struggles out of her clothes and into a clean shirt and jeans. She emerges from the stall to see an older woman leaning into the sink, eyes wildly meeting her own reflection. The woman is empty-handed, no purse or bag in sight, and dressed in a parka far too warm even for this cooler weather. Her gaze darts to Clare.

"I'd like you to leave," she says.

"Excuse me?"

Something adjusts in the woman's face, a snap to focus. She smiles. "Long trip?"

"Not really," Clare says.

"Coming or going?"

"Both," Clare answers.

The woman grimaces. Clare won't engage any further. Back in the terminal travelers shuffle like zombies, eyes up at the blinking arrival and departure screens, searching for direction. Clare finds an empty row of benches and scans the terminal for the rental car kiosk. She will have to hope that the false identification she and Detective Somers secured passes muster. Clare pulls her cell phone from her backpack and thumbs in the number from memory. Somers answers after one ring.

"You're there," Somers says, no greeting.

"Just arrived. I'm at the bus terminal. About to rent a car. You're sure the ID will work?"

"That's police-grade fake ID," Somers says. "It better work. Ready to get started?"

"Yes," Clare says, forcing the word. "Yes."

The familiarity of Somers's voice offers Clare some comfort. Hollis Somers, the police detective she'd met working on her last case as a private investigator. Somers, the detective who'd come up with police funds to hire Clare to travel

10

to Lune Bay and look for Malcolm. Somers has yet to offer any explanation on how she's able to pay Clare, and Clare hasn't asked. The money is a means to an end; she is here to find Malcolm. Clare holds a finger to her other ear to block out the din.

"You know Malcolm better than anyone," Somers says. "You're the best person to find him. You know that, right?"

Clare doesn't answer. She withdraws the case folder from her backpack, all its contents neatly printed and ordered, color coded. This, her third missing persons case. Two cases worked with Malcolm Boon and now this one on her own, searching for Malcolm, the very man who hired her to do missing persons investigations. Whatever of Malcolm's past Somers had been able to glean, his secrets and lies, Clare has them all curated into one file. It's been eight days since Malcolm Boon bid Clare goodbye before their last case was even solved, disappearing himself, fearful of the past catching up to him. It's been six days since Clare left High River at the conclusion of that case. Six days since Detective Somers handed her Malcolm's file and encouraged her to head to Lune Bay to begin the search.

"Listen," Somers says after a long pause. "You know what you need to do. You're good at this work."

Am I? Clare thinks.

"You know you are," Somers adds, as if reading Clare's mind. "Start at the beginning. Turn over stones until you find the rot. Just please don't risk your life."

"Yeah," Clare says, rapping her fingers over the folder.

"We're working together on this. I'm not far away."

Working together. Clare distrusts that notion now. Working together, and yet Clare is here alone. On both their previous cases Malcolm had said the same thing—*we're working together*—and yet Clare had both times been the lone foot soldier while Malcolm observed from afar.

"I still don't totally get why you're giving this case to me," Clare says.

"Because you helped me on the last case," Somers says. "We've gone over this. You need closure on this guy. Now it's my turn to help you. Okay?"

"Okay," Clare says.

"What do you need?" Somers asks.

"Nothing. Give me a day to get my bearings. I'll touch base with you tomorrow."

"You going to follow our plan?"

"Yes," Clare says, a lie.

"Remember. No huge risks."

"I should go." Clare's tone is curter than she means it to be. "I just need to get my bearings."

"Right," Somers says. "Keep me posted."

Clare ends the call without a goodbye. In the folder is a map marked with the places Clare is supposed to go, the landmarks of Malcolm's former life, the whereabouts of those who knew him, who knew his wife, Zoe Westman, herself missing for well over a year, a case unsolved and abandoned by this city's law enforcement. *Go to the police first*, Somers told Clare. *Find the detective assigned to the case.* Of course Somers would insist on a police-first approach, one detective certain that her fellow officers should be the best source of help. In only two cases, Clare has learned that's not always true.

At the bus station's ticket counter, the woman from the bathroom yells at the agent. Across the row from Clare, another woman cries, her body slumped against a stroller where a young boy sleeps. She looks at Clare, her eyes filled with anguish, fear. Behind the woman, a poster reads TRAVEL INTO FALL!

Fall, the last season that ties to her home. This time last year Clare was still in her home with her husband, Jason, enduring his wrath, plotting her escape. When fall ends it will be a year since she left him, since she escaped her marriage. Every season after that will no longer mark her first year away. Clare, a missing woman herself. A missing woman who now searches for missing women. *What are you running from?* Clare could ask the woman crying on the bench. *Who are you running from?* Instead Clare stands and dusts herself off, walking past the woman without looking her way. By now Clare knows better than to absorb someone else's pain.

At the rental car counter, Clare presents her identification and secures the rental without incident. The clerk leads her to a small parking lot and a car only big enough for Clare, her duffel bag in the hatchback, and her backpack on the passenger seat. Clare turns the ignition, then sits in the quiet of the car to catch her breath. Her body's wounds emit a constant dull ache. She will check in to the hotel later. First, she will drive to Malcolm's marital home.

Clare reverses out of the parking space and onto the wide road. The outskirts of Lune Bay look like any other town, box stores and fast-food restaurants. But as Clare descends towards the water, the real Lune Bay begins to form. Modern houses perched on hills to catch any ocean view, winding streets bookended by coffee shops and bakeries. Zoe's father, Jack Westman, was the developer who upgraded this once humble village to a suburban utopia. Clare follows the pings of the car's GPS until she lands on a road ablaze in sunset light. She pulls over and looks westward. And there she sees it, where the road drops away: the straight line of the ocean, a ball of sun hovering just over its horizon. The shock of colors takes Clare aback. A town hovering on the edge of the sea. She lowers the car window and inhales, the texture of the salt air still so novel to her. Clare could almost laugh at the fact that this sunset makes her angry, its beauty like an affront. What is she angry at? Jason? A husband so vicious he gave her no choice but to run? Malcolm? The man who lured her into investigation work, then abandoned her? All Clare knows is that these days the anger simmers below the surface always, its cause and its targets indecipherable. Clare takes another deep breath. Focus.

You can do this, she thinks. You are good at this work. You have a plan.

She taps at the GPS again. Northshore Drive. Two miles from here through the center of Lune Bay and then along a cliffside road. This strange city, home to Malcolm before Clare knew him. Can she conjure what his life might have been like here before his wife disappeared? The network they would have built, the connections to his wife Zoe's family, the Westmans. A family name tied to Lune Bay at every corner, but tied murkily to crime too, bribes and shady dealings, Jack Westman's murder five years ago, and then Zoe's disappearance three years later. Can Clare fathom Malcolm's panic after the police pegged him as the only viable suspect in his wife's disappearance? A panic that led him to flee Lune Bay too.

You are the best person to find him, Somers said. *You know him better than anyone.*

No, I don't, Clare thinks now. All she has is a plan. The plan is to be detached, assertive, to reconstruct Malcolm's world as she searches for him. There is a gentle flip in Clare's chest, her heart's way of warning her.

The GPS pings and Clare makes a sharp turn down a winding residential street. The lots are large, houses hidden behind brick walls or wrought iron fences lined with tall shrubs. In the space between two houses, Clare catches a quick sight of the water. The ocean is too close. Here, you could just wander off a cliff and never be seen again.

Northshore Drive. Clare slows at each house, peering out the windshield to read the numbers. She reaches the dead end and sees it, two silver digits nailed to a tall tree. 28. The house itself must be down the hill. Clare parks and yanks the emergency brake.

The light has faded still. Clare sits in silence for a moment. No. There is no time to think. She retrieves her gun from her backpack before stuffing the bag into the passenger footwell. Clare checks the weapon, then tucks it into the belt of her jeans, the cool metal a familiar comfort against her skin. When she opens the car door she is struck by the coolness of the air.

The driveway follows a steep incline to a wrought iron gate marked with an *H.* Malcolm Hayes. Malcolm Boon's real name.

The gate is unlocked. Clare passes through and turns the last corner. The house is perched on a rocky hillside. She can hear the ocean though she cannot see it, the shifting hum of crashing waves. In the photographs from news stories this house had looked much different. The Glass Box, it was called. An architectural marvel that glowed against its backdrop. A home built by Malcolm Hayes and his wife, Zoe Westman, only a year before she went missing. The last place anyone from Lune Bay saw either of them alive. Clare straightens up and takes a deep breath. *Start at the beginning,* Somers said to her. For Clare, the beginning is not with the police officers investigating this case. The beginning is here.

The windows of this glass house are black with darkness. A small, rocky moat of sorts separates the house from the path that curls off the driveway. Clare takes the small bridge to the front door. This house feels somehow inharmonious with what Clare knows of Malcolm—it's too modern, flashy. Not like him at all.

Clare knocks on the large metal door. Nothing. She knocks once more, waits, then crosses the bridge again and circles around to the back of the house. Every few paces she stops to call out a hello, her voice drowned by the hum of the ocean not yet in her sight. There are no neighbors visible here, just this isolated glass house carved into a wall of rock.

When Clare reaches the rear deck, she is again astounded by the ocean. She spins in a slow, full circle to check the surroundings. No one is here. The house is dark. This deck is all glass too, even its floor, so that the rocky cliff is visible underneath her feet. It gives her vertigo to look down, and so Clare fixes her gaze on the horizon. The sun has recently set, the last pink of the sky casting everything in a hazy light. The edges of the deck are marked by a metal and glass railing. Clare peers over. She can still make out the frothing white waves a hundred feet below. She grasps the railing and shakes it. It holds firm. It'd better, she thinks, because you'd never survive that fall. Clare arches her back to feel for her gun.

It was only this morning, before she boarded the bus, that Clare found herself at the back of a sporting goods store, the fake ID provided by Somers in hand, the young clerk more than happy to help a woman who knew her weapons well. The gun was an easy purchase. Clare tracks a seagull circling among the rocks below. Even in the dying light she knows she could withdraw the gun, aim, and strike it. She was still just a girl when her father started her on moving targets, skeets and tin cans tossed into the air. She knows Somers would not approve, but then, Somers would have no idea just how well Clare knows the feeling of a gun in her hands.

At the back, the house's stucco foundation is washed gray by the salt off the sea. To one side is a rock garden. Its flowers bloom, the soil around them weedless and black. Malcolm and Zoe may not live here anymore, but someone tends to this place. It is not abandoned. It takes Clare a minute to notice that the sliding door is open an inch. There is a screen door too, and she tries it and finds it locked, but the screen itself has a tear, and Clare is able to edge her arm through it and unlock it from the inside. She cups her hands to the glass and looks in. A kitchen devoid of color and life.

No huge risks, Somers said.

This *is* risky, Clare thinks. Stupid. And yet, I'm here.

The patio door slides open with a whine.

"Hello?" Clare calls into the space. "Hello?"

Clare presses the door closed behind her and the sound of the ocean vanishes. Instantly there is a shift in the quality of the air, the breeze replaced by thick humidity. This kitchen is stark, the floors cement, the counters and cupboards white and angular. It's the sort of room you'd find in the pages of an architectural magazine. Clare stands still, listening. Of course Malcolm is not here. He would never be so reckless as to return to his home. All she wants is evidence of Malcolm's former life, his marriage. To paint a picture. This showpiece house is nothing like what she would have imagined of him, the calm and reserved Malcolm she thought she knew.

In the living room the furniture is spare, a long leather couch and a wooden coffee table facing a gas fireplace embedded into an otherwise bare wall. Everywhere the walls and the floor are white. Ghostly. Clare is losing light fast. She closes her eyes in an effort to animate this space, to imagine Zoe and Malcolm in this room, drinks in hand, talking or arguing. Were there mundane aspects to their marriage? Or was Zoe always craving adventure, conflict? Though Clare calculated last night that it's been two months since she first met Malcolm, he is still unknowable in so many ways.

She climbs to the second floor. At the top of the stairs is a square landing with only three doors, all open. Straight ahead is a bathroom, and then a guest bedroom with nothing but a queen bed. Clare turns left first and finds herself in the master bedroom. The mattress has been stripped, the blinds open, the ocean vast out the large window. Clare enters the walk-in closet and uses the light on her phone to illuminate the space. It is split into his and hers sides. A smattering of clothes hang, the shirts on Malcolm's side ordered from dark to light. Clare leans into them and inhales. Dust tickles her throat. She must stifle a cough, annoyed at herself for thinking these shirts might still bear Malcolm's scent. Clare opens and closes the drawers. Most are empty, but in the bottom one on Zoe's side she finds a framed photograph. Clare holds her phone over it.

In the photo a family of six stands on a beach, each in khaki pants and a white shirt. The Westman family. Clare's gaze is drawn immediately to a younger Malcolm on the far left, his posture tense, his expression serious. Zoe is not beside him but instead at the opposite end of the group. The woman next to Malcolm holds a young girl on her hip. The little girl is beaming, her eyes fixed on Malcolm. Jack Westman and his wife, Colleen, are centered in the frame, arms around each other. Zoe and Malcolm are the frowning bookends to an otherwise happy family portrait.

The details of Jack Westman's death are easy to come by, a prominent businessman shot dead five years ago in his favorite restaurant as his wife and daughters sat with him eating dessert. Clare draws the photograph closer. It must be Charlotte Westman who stands next to Malcolm, Zoe's younger sister. She is taller than her sister, heavier set, her curly hair blown sideways to shield her face.

Clare uses her phone to take a picture of the photograph. She returns the frame to the drawer and enters the master bathroom. It is cavernous, tiled from ceiling to floor with marble. At its center is a large stand-alone tub, a floating vanity under the window and a shower open to the space. No glass enclosure. Clare returns to the bedroom and stands at the window as the last light fades. So far, this house has offered her very little. It feels nearly devoid of any history, any context, any sense of its owners. Perhaps not so inharmonious with Malcolm after all.

Wait. Clare holds still. What is that sound?

The room washes with light.

"Turn around," a woman's voice says behind her. "Slowly. Now. Turn around."

Clare obeys, her hands lifting instinctively. She must squint to adjust to the brightness of the track lighting. In the doorway stands a woman about Clare's height and age. Her hair is the same curly brown. This woman wears a black T-shirt and black pants, an outfit that would have rendered her nearly invisible in the dark. And she has a gun. She holds it up, aimed right at Clare's head. This woman's hand is steady, her stance firm as she steps closer.

If I reach for my gun, Clare thinks, I'm dead.

"Please," Clare says. "Don't shoot me."

Now the woman is within a few feet of Clare, her expression blank. At closer range, Clare recognizes her. Charlotte Westman, Zoe's sister, vastly changed from the photograph Clare examined only moments ago. Too thin, much aged.

"You're trespassing," Charlotte says.

"I know," Clare says. "I know I am. But I know Malcolm. He's . . . a friend. Malcolm Hayes. I know him."

A flicker crosses Charlotte's face, a small register of surprise. She lowers the gun by an inch. But just as quickly her stance rights itself, and she steps to within point-blank range.

"You're on private property. I should shoot you."

Clare inhales deeply and holds her eyes closed. Why does she feel so calm? Charlotte edges the gun closer to Clare's skull. When Clare pushes back against the wall, the numbness she feels is broken by the pressure of her own gun against her spine.

"You could shoot me," Clare says, popping her eyes open. "But you shouldn't, Charlotte. You really shouldn't."

"Shut up," Charlotte says. "Shut the fuck up."

Charlotte's finger is not on the trigger. This gives Clare a split second.

"Charlotte," Clare says again. "You're Zoe's sister. I know who you are."

And then Clare reacts. She grabs the barrel of the gun and spins her hip into Charlotte until she's able to yank the weapon free. A scramble ends with Clare holding the gun, their positions reversed, so that Charlotte is against the wall, her hands in the air. Clare clicks the safety open and threads her finger through the trigger loop.

"I get the feeling you've never actually fired a gun," Clare says. "I promise you that I have."

"Go ahead," Charlotte says, her voice low. "Go ahead. I don't fucking care."

At this Clare takes several steps back until she is on the opposite side of the master bedroom. She thinks of Somers, her calmness, her professionalism. What would Somers do if she were here? She would not let her anger get the best of her, Clare thinks. She would assess, de-escalate. She would do her job. Clare keeps the gun pointed with one hand, then fishes a card from her back pocket and flicks it across the room. Charlotte watches stone-faced as it flutters to the floor.

"The back door was open," Clare says. "I let myself in. My name is Clare O'Kearney."

This name. Before she'd embarked on this case, Clare had allowed Somers to select her alias from a list of *O'* names they'd found online. *It means warrior,* Somers had said. *Let's give you a name that means warrior.*

"Like I said, I know Malcolm. Personally. I can explain." Clare points to the card on the floor. "I'm an investigator. And I'm looking for him. I'm looking for Malcolm."

"Stop saying his name," Charlotte hisses.

21

"Malcolm's name?"

"Fuck you."

The venom in her voice, the wildness in her eyes takes Clare aback. What is it about her brother-in-law's name that stirs such anger in Charlotte Westman? In the week between cases, Clare had sometimes enacted scenes like this one, trying on reactions, personas. The cold, detached investigator. And then a warmer version, like Somers, professional but disarming and friendly. Neither felt right. I have no persona, Clare remembers thinking. And now Clare must tamp down the urge to say sorry for not doing as she's told, for taunting Charlotte. This is her missing sister's house. She may well know more than anyone else. Clare needs Charlotte Westman on her side.

"Can we make a deal?" Clare says. "I put down the gun, and we talk? It's possible that we want the same thing."

The words hang in the air, Charlotte breathing hard, eyes diverted to the window. Is she waiting for something? Someone? Clare clicks the safety back on and lowers the gun, tucking it into her pants next to her own.

"You've probably been through a lot," Clare continues. "I might be able to help you."

Charlotte slides down the wall until she is slumped on the floor, her face buried in her hands. She begins to weep. Clare keeps her distance, silent. Whatever she knows of this woman's story has come only from news articles, a family destroyed by her father's murder, a sister missing. Who knows what else she's lost? Enough to bring her to this house with a gun, enough for one gesture of goodwill to make her crumble. Clare can't begin to understand these tears. She can only wait them out.

C lare sits on the floor across from a crying Charlotte Westman. The dark and tattered clothes Charlotte wears do not align with the photograph filled with well-dressed Westmans; a photograph where she'd been smiling so brightly, her daughter on her hip, her brother-in-law Malcolm at her side. Now her hair is unbrushed and wild around her pale face. But most telling to Clare are the small lines and dots of pink scar tissue in the bend of Charlotte's elbow. Scars that have not yet faded to silver. What drugs are your weakness? Clare thinks to ask her. Takes one to know one. Instead she clears her throat, her thumb running the bumps of her own scars hidden under her shirt. From her low vantage on the floor Clare can see the dust bunnies under the master bed. It's been a while since anyone lived here.

Finally Charlotte wipes her eyes with her sleeve and looks up, her expression returned to one of hardened rage, her eyes rimmed red. When Clare points to the card again, Charlotte crawls to collect it from the floor between them.

"Why don't I start at the beginning," Clare suggests. "Tell you why I'm here."

"Why don't you give me back my gun," Charlotte says, not a question.

"You mean the gun you just pointed at my brain? I'd rather not."

"Fine," Charlotte says. "If you're going to hold me hostage. Fuck. Just start."

Hostage. The word troubles Clare. She'd pictured this going so differently. She'd pictured entering this home and finding some clue, big or small. Some place to begin. Her head aches. She is tired. She swallows to gather herself.

"Okay," Clare says. "Like I said, I'm an investigator. I know Malcolm because I used to work for him." Clare pauses to gauge her reaction, but Charlotte only stares at her, deadpan. "I know that he left Lune Bay, took off or whatever, after he became a suspect in your sister's disappearance. Well, he's spent the past few years searching for missing women—"

"Wait. What? Is this some sort of joke?" Charlotte searches the room, as if expecting someone else to appear. "You're joking, right?"

"No," Clare says. "I guess it became his vocation. Maybe because of what happened to your sister? I don't know. Anyway, he hired me about two months ago to work with him. To help him investigate women who'd disappeared."

A simple enough version, Clare knows. It's the truth, just not all of it. What Clare won't tell Charlotte is that she was initially one of the missing women Malcolm signed on to search for, that her husband, Jason, had hired him a few months after Clare ran away from her life. She won't tell

Charlotte about Malcolm's offer to hire her instead of turning her in to her abusive husband. Clare still can't yet tell the full story to anyone.

"I knew nothing about Malcolm when I met him," Clare continues. "He said he'd been married, but otherwise he was very cagey about his past. But when we were working our second case together, I guess something or someone started to catch up with him. I don't know what, he never told me. I was working that case with a police officer, a detective actually, and she helped me dig up some details about his life. Some things I didn't know—"

"Oh my God," Charlotte says, laughing bitterly.

"What?"

"Let me guess. You fell in love with him."

No," Clare says, surprised by the bark in her tone. "What? No. Not at all."

"Yes, you did. Oh God, I can totally see it. He was this man of mystery, this big-hearted, broken guy searching for missing women. And he kind of *saved* you, right? Or something like that? He pulled you out of the darkness and into his little world."

At first Clare is too stunned to speak, anger gnawing in her gut. It is not that Charlotte is right, it's that she is so flippant. You know nothing about me, Clare would like to say. Instead, she shakes her head and forces a small smile.

"That might make for a better story," Clare says. "But no. I worked for him. I knew nothing about his past, like I said. I think after he left Lune Bay, he needed to do something. Maybe he felt tied to missing women cases somehow, because of your sister, his wife. Maybe that's why he set up his own . . . why he started investigation work himself." Clare can detect the falter in her voice. How improbable a story it seems when she tells it aloud. "Something to keep busy, I guess?"

"To keep busy? Jesus Christ." Charlotte holds Clare's card aloft and studies it again. "Investigator. And you believed him? You bought that story? That's rich. Did he make these cards for you?"

Clare's chest aches. A lump climbs up her throat, tears forming behind her eyes. She feels strangely exposed. This back and forth is muddling her. She bites hard at the inside of her cheek, the pain refocusing her.

"I know Malcolm didn't give me the whole truth," Clare says. "That's why I'm here. That detective I met on my last case? Her name is Hollis Somers. It turns out Malcolm had a connection to the last case we worked together. So he disappeared again. Told me he needed to go. And after he left, Somers and I learned that there was more to his story than he'd let on. A lot more. This isn't Somers's jurisdiction, but her feeling was that the cops here weren't doing much to solve the case of his missing wife. That as far as they were concerned, it's gone cold. So we agreed that I'd come and see what I could find out about Malcolm, and even about Zoe. Test the waters a little."

Charlotte wears the hint of a smile, nodding at Clare as though she were a child weaving a tall tale. Clare thinks of Malcolm at the end of their first case, confessing the basic details of his life. A missing wife. *You look like her*, he'd said. In her case file Clare had itemized every detail Malcolm provided about his life. It occurs to her now that little of it might actually be true.

"You must be worried about your sister," Clare says. "It's been nearly two years."

"It's been a year and a half. And my sister's not missing. She's dead."

Clare works to mask her surprise, to hold her expression steady. "How do you know that?" she asks.

"Because there's no way she came out of this alive. She pissed off way too many people. Your boyfriend Malcolm included."

"He's not my—" Clare stops herself. Charlotte is trying to get the best of her. Clare withdraws the gun from her belt and inspects it, turning it over in her hands, a show of power. "Why don't *you* start at the beginning, then, Charlotte? You say your sister's dead, but you're keeping some kind of tabs on her abandoned glass house?" Clare waves an arm about. "Do you keep cameras here? Motion detectors? You sure got here pretty fast after I did."

"We've had problems with trespassers."

"Who's *we*?" Clare asks.

The question is met with a stony gaze.

"Locking the door might help," Clare says, allowing a pause. "I'm guessing you're playing the vigilante now, the sister dressed in black, looking to avenge? You've got a bone to pick with someone. Maybe I can help you. Your sister pissed a lot of people off, you say. I'm sure there's more you can tell me about that."

Charlotte keeps her chin up, her back straight against the wall, all signs of her tears gone. She says nothing. We are the same, Clare thinks. At war with ourselves—one part of us in pain and the other ready for revenge. Clare works to call up the details on Charlotte Westman she'd collected in the file. Younger than Zoe by barely a year. Never went to college. Married young, divorced young too. She has a daughter who, if Clare remembers correctly, should now be about ten. A lot in Charlotte's life has gone wrong, Clare thinks. Hostility is not the right angle to take with her. Clare will try a different tack.

"Charlotte," she says, calmer. "Listen. This was a terrible way to meet. But I think you and I probably want the same thing."

"Yeah? What's that?"

"I've read about you. I know your life hasn't been easy. You have a daughter. But five years ago your father was murdered and everything went to shit. Then your mother dies, of what? Heart failure? And your sister vanishes three years after that. I believe you lost custody of your daughter. So now you're alone."

Clare pauses. Charlotte's hands open and close into tight fists. She cracks a knuckle, breathing hard through her nose.

"Malcolm isn't my boyfriend," Clare continues. "I came here to find him. To figure out what happened. And when you try to tell someone's story, you should start as close to the beginning as you can get, right? The first sign of trouble is a good place to begin? In this case, the first signs point to your family. My guess is that you were collateral damage in all this. That you paid for other people's sins. Your dad's maybe? Even your sister's."

"You know nothing about me. Or my family."

Clare clicks open the gun and allows the bullets to pour onto the floor. She picks them up in a fist and jams them in her pocket, then slides the gun across to Charlotte. It's a risk, but the way Charlotte had held the gun, the safety still on, Clare can assume she doesn't have any spare bullets. Charlotte leans forward and snatches the weapon from the floor.

"Collateral damage," Clare says again.

"That's what my lawyer said to me," Charlotte says, her voice low. "Four years ago. Collateral damage. My ex-husband got sole custody of my daughter and moved her across the country. I have zero visitation rights. Nothing. Everything I owned . . . my house, my car, was repossessed, because my father co-owned it all. This house is technically still a family asset, but it's frozen. Because where the fuck are the owners? Jesus. You have no idea what's happened here, Clare. I warn you, run while you can. There hasn't just been *damage* to me, to my family. It's been complete and total obliteration."

"So what do you want, then?" Clare asks. "Why are you here in this house?"

"Let me tell you something." Charlotte studies the card again. "Clare? Is that your real name? My brother-in-law Malcolm? He's not the good guy in this story. If you dig a little, you'll see what I mean. I'd warn against it, but who am I to stop you? And if you think you're going to find him, to save him or whatever, you're in for a big surprise. There will be no happy ending."

It takes effort to hold Charlotte's steady gaze.

"What about your sister?" Clare asks. "You say she's dead. Do you really believe that?"

"You want a place to start?" Charlotte says. "Talk to the cops around here. There's been about eight of them assigned to the case since my dad died. And nothing's come up. Nothing. The newest detective? His name is Patrick Germain. I'm pretty sure he made detective barely a year ago. The so-called journalist who works the case knows more than the cops do. It's all too fishy, you know?"

"I know."

"Yeah. So you do whatever you want. It's a fucking quagmire, Clare. Go find Germain if you want. Get yourself caught up in this mess. But leave me alone. I don't want any part of it."

When Charlotte hoists herself to standing, Clare does the same. Charlotte gestures for Clare to leave the room first. They descend the stairs together, the hallway lit. When they reach the front door, Clare turns to speak, but Charlotte waves her off, shaking her head no. Outside, once she's alone again, Clare's heart begins to race. *Don't risk your life*, Somers said. And yet in only her first stop Clare found herself at gunpoint. An omen, she knows, that this place is not safe.

The bathroom mirror is fogged. Clare clears a streak across it with her palm and scrunches her hair to draw the water from her curls. She leans in to examine herself. She looks almost healthy, a peach tone to her cheeks, the circles under her eyes faded from dark purple to something gentler. Clare points her index finger and presses it into the scar at the exact angle the bullet entered her shoulder about six weeks ago. It is still tender, the damaged nerves sending a tingling shot down her arm. With her thumb and finger Clare marks the distance from the wound to the top of her breast, her heart. Two inches, maybe three.

Her first case ended with Clare taking a bullet to the shoulder. The wound is now settling into being only a nuisance, an unsightly scar. The pain still comes and goes, though Clare has stopped taking medication for it. It is better to endure the ache than to risk the urge those pills bring her.

Chance is a funny thing. Fate.

Had Clare turned just slightly to the left as the bullet came at her, it would have hit her heart and not her shoulder. *You're here and then you're not*, Clare's mother used to say from her hospital bed, inuring herself against her own impending death. It often comes down to chance.

This hotel room is soothing in its blandness. The carpet, the faded comforter, the landscape paintings on the wall. The cheapest place to stay near the center of Lune Bay, a relic from before the Westman money flowed into town. The walls of her room are thin enough that Clare can discern the dialogue from the sitcom playing in the next. In less than an hour, Clare has managed to overtake the entire space, her belongings scattered, the desk covered with papers and photographs, the details of Malcolm's file. Her cell phone rings at full volume. Clare yelps, startled. She collects it from the dresser and swipes the screen to take the call.

"Somers," she says, breathless. "Hi."

"That's Detective Somers to you."

"Yeah, yeah."

"You all right?" Somers asks.

"I'm fine."

"Okay," Somers says, unconvinced.

In the silence Clare tries to evoke an image of Somers, her exact looks. Her braided hair pulled half up, glasses only when she needs to read. Clare lies on the bed.

"I went to Malcolm and Zoe's house as soon as I got here. Seemed like a logical first stop."

"Don't tell me you—"

"The back door was open."

"Jesus, Clare. I told you, nothing risky. Don't be stupid."

"Yeah. Well, Zoe's sister, Charlotte Westman, showed up with a gun."

"Oh Christ," Somers says. "I'm about to pull you off this case."

"No, no. I was able to talk her down." Clare will withhold the details, the gun held at point-blank range, the wrestling match it took for Clare to retrieve it. "She's very angry. You remember her from the file? She lost custody of her daughter. Drug problems, I think. She was with her dad when he was murdered. Seems to me like she's lost everything since then."

Through the receiver Clare can hear Somers flipping papers. Writing things down. She feels a surge of something she cannot decipher, a sense of authority. She feels useful, in control.

"She mentioned the cops on the case," Clare continues. "There's been a string of them. I mean on her father's murder case, which seems to have been merged with Zoe's disappearance, even though they happened almost three years apart. I get the murder happened five years ago, but Zoe's only been missing eighteen months. Feels weird that they're lumped together."

"They're lumped because they're connected," Somers offers.

"Right. But there doesn't seem to be much focus on either anymore. Apparently, the current detective is a rookie."

"That's not good," Somers says. "There are two reasons cops stop working on a case. One, it's truly gone cold. No eyewitnesses, no hard evidence, no DNA, no weapon. You nudge those cases to the back of your desk and hope someone walks in one day and confesses."

"And the other kind?" Clare asks.

"The other cases get nudged to the back of your desk for you. You're given no choice in the matter. You understand?"

"Right." Clare sits up and twists a finger through her damp hair. "The detective's name is Patrick Germain. I looked him up after I checked in to the hotel. From what I can see he was a beat cop this time last year. My plan is to give him a call."

"I don't recognize the name," Somers says. "I'll do some recon."

"There's one reporter who keeps writing about the Westmans. A rogue freelancer. A guy named Austin Lantz. I emailed him—"

"Listen," Somers interrupts. "I know you're in the thick of it down there, and I appreciate what you're doing. But I wanted to give you a heads-up."

Something in Somers's tone tightens a vise around Clare's chest. "A heads-up about what?"

"I've been getting calls at my desk."

"What kind of calls?"

"Hang-ups, mostly. A couple of times a woman said hello and then hung up. I'm pretty sure it's been the same woman every time."

"So? What does that have to do with me?" Clare asks. "Can't you trace it?"

"The calls come from a blocked number, but after the third or fourth time I asked a guy in tech to set up a tracer on my phone. Over the years I've had a fair number of threats against me. Some donkey I put behind bars gets out and thinks it's a good idea to make a few crank calls, scare me. But sometimes the calls feel . . . different."

"And?" Clare prompts her. "Why are you telling me this?"

"My tech guy was able to triangulate a general area. These calls were coming from east of here. A long way east of here. Cell towers within a small radius of each other. One was even from a pay phone."

"Where?" Clare asks, though she suspects the answer.

"Your hometown."

Clare blinks fast. She tries to picture the stretch of her hometown's main strip where the pay phone still stood, the very one she'd use to call her mother to come pick her up after spending a Friday night wandering up and down the block with her teenaged friends. She can summon its exact location next to the hardware store, the feel of the heavy receiver in her hands, the winter nights when she'd turn her back to the wind and press a gloved finger to her ear so she could hear her mother on the other end.

"Are you sure it was a woman?" Clare asks.

"Unless it's a man pitching his voice." Somers pauses. "No. It was a woman. The *hellos* were weird, taunting or something. Drawling it out. Sarcastic. But every time I tried to engage, I'd hear the click before I could say anything beyond hello."

"And she never said anything else?"

"Once," Somers says. "She said hello and then she paused. I spoke into the silence, asking the obvious questions. Who are you, why are you calling, yada yada. I wanted to keep the line open as long as possible so my guy could calibrate the location. She said hello again, but this time she added my name. 'Hello, Somers.' Upbeat, like we were old friends."

Now Clare's mind spins. A woman. If it were a man, the answer would be obvious: Jason. There's Grace, her childhood friend, who might have traced or followed Clare here after running into her, who might have been indoctrinated even more by Jason, since Clare saw her over a week ago. But Grace wouldn't stoop to such a tactic. Would she?

"Any chance it might be related to you?" Somers asks. "You have any reason to believe it could be?"

Clare doesn't answer.

"Listen." Somers releases a long sigh. "Maybe your husband's got himself another woman. One who's willing to do his dirty work. They figured out our connection somehow and now they want to toy with you a bit. In my years as a cop I've met my fair share of women willing to play their man's game. I've even met a few who take over and win it."

"It's possible," Clare says, her voice a croak. "Maybe."

"I'll confess something to you," Somers says. "I made a call to the detachment over there. One of the guys here has a cousin who's married to a cop out your way. It's always six degrees with cops, you know? Anyway, I asked him to do a head count. Make sure your husband was still in town, minding his own business."

Minding his business. Clare can so easily recall the simplicity of Jason's life, his truck and his short commute to the factory, the tediousness of his day on the assembly line ramping him up by the time he arrived home to her, sometimes by way of the bar. And then Jason would pace the kitchen as Clare kept a safe distance, another drink in his hand, spewing the same diatribe about life owing him more, about the world's failure to recognize how capable he was of bigger things. That he'd find bigger things if they didn't find him.

"And?" Clare asks.

"He's there. Jason. Your husband."

"Ex-husband."

"Yeah. Sorry. Anyway, he's there. My guy got some pictures

of him coming and going. I didn't ask for much beyond that. Just a visual. Guy sent me a few pictures as proof."

Clare breathes heavily into the receiver, her cell phone warm on her ear. Her throat aches with the effort not to cry.

"Hey," Somers says, ever calm. "Let's not get ourselves twisted into knots. I've been going through my old cases. Checking on my lady friends, which ones have been released recently, who might have had ties to that region. That's the most likely scenario for these stupid crank calls. I've put more than one woman behind bars in my day. The more likely answer is that it has nothing to do with you at all. I just thought I'd ask."

"Yeah," Clare says.

In the ensuing pause Clare feels a stab of sadness. She wishes Somers was here with her, that they were actually working this case together, in person. She wants to believe she can trust Somers over everyone else, but even that feels like an impossible feat.

"I've got to get going," Somers says. "No catastrophizing, okay? Just keep working the case. I'll keep my eyes and ears open. No one's coming for you that we know of. Not yet. Let's not panic."

With a quick goodbye Clare hangs up and splays backwards onto the bed. She refreshes her email, a response popping up from the reporter she contacted.

I'll be at The Cabin Bar tonight until late, 14th and Burns Rd

Austin Lantz. Clare opens her browser and looks up his name. Hundreds of results pop up, long- and short-form articles on the Westmans, on Zoe and Charlotte. Clare recognizes some of the articles from the file she and Somers curated.

The clock on her phone reads 9:43 p.m. Clare forces herself to stand up, get dressed. She will keep working. Push through the fatigue. At the bathroom mirror, she leans in and stares closely at her reflection. It feels like looking at a stranger, her face creased with worry.

No one's coming for you that we know of. Not yet.

But there'd been a lilt in her voice as Somers said it, as if it were taking some effort to make the words ring true.

This bar is cozy and dimly lit, empty even for a Tuesday night. A neon sign over the bartender's head reads WELCOME TO THE CABIN. She spots him seated at the bar just as his email said he would be. Austin Lantz looks different in real life from his pictures online: lanky, younger than Clare, a flannel shirt far too warm for the stuffy air of this bar. She studies him from the door until he checks his watch and twists, anticipating her arrival. Austin smiles and lifts the beer he holds in a *cheers*, gesturing at Clare to join him.

Clare strides his way. This job requires a confidence, an extroversion deeply unnatural to her. She places a card in front of him without a hello. He offers her a card in return—AUSTIN LANTZ, FREELANCE JOURNALIST—and extends his hand. His handshake is flimsy.

"Have a seat, Clare," he says.

She sets her backpack in the footwell of the stool and sits. The bartender wanders over.

"You here to drink? Or is this Austin's office for tonight?"

"I'll have a drink," Clare says. "And maybe a menu?"

"Sure," the bartender says. "Let's start with a drink."

"I'll take a whiskey," she says. "Neat."

Clare will not overthink this. She never had troubles with alcohol the way she did with other vices. She never loved the burn down her throat or the loss of inhibition, the time and effort it took to get drunk versus the ease of the pills or tabs that dissolved discreetly on her tongue. Jason was the drinker between them, and watching him descend to the mean, sputtering, slurring version of himself was enough for Clare to keep her distance from their liquor cabinet. But here, miles and months away, as she watches the bartender select a bottle from the row and pour a shot into a tumbler for her, Clare feels oddly elated. It's just one drink. Once the tumbler is in front of her, she lifts it to clink Austin's beer bottle.

"Thank you for meeting me," she says.

"I love that there's a PI on the case now."

"You've been tracking this story for a long time," Clare says.

"I wrote my first article on it in journalism school. Covered Jack Westman's murder. So yeah. I've been at it for five years." He swivels his stool to face outward. "This building was a Westman property. Most of Lune Bay was at some point or another. Zoe Westman ran this bar for a while after she moved back to town. Did you know that? She had her engagement party here."

"To celebrate her engagement to Malcolm Hayes," Clare says. "I've seen photographs of that party."

"That was a big social event in Lune Bay. The Westmans were local royalty back then."

Clare found the photos of the engagement party online, Malcolm so young and handsome, his dress shirt unbuttoned low on his chest, his hair longer and wavy. What surprised her most was the way his chin lifted to the camera, a drink in one hand, daring the picture to be taken. It seemed impossible that the young man in that photograph was the same stiff and inscrutable man she'd meet eight years later. Clare recognized other people too; Zoe of course, Charlotte, the Westman parents. All these characters in Malcolm's origin story.

"Why don't we exchange what we know?" Austin suggests, facing Clare again.

"I've already read most of what you've written," Clare says. "I think I know what you know."

"Ha! So you think a reporter writes down all his secrets?"

"Isn't that exactly what a reporter's supposed to do?"

"Maybe. I'll tell you that I couldn't find anything on Clare O'Kearney, Private Investigator."

"No," Clare says, a ringing in her ears. "You won't find much on me."

"I'd say that means you're using an alias."

"If I were, I'd probably have a good reason to, right? Keep a low profile, that kind of thing."

Austin smiles. The bartender returns with a menu. Clare scans it quickly and orders a burger. She can't remember the last proper meal she ate, her stomach hollow with hunger. And she must eat if she's going to keep drinking.

"You want any food?" she asks Austin.

"He's too cheap to order food," the bartender says, taking the menu. "I force him to order at least one drink."

"Come on," Austin says. "You know you love my company."

Clare must remind herself to take small sips of the whiskey. She watches Austin over the edge of her glass, his easy banter with the bartender. His eyes are a sharp blue, his jaw patched with the attempts to grow a beard. Much of his presentation is about making himself appear older than he is. One arm rests on a leather notebook thick with earmarked pages. Clare bends to her own bag and extracts her notebook. In the days in between cases she'd thought of every way she could to formalize this work. She'd sat in a motel room with papers scattered, watching rerun detective shows into the early hours. Anything she could think of to authenticate herself into this role. She writes today's date at the top of the page, then the name *Austin Lantz*, underlining it twice.

"Can you tell me everything you know about Malcolm Hayes?" she asks. "Any secrets, as you say, that you didn't include in your articles?"

"The guy was a creep. I'm pretty sure he offed his wife."

"There's no proof of that."

Her tone is measured. If she is biased, Clare must not reveal that to Austin.

"A woman goes missing, they can't find a single trace, and as soon as the cops lean on him, the husband vanishes? I'd say that's as close to a confession as you'll ever get."

Not necessarily, Clare thinks. She too disappeared from her life nine months ago, never reaching out to those left behind, instead allowing them to believe whatever they chose to believe. Clare knew they'd think she was dead, that her brother, Christopher, and her best friend, Grace, would assume the worst. No doubt they believed that if Jason hadn't killed her, then she'd probably overdosed, done herself in. Clare knows better than anyone else that it's possible to vanish, alive and well.

"Did you ever meet Malcolm?" Clare asks.

"I met him. I know him."

"What do you mean, you *know* him?"

"I've researched his life. Take a walk down to St. James Cemetery. In one corner you'll find Malcolm's whole family, dead. Plane crash. He didn't grow up here. His father was a bigwig in Newport, which is a few hundred miles up the coast. But his parents were from this area, so they're buried here. About a hundred yards away, you'll find the Westman plot. I've talked to people who knew Malcolm back in the day. They say he was stone cold after his family died. His family died in a plane crash and he just iced over. Sound like a normal guy to you?"

"But you don't actually know him," Clare says.

Austin says nothing. Clare knows she can't fully trust the version of Malcolm offered to her by those here in Lune Bay. She has often thought of what people in her hometown might have said about her after she left, how they might have described her as bitter, cruel, detached, a drug addict married to an angry drunk. Clare drains her whiskey and orders another one. Fuck it. She needs it.

Austin flicks her empty glass so it edges down the bar.

"A PI with an Irish name drinking whiskey," he says. "That's very on brand."

Clare smiles tightly. "Beer's not my thing."

"Was it your husband's thing?" Austin asks.

"Excuse me?"

Austin lifts Clare's left hand from where it rests on the bar and gently rubs at the base of her ring finger. "You see right here? The little dent in the skin? It's almost faded. Almost. Your wedding ring might have gotten a bit tight over the years. Literally, I mean. My mom still had that dent two years after leaving my dad and chucking her wedding ring. It drove her nuts."

"That's pretty observant," Clare says, a heat in her cheeks.

"That's my job."

"Yeah, well. My husband's long gone. He's not relevant to this."

"Fair enough. Then why don't you tell me who hired you to work this case?"

"You don't need to know that either," Clare says.

The bartender returns with Clare's food and a refill on the whiskey. Clare pours a pat of ketchup next to the fries and folds one into her mouth.

"You want to hear something funny?" Austin asks. "I was supposed to be on a blind date tonight. It was a setup. My mom says I don't date enough. She thinks I take my work too seriously. So she and some friend from her book club matched me with this woman's niece. Anyway, I got a text about an hour ago that my blind date wasn't coming. She said her dog was sick, but I'm guessing she googled me and figured me to be some kind of crazed person fixated on an unsolved murder. Or maybe she peeked into the bar and didn't like what she saw."

He's fishing and Clare knows it. "That's too bad," she says.

"But then your email came through about five minutes later." Austin shrugs. "These things have a way of working out."

Clare says nothing. She leans over the bar to bite into her burger, a graceless task that seems to amuse Austin. Does he believe that she's flirting with him? How is it that some men can see anything they want in nothing at all?

"I'll make you a deal, investigator Clare," he says. "Question for question. A little game of get-to-know-you."

"Okay," Clare says. "I go first. When did you meet Malcolm Hayes?"

"Twice, I think. First time was right after Jack Westman's murder. I tracked him down, tried to get him to talk to me.

Second time, a few years later, maybe? Definitely before Zoe vanished. He finally agreed to an interview, then sat through the whole thing stone-faced, like he was mocking me. After Zoe went missing, I stalked him for a while. Camped out in front of their crazy cliff house. Confronted him a few times, but what's he going to say? Then he was gone. I tried to track him, but he had every one of my sources stumped. I'll give the guy credit: he knows how to disappear."

The bartender brings Austin another beer and swipes the first one from his grasp. Austin makes a show of protesting, then takes the cold bottle and clinks the top of Clare's whiskey glass.

"My turn," he says. "So what's your skin in this game?"

"What do you mean?"

"Do you know any of the Westmans? Any of the missing women?"

"Women?" Clare asks. "Women, plural? As far as I know, there's only Zoe."

"Ohhh." Austin drawls the word, then taps a finger to his temple. "See? Secrets. You haven't made that connection yet. I've been working on this big piece. An exposé, you could say. My mom tells me the Zoe Westman case is dead, no pun intended. But did you know that in the years before Zoe Westman vanished, at least two other women went missing in this town? Possibly even more. Women who knew each other, ran in the same circle. The Westman circle. But not the kind of women who'd raise serious alarms with the police. Women they figured just took off with boyfriends. One of them had developed a pretty bad prescription drug habit. I don't even think any of them made the front page when the missing persons reports were filed, if they made the papers at all. But I've been piecing things together." He touches finger to thumb. "Connections people haven't made before. I wrote one piece about one of the girls' dads. He's been on the hunt for his daughter, but the cops have him labeled a conspiracy theorist. No one wanted to print the story. It's online on this niche crime blog. I'll send you the link."

"That's a big share, Austin. Thank you."

"Hey, I like the fact that you're a PI," Austin says. "But wait. We're getting out of order here. The question is still mine. You never answered. What is your skin in the game?"

"I was hired to come here," Clare says, her tone unconvincing. "That's it. I work alongside a detective named Somers. Hollis Somers. You can look her up. She's not based in Lune Bay, obviously. We worked a case together a while back."

It occurs to Clare that she should tell him the truth about Malcolm too, given she's told Charlotte. It is not her secret anymore. But something holds her back.

"My turn," she says. "Do you know Charlotte Westman?"

"I know her well," he says. "Really well these days, actually. She's been crashing at my place. She got evicted a few weeks ago. It's tight quarters, but we manage."

"Isn't that a conflict of interest? Or a . . . breach of ethics or something?"

Austin tilts his beer and shrugs. "I'm not a lawyer. She's a source. And she's fallen on hard times."

Her burger finished, Clare drains her second whiskey too fast. It burns down her throat. What time is it? Clare takes her phone from her pocket. 11:00 p.m. She is suddenly very tired.

"My turn," Austin says. "What's your real name?"

Despite the tightness in her chest, Clare angles her head and stares at Austin until he blinks.

"Clare," she says. "My real name is Clare."

"Ha. Right. Well, Clare," Austin says. "We've barely scratched the surface. But I'm feeling like this has been a little uneven. Maybe another whiskey will make you more amenable to sharing?"

"Maybe," Clare says, finishing her drink before standing up. "But I'm meeting the detective assigned to the case tomorrow. I need to get some sleep."

"Germain?" Austin laughs. "Good luck. That guy couldn't find his own ass in his pants." He reaches for her arm, brushing it lightly. "Come on. One more drink never killed you."

What's making Clare uneasy is how much she wants to capitulate, to drink with this guy who believes something is forming between them, to use her wiles to gain the upper hand. But she feels a little dizzy, and she cannot afford to lose her inhibition. Clare shakes her head with a contrite smile and collects her bag. Austin places his hand on the small of her back and directs her to the bar's entrance. He stops just short of the door, pouting.

"This evening turned out pretty well," he says. "Wish it didn't have to end so soon."

"I appreciate you meeting with me."

He leans one arm on the door, posed. Clare smiles again, embarrassed by his efforts to be coy. Austin Lantz seems like a boy working hard to play the part of a man. Still, she knows there's a mild slur to her words and he's interpreting that as an invitation.

Outside, the cold air is a shock to Clare, a misting rain coating her. She hadn't realized how sweaty she'd gotten inside. She walks to the nearest corner to gather her bearings. Her breaths are quick, short. She knows this feeling too well, the exhilaration of the whiskey, the desire for one more. She must keep walking.

WEDNESDAY

The restaurant is a shabby BBQ spot. It's busy inside, but the older hostess breaks into a big grin and offers Detective Patrick Germain a warm hug. She looks to Clare with the curiosity of a nosy aunt. Germain shakes his head to stave off her implied question.

"Work meeting," he says.

When Patrick Germain smiles, he looks almost bashful, his strong and squared jaw still somehow boyish. He is taller than Clare by only an inch, and though he's made detective, he can't yet be thirty. The hostess laughs, then leads them to a small booth at the back, empty, as if she'd been waiting for Germain to arrive. They sit and Germain hands Clare a menu.

"The ribs are the best in five hundred miles."

"It's not even nine in the morning," Clare says.

"Never too early for ribs. This place is open twenty-four/seven. You a carnivore?"

"I guess so," Clare says.

Germain sets the menu flat on the table to study it. Clare spots a small tattoo on the inside of his wrist, a sideways eight. The infinity symbol. The waitress comes over and Germain orders for both of them. Ribs, coleslaw, water.

"So." Germain opens a notepad. He copies her name from the card she's given him. "Clare O'Kearney. What's your date of birth?"

"Why do you need my date of birth?" Clare asks. "We're just talking."

"It's standard procedure."

"With a witness maybe," Clare says. "Or a suspect."

"Okay." Germain clicks at the tip of his pen. "But not with"—he studies the card again—"not with an investigator?"

"Listen," Clare says. "I appreciate you meeting with me. I know you haven't had the best of luck with this case."

Germain leans back in the booth and lets out a long sigh. Clare has come to understand that the greatest puzzle in this work is deciphering what to share with whom. She knows better than to trust just anyone. In their phone call yesterday, she'd told Germain the basic facts of her relationship with Malcolm. Still, her guard will stay squarely up. Germain raps his fingers against the grainy wood of the table.

"The way I see it," Germain says, "this case was given to me as a hazing ritual. A murder five years cold, a missing woman gone eighteen months with zero leads or clues. Two cases that shouldn't even be on the same file but are. And the woman's husband, the prime suspect, gone too. Malcolm Hayes's trail has been as cold as ice, until you show up and say you've been playing PI with him for the past few months."

"I'm trying to be honest with you from the get-go."

Germain eyes her. "I appreciate that. Because, let me tell

you, it feels like the witnesses change their story every time you sit them down. And the early police files are . . . thin."

"Thin as in you don't think your fellow officers were doing their jobs?"

"I make a point to never speak ill of my colleagues. But one guy who worked the case was an old boyfriend of Zoe's. He knew Malcolm too, for chrissake. That kind of stuff is bound to happen in a small place like Lune Bay, but this one had conflict of interest written all over it. Lots of rumors that that particular cop was dirty too. There were other lead detectives too. Let's just say a few old-timers were offered very convenient retirement packages around the time the case started to go cold."

Clare nods. In her hometown these sorts of rumors plagued the local department, the notion that certain cases could get pushed aside if the suspect had the right connections. Even Clare had been a beneficiary, avoiding formal arrest on drug charges because her father was friends with the officer's brother. She sips at her water. Germain seems almost at odds with himself, a day's growth on his beard, the tattoo, nails bitten to the quick, but then a pressed shirt and a tie. He seems more a miscast actor playing the part of detective than the young phenom Lune Bay's public relations team declares him to be.

"So," Germain says. "You call me out of the blue and tell me that Malcolm is your employer—I guess that's what you'd call him, right? And you've seen him as recently as last week, which means he's alive, unless he drove off a cliff in the meantime. *And* you're a private investigator working alongside a police officer from wherever. That's a mouthful."

Clare smiles. Germain is studying her closely. Before leaving the hotel this morning, Clare had taken advantage of the well-stocked bathroom, the fruity shampoos and fancy hair dryer. She'd taken time she never takes anymore, putting effort into the curl of her hair, applying mascara and lip gloss she'd picked up in a drugstore along the way. Selecting jeans and a black sweater. *Those looks of yours are currency*, Clare's mother used to say. *Spend wisely*.

"I said I worked for him, yes," Clare answers. "Now I'm looking for him, yes. And that police officer from wherever? She's a detective. Just like you."

"And you really saw him a week ago?"

"Roughly a week ago. Yes."

"He's wanted in connection with the disappearance of his wife. You're aware there's been a warrant for his arrest in place for a long time?"

"I'm aware now," Clare says. "I wasn't a week ago."

"And your detective friend wasn't aware either?"

"By the time she was, he was gone," Clare says.

Clare clears her throat and again takes Germain through an abridged version of her history with Malcolm. His hiring her, the cases, the relationship with Detective Somers that Clare formed on the last case. The story flies from her like a rock skimming over deep water, all the details about her escape from her marriage nine months ago, about her husband, Jason, and her own demons, left under the surface.

"Why does Detective Somers want you here?"

Clare shrugs. "I guess she doesn't like unsolved cases."

"Hm. Okay."

Before Germain can continue, the waitress arrives and sets an oval platter of ribs and coleslaw between them. She returns seconds later with napkins and wipes, plates and forks, then the cutlery, everything dropped in front of them unceremoniously. Germain busies himself arranging the food for them, his face locked in a concentrated frown. Clare attempts to nibble a rib without streaking her face with sauce.

"I called you," Clare says, "because my guess is that you haven't had a real lead in a long time. I figured maybe we could help each other."

"I'd consider *you* a lead." Germain bites at a rib. "I mean, hey. A stranger shows up with a glossy PI business card and tells me she was in touch with one of my suspects as recently as a week ago? A suspect who disappeared deep into the ether? A guy with big ties to the Westman family? That's a monster lead, if you ask me."

For a moment, neither of them speaks. Germain sucks on the bone in a way that turns Clare's stomach.

"And this stranger," he continues. "You, I mean. You claim you didn't know who he was. That you had no idea that this guy you were apparently working with was a suspect in one of the biggest missing persons cases Lune Bay has ever seen."

"Lune Bay isn't exactly cosmopolitan. And he gave me a fake name."

"He gave you his real first name."

"There are a lot of Malcolms in the world," Clare says.

"You think? Johns, maybe. Michaels. But Malcolm?" Germain scratches his head, feigning contemplation. "I don't know about that."

"Yeah." Clare rips open a wet napkin and uses it to rub her hands clean. "I guess we've both had our failings with—"

"Don't you read the news?" Germain interrupts. "Most PIs should. Zoe Westman is somewhat of a household name, at least around here. Not to mention her father was shot to death in a restaurant. Jack Westman? Surely you'd heard of him. One of the biggest developers on the coast? Lots of money coming in and out of strange places. A business partner in jail for tax fraud. Your friend Malcolm was in deep with what is essentially a local mafia family. A lot of people would have recognized him from the papers."

"Not where I'm from," Clare says. "And he's obviously good at going undetected, or you'd have caught him by now."

Germain frowns, allowing for a pause in the tempo of back and forth. He is not wrong, Clare knows. After his true identity was revealed to her, it amazed Clare how much information on Malcolm she could find online. A better sleuth probably would have uncovered Malcolm's backstory, the Westman connection, without his full name at hand. Clare's leg bounces under the table. At one point in this exchange, she'd felt almost confident. But now the effort to wrest control of the conversation is rankling her. He might be young, but Germain is a natural at cutting her down to size.

"Look," Clare says, meeting his eyes with as steady a gaze as she can manage. "I'm the first to say that I'm new at this work. But I'm good at it. I've had success. I won't get in your way. I can fly under your radar, or maybe we can help each other."

The waitress returns and removes the platter and their dishes. Clare watches Germain closely as he chats with her, his easy smile, the effusive way he compliments the food, touches the waitress's arm. He knows his charm is a useful tool, a way to get him what he wants.

"You were saying," Germain says once the waitress has left. "About flying under my radar? I appreciate that, I do. But I think I'd prefer to keep you square in my bull's-eye."

"Or we just avoid each other altogether," Clare says, arms crossed. "I've got other people I can align with."

"You mean Austin Lantz?" Germain offers a hearty laugh and crosses his arms behind his head. "The self-declared expert on the Westman family. That's funny."

Clare's jaw tightens. "Were you spying on me?"

"No. You called me, remember? He's just the obvious guy to align with. It's almost a cliché. The obsessed reporter."

"He doesn't have the best things to say about you," Clare says.

"Because it bothers him that I won't give him the time of day," Germain says.

"He claims other women have gone missing too," Clare says. "From Lune Bay. That it's not just Zoe."

"Right." Germain leans forward. "That's one of my favorite conspiracy theories. Of course he's peddling it. Finds the name of a few women who had tenuous connections to each other—which everyone in Lune Bay has, by the way—women who left town for whatever reason. Maybe their overbearing parents filed a report because their daughters stopped taking their calls. And Austin tries to tack them on to the Westman case. Man, he'd love that to be true. He wants this all to be one big monster plot. Did he tell you that he used to be Jack Westman's personal driver?"

"No," Clare says. "He didn't."

"Yeah. See? So his whole 'reporter' thing is a little much. He'd tell you he was only driving to put himself through journalism school. Still, there's a bit of shitting where he used to eat going on, isn't there? He quit right before Jack Westman was killed. His brother hit the jackpot in the tech business, and now he funds Austin's little reporter escapades."

Clare fiddles with her napkin. She does not want to feel daunted by Germain, outfoxed.

"Well," she says. "That's good intel. Thank you."

"We can be cordial, can't we?"

When the bill arrives Germain hands the waitress his credit card without looking at it. He smiles, offering a détente between them, a declaration of his own victory. Clare knows her silence does her no favors, that Germain is all but toying with her now. But her exchanges with Austin turn over in her head, the whiskey that may have dulled her. She is angry at herself once again.

"Where are you staying?" Germain asks.

"Downtown."

"Oh, come on. It's not hard for me to find out where."

"The Caledonian. Not easy to find cheap digs around here."

"No, it isn't," he says, sliding out of the booth. "Clare O'Kearney. I hope we can keep talking."

"I do too."

Germain saunters to the front to engage the waitress again. Clare watches him. She'd figured on the upper hand in this exchange, but even a relative rookie like Germain is still more experienced than she is. The food has her tired though it is still early morning. She feels flustered, uncertain. But the day is young, and the list of leads to follow grows longer and longer. She must dig deeper on the Westmans. She must keep her focus at all costs, avoid distractions like the whiskey last night. As she follows Germain back through the restaurant and out to his car, Clare reminds herself to remain vigilant. You can still slip, she thinks. You are still you, and you always will be.

A wrought iron fence with a rounded gate marks the entry to St. James Cemetery. The online search for the graves had been a simple task. *Take a walk down to St. James Cemetery,* Austin said to her last night. Though he was being facetious, Clare needs a chance to regroup, to stand in the morning sun. She follows the narrow road down a winding hill, the older gravestones towering high and tilted, the carved lettering mossy and faded. By the time Clare circles to the bottom of the hill the headstones are no longer stone but dark marble, the dates of death flashing white with their more recent etching. She consults the screenshot of the map on her phone, then takes a final left before spotting it.

HAYES. ALISON, BRIAN, CAMILLE.

It feels almost intimate to be standing here. The dates of death are all the same, Malcolm's parents and his eleven-year-old sister killed in a plane crash twenty-five years ago, when

Malcolm was just a teenager. Clare reaches down and rests her hand on the cool marble of the headstone. She tries to envision Malcolm here, as a young man or as his current self, the grief that might overcome him. Or maybe the tragedy struck at an age where Malcolm went numb instead. *Stone cold*, Austin said. It tells Clare something about how little she knows Malcolm that she cannot predict what his reaction to such a loss might have been. She takes a photograph of the gravestone, then looks to the map again and circles back to the path in search of her next stop.

It's quiet here. Clare takes a deep breath. Her mother had not wanted a burial in a place like this. She'd asked for cremation instead, her remains to be sprinkled into the creek that marked the far boundary of their farm. But the urn sat unattended for so long on the mantelpiece that Clare knew her father, wrapped in his own obstinate grief, would not be able to bring himself to honor his dead wife's wishes. So one day, the October before Clare left, she'd gone to her childhood home in the late daylight hours when she knew her father would be in the fields. She hooked the urn under her arm and walked the path of sheared grass to the trees and then the creek. Clare remembers how badly her head hurt as she worked to unscrew the urn's lid, those early days of sobriety leaving her shaky. What she remembers most is the way her mother's ashes dropped from the urn as she overturned it, not in a wispy trail but in chunks that only dissipated into blackness when they hit the cold water of the creek.

In the far corner from Malcolm's family, Clare finds the next plot in her search.

JACK WESTMAN

AGED 62 YEARS

ALL THAT IS LOVED IS NOT LOST

Jack Westman. Murdered while celebrating his wife's birthday at a local restaurant. Next to his grave is that of his wife, Colleen, dead of heart failure a year later. Was it an act of marital defiance on the part of Zoe's mother, Clare wonders, to be buried in a separate plot adjacent to her husband? Clare crouches before Jack Westman's headstone and traces the words with the tip of her finger. Someone planted perennial flowers at the base of the graves, then left them to be choked by weeds.

Up the hill a stream of cars follows a hearse down the road. A woman walking alongside them wears a flowery sundress under a cardigan, not an outfit for a funeral. When Clare locks eyes with her, the woman cuts off the path. Clare wants to move on, to walk away, but her feet are bolted in place, sunken into the grass softened by last night's rain. On approach the woman lifts her hands and smiles to disarm Clare. Clare searches her face for something familiar. The woman is tall, her dark hair tied back in a tight ponytail. She walks straight to Clare.

"Are you Clare O'Kearney?" she asks.

A wave of dread overtakes Clare. "Yes. Did you follow me here?"

"Kind of. Yes, I did. I'm not trying to freak you out. I don't . . . I'm not a threat, I swear."

"Tell me who you are," Clare says.

"Kavita Spence." She bites at her fingernails. This woman is afraid. Anxious. "I was with Charlotte Westman at the house last night. When she confronted you. Well, I was up the road in the car. We followed you after to the Caledonian. I came back to the hotel early this morning and waited for you to come out. Charlotte doesn't know—"

"Why are you following me?"

"I'm sorry. I should have said something to you at the hotel. But I was too freaked-out. I was afraid you'd make a scene. Please. Can we talk? I just want to talk to you."

"After you tell me exactly who you are," Clare says.

Kavita points to the gravestone in front of Clare.

"I was working at the restaurant the night Jack Westman was shot."

A silence hangs between them for a moment as Clare absorbs this revelation. Some of the articles had mentioned the bystanders, the bartender and restaurant owner, Roland Song. Waitresses, hostesses, other patrons. But never by name.

"We can talk here," Clare says.

"Okay," Kavita says. "Okay. Sure."

"Where is Charlotte now?"

"She doesn't know I'm here," Kavita says. "I knew Zoe from school. She got me a job at Roland's restaurant. Charlotte and I, in the past few years, I can't really explain it. We've banded together, I guess. Misery-loves-company kind of thing. But I feel like she's losing it. And when she got back into the car yesterday she threw this at me." Kavita pauses and extracts Clare's crumpled business card from the pocket of her cardigan. "Made it seem like you were a problem we needed to deal with. But I kept thinking last night, What if you're not? What if you might actually be able to help us?"

Us? Clare thinks. This woman is so different in demeanor from Charlotte Westman, so unsure of herself. She wraps her cardigan tight and shivers despite the sun. Clare directs them to a nearby stone bench. They sit at the greatest distance from each other that they can muster.

"I'm here to find the truth about Malcolm Hayes," Clare says. "Zoe's husband. Do you know him?"

"I didn't know him well. I met him a few times. He was pretty quiet. Always seemed preoccupied. Or sad."

"Okay. And you were working the night of the shooting?"

"Yes," Kavita says. "Malcolm wasn't there."

"Can you tell me what happened?"

Kavita presses her hands into prayer and pins them between her knees, shoulders hunched.

"I was back in school doing my master's degree," she says. "I needed a few shifts a week somewhere to cover rent. This was maybe my fourth or fifth shift. I'd literally been working there for two weeks. I was standing maybe twenty feet away when he was shot. The shooter walked right past me on his way in and on his way out."

"Do you remember any details about him?"

"The police interviewed me for a few hours the night of the shooting. I've probably been interviewed another five times since. Every time they put a new cop on the case, they call me again. I tell them everything I remember."

"Which is what?"

Kavita grimaces, then shakes her head. "It's all really messed up, right? I had a therapist once who told me I'll never remember it exactly right. That's the nature of trauma, she says. You become this unreliable narrator in your own story. So that's the problem. The last cop? Germain? He accused me of changing my story. But I'm not changing anything. My brain has fucked it all up. It's changing the story for me."

Kavita speaks too quickly, her voice rising, so that the people gathered for the burial up the hill begin to turn in search of the commotion. Clare wants to reach out and touch her elbow, tell her to lower her voice. But she knows better. *The witnesses change their story every time you sit them down*, Germain said this morning. Maybe, Clare thinks now. But not all shifting stories are by design, Clare thinks as she watches Kavita. Sometimes memory does it for you.

"You say you think I can help," Clare says.

"Charlotte thinks you're a problem. But I feel like a set of fresh eyes can't be bad, right? Zoe's been gone for what, two years?"

"Eighteen months," Clare corrects.

"I just think there are answers out there. No one seems to care much anymore."

Austin's words from last night return to Clare, the exposé, the other women he claims have gone missing from Lune Bay too. *Not the kind of women who'd raise serious alarms with the police.* Clare's cursory search this morning brought her no leads. She thinks to ask Kavita about them now, but she appears so tightly wound, trembling, that Clare must parse the questions.

"Do you think Charlotte is worried about Zoe?" Clare asks.

"I don't know. She's lost in her own problems. If Zoe is dead, if she can prove that Zoe is dead, then I guess she inherits that stupid house. Charlotte is beyond feeling the pain. She's focused on herself."

"Okay," Clare says, soothing. "But you care. About the shooting going unsolved. About Zoe."

Kavita scratches hard at her arms. "Zoe didn't have much of a soul. She was trying to keep the family business afloat, making some pretty bad choices. Honestly, this isn't about her for me. The shooting fucked up my life. It took everything from me. I know what I saw. I just want the story to be straight. I want to go speak to Roland."

"You mean the restaurant owner? Roland Song?"

"Yes," Kavita says, biting again at her fingernails.

"Why?"

"I tried to talk to him once, a while ago. To sort out the truth, or the facts or whatever. Compare stories. He was there too. Behind the bar. I've tried to talk to Charlotte about it, but she's a steel trap. She won't say anything. She just tells me to drop it. I tried to talk to Zoe too before she disappeared. They were all just shut down. Or they'd contradict the way I remembered things. They'd say the shooter came in from the back, but I know that he walked right past me. I guess they just made me feel crazy. And Roland, he just brushes me off. And now it's been five years. People don't care anymore. They've moved on. But I just need some kind of closure. Even if it just means saying my piece. So I'm hoping you'll come with me. Maybe Roland will act differently if someone else is there." Kavita pauses and looks to the sky. "Like an intermediary or something. In case I get all turned around."

"Okay," Clare says, checking the time on her phone. "When?"

"Now?"

What a strange morning, Clare thinks, eyes back to the gravestones. This woman following her here, more a crumb dropped in her lap than a threat. Or perhaps, Clare wonders, some kind of decoy.

Kavita gestures to the graves. "I've come here before," she says. "I look at the stones and let the scene replay. And it does, like a dream. And I never know if I'm adding new details, making things up, or remembering. It's not like standing on top of this grave is going to clue me in to something I've missed along the way. Like the spirits are going to whisper their secrets. But whatever. What else can I do? The truth is impossible."

The truth. For a moment, they sit side by side on the bench, absorbed in their own thoughts. A scene comes back to Clare, a restaurant with Malcolm shortly after he'd offered her a second case to work. Clare sat groggy at the table as a waitress filled their coffees and brought them eggs. What she remembers most is feeling surprised by how chatty Malcolm seemed that morning. He was outlining the details of the next case. *If I've learned anything in this line of work*, he said, *it's that memory is the enemy of truth. People will remember the same moment in completely different ways. So you gamble on who to trust.*

"Can I ask you something?" Clare says. "Are you scared?"

"I am," Kavita says, a crack in her voice. "I can't stop being scared."

"Of what?"

For a moment Kavita says nothing, her eyes glassy. Then she inhales deeply, righting herself, wiping a finger under her lashes to gather any tears before they fall.

"I don't know," she says. "Everything."

"Are you afraid of the Westman family?"

"No. Not if Charlotte is all that's left of it."

All that's left of it. What Kavita might mean is that this fear hinges on whether Zoe is still alive.

"Okay," Clare says. "Okay. I'd like to help you. I can try to help you. I've got some time this morning. We can go to Roland's."

"That would be good. Yes. Thank you. That would be good."

Clare points Kavita up the hill to her rental car. She studies the young woman's gait from behind as they climb, Kavita's arms dull at her sides. Defeated. This is a detour. Clare had a plan for today, but every case has taught her that the detours often prove the most fruitful. All these Westman characters might seem secondary in Malcolm's story, but Clare isn't so sure. Something tells her that Jack Westman's death and its aftermath played a direct part in Malcolm's fate too. Whether he was a key player or collateral damage, Clare can only guess.

The map app on Clare's phone dings their arrival at Roland's Restaurant. She parks, Kavita silent beside her in the passenger seat. This is Lune Bay's oceanfront downtown, a stretch of colorful buildings of different heights and sizes, planters sprouting large trees. A perfectly designed and curated strip meant to feel quaint, the ocean a blast of blue behind it. Roland's is housed in a single-story brick building that backs directly onto the water. In her file on Malcolm there were several articles about this place. "Businessman Jack Westman Dead in Brazen Restaurant Shooting." In the years since, the restaurant's signage has been updated, but nothing else has changed.

"We have two options," Clare says. "We go in there as friends and strike up a chat. We don't tell Roland who I am.

I try to ask questions. We see how we can steer the conversation."

"He might not let us in," Kavita says flatly. "The restaurant isn't open for lunch. What's the other option?"

"That we tell him upfront why we're here. I give him my card and ask him questions."

"Will that work?"

"It might."

Kavita says nothing, her eyes fixed blankly ahead.

"Let's go with option two, then," Clare says. "I think a direct hit is our best bet."

Kavita exits the passenger side and circles the car to cross the street. Clare must dart to catch up. Kavita stands immobilized in the entranceway until Clare reaches around and tugs at the door to find it locked. CLOSED, the sign reads, a white menu with embossed calligraphy framed at eye level. Clare cups her face to the window to peer inside. An older man shuffles behind the bar, counting the bottles on the row of shelves behind him. Clare recognizes him from the restaurant's website. Roland Song, the owner. She knocks and makes an unlock gesture when he looks her way.

Can you let us in? she mouths to him.

The man dries his hands on a towel and comes to the door.

"We don't open until five," he says. "Brunch on weekends only."

"Mr. Song?" Clare asks, handing him a card. "I'm wondering if we can speak to you for a minute."

"About what?" he asks. He registers surprise when he catches a glimpse behind Clare. "Kavita?"

"We'd like to speak with you," Clare says.

"A PI?" he says, regrouping with a forced smile. "That's a

first. I've seen lots of cops and reporters, obviously. Last week
I had a novelist show up. He wanted me to reenact the scene
for him. You know, for inspiration. You ever get any of that,
Kavita?"

Kavita shakes her head, eyes down. Roland steps aside and
waves them in. Inside, the restaurant is small, tables for two
with white linens spaced at close distance. At the back Clare
spots the booth where the shooting happened, reupholstered
but otherwise unchanged from the crime scene photographs.
And behind that, a wall of glass overlooking the ocean glitter-
ing in the midday light. A patio door marked with a CLOSED
sign, the chairs and tables on the outside deck stacked in a
corner. Clare takes Kavita by the arm and leads her to a seat at
the bar. Roland's hair is gray, aging him at first glance. But up
close Clare guesses he might only be fifteen years older than
she is. Late forties.

"You look good, Kavita," he says. "It's nice to see you."

"Yeah. Thanks, Roland."

An awkward silence passes between them. Now that they
are sitting still, facing each other in broad daylight, Clare
notices the stains on Kavita's cardigan, the small moth holes
along its sleeves. Her hair looks unwashed, the beds of her
nails dirty. Clare can guess that Kavita did not look this way
when she worked here, that the years since have ravaged her.
Fucked up her life, as she said.

"You hungry?" Roland asks.

"I just ate," Clare says.

"My best cook's already clocked in. Lots of deliveries today.
Can I get him to whip you something up?"

"No," Kavita says.

Kavita appears to be trembling on the stool. She looks on
the verge of tears.

"Okay," Roland says. "You won't eat. And you show up here with a private investigator? Not sure what this is all about."

"Clare is working the case," Kavita says, shaky.

"Is that so?" Roland turns to Clare.

"Not directly," Clare says. "I'm looking for Malcolm Hayes. Zoe Westman's husband. Kavita and I crossed paths earlier today. I'm just doing some due diligence on his former connections. The Westmans were regulars here?"

Roland takes the cloth and begins wiping the counter again. "The definition of regulars."

"Can you expand on that?"

"They were in here twice a week for dinner, every week. Family dinner when the girls were younger. They liked the familiarity, the view. Jack Westman sold my father the land to start this place. The Westmans were part of the restaurant's inception forty years ago. I watched those girls grow up. Zoe and . . ." He snaps his finger. "My God. What's the sister's name?"

"Charlotte," Kavita says. "You know her name."

"Right. Charlotte. I'm an old man, forgive me. For some reason it escapes me to this day. Always did. It's terrible."

Kavita shoots Clare a sidelong glance. That's a lie, her look means to say.

"She wasn't quite as dynamic as her older sister," Roland continues. "Charlotte was the quieter one? She and Zoe's husband seemed to get along well, the Malcolm guy you're talking about. I remember that. They seemed tight. Not sure how Zoe felt about that."

It occurs to Clare that she should have her notebook, that she should be writing all this down. But it feels too forced, restricting the flow of conversation. She will have to log it all to memory instead.

"Was Malcolm here that night?" Clare asks.

"No," Roland answers. "It was just—"

"All I want," Kavita interjects, "is for you to tell us what you remember from that night. Tell us the story. It would help me a lot to see things from your perspective."

Roland straightens, glancing at Clare. "The story? What is this, Kavita? It was five years ago. And you were there."

"I know I was. But I feel like I don't remember it properly. There are these holes for me. All this crazy stuff that's happened since. You know? I've been in therapy for the past while because, well. Because things are difficult. My mind is screwing with me. I don't know. I don't want to say I have PTSD, it's not that serious. But I can't focus."

"Hey." Roland puts on a soothing tone and sets his hand on hers atop the bar. Clare notices Kavita's fist clench under his grip. "It was terrible, what happened. Terrible. But it's been a long time. You're young. You were so young. Let it go."

"I can't," Kavita says.

Clare watches this exchange, Kavita's anxiousness against Roland's shifting demeanor. She can't pinpoint the source of the insincerity between them.

"Please?" Kavita says.

Roland releases a long sigh. "What is there to say? It was a weeknight. What? A Tuesday, I think? Colleen's birthday, wasn't it?" He pauses, but Kavita says nothing, so he directs the story to Clare. "Colleen Westman, Jack's wife. Zoe and Charlotte's mother. See? Charlotte. I remembered. It was Colleen's birthday. Some milestone. Probably sixty. And the family was sitting in that booth, minding their own business. And I was here at the bar. And, Kavita, I remember you over at the hostess stand. At the computer. Maybe you were printing their bill, because I know Jack was eating tiramisu when it happened. I remember giving my statement and spelling that word for one of the cops. *T-I-R-A-M-I-S-U*. And the shooter came in through the patio door. I didn't even notice him until the gun was pulled. Frankly, I don't even know if I noticed him until after the first shot was fired. Then I ducked? By the time I stood up the shooter was gone and Jack Westman was dead. Slumped against his wife."

Both Clare and Roland watch Kavita, but she looks down at her worried hands, thinking. The patio door would offer easy access to the restaurant, Clare can see, especially at night. Now, beyond the patio, the ocean's color is a muted gray, the sun gone behind low and swirling clouds.

"What more do you want me to say?" Roland says after a minute.

"Do you remember what the shooter looked like?" Clare asks.

"No. It was a crazy blur. Wasn't it, Kavita? He had a hoodie on. Some people said glasses. I don't remember glasses. I remember a dark hoodie. Navy blue or black. He wasn't a big guy. Pretty compact frame."

On the barstool next to Clare, Kavita shifts back and forth, unsteady.

"How did he manage to get out?" Clare asks.

"People were frozen," Roland says. "Terrified. By the time my brain had registered what happened, he was gone. Some of the kitchen guys tried to chase him, but he was too fast. There are nooks and crannies around here. He probably had his getaway route well mapped out." Roland pauses, frowning. "I can't even count the number of times I've been interviewed by the police. Dozens. Hundreds. We all wanted them to catch the shooter. I closed this place down for a week so they could scour it. I've been an open book."

"You don't have security cameras?" Clare asks.

A cloud passes over Roland's face, the shift so instant that it sends a chill down Clare's spine.

"I do now," he says.

"Did you keep up with the Westmans after it happened?" Clare asks.

"Sure." Roland addresses Kavita. "You remember Colleen? Zoe's mom? Her daughters brought her back in for dinner a few times after the shooting. I guess some ill-advised attempt at normalcy, reclaiming the space, as the kids say these days. But in my all days I've never seen the life drained out of someone the way it was with Colleen Westman. She was catatonic. I never even heard her speak. Then her heart gave out. That's what happens when you let this kind of thing get to you. It burrows its way deep into your system, your gut, and some kind of rot sets in. You need to find a way to move on, Kavita. This could kill you if you're not careful."

There is something in his tone, a sharpness, words of warning. *This could kill you.* Kavita is flushed, her breaths short, as if on the verge of a panic attack. Roland must notice because he collects a glass and fills it to offer her water.

"I'd like to ask you about Malcolm Hayes," Clare says to Roland. "About Zoe's disappearance."

"I don't know anything about that. Like I said, he wasn't around much. After Colleen died, I only really kept up with Zoe. Tragic what happened there. I'll say that any guy who disappears after his wife does looks pretty guilty to me."

Clare nods. Next to her, Kavita has already drained the water, her breathing still too fast.

"Listen," Roland says. "Delivery trucks are going to start pulling up here. I need to get back to work."

"Yes." Clare points to her business card on the bar. "I appreciate your time. You can call me if you think of anything else."

Back outside, the temperature has dropped without the sun to warm them. Clare chases Kavita across the street, pressing the key button to unlock the car. They sit in silence in the tight space of the rental car, Clare waiting, gauging.

"Did that help?"

"No," Kavita says. "I know he came through the front door. Not the patio."

"That's a perspective thing," Clare says. "Eyewitness accounts are tough. You can both be right, or wrong."

Kavita says nothing. Clare turns the ignition and adjusts the vents to allow the heat to hit them both. She feels inundated, her brain struggling to compute everything that's unfolded. Just try to channel Somers, Clare thinks. Her quiet way, her calm.

"We could speak to Charlotte," Clare offers. "She was there too."

"Yeah," Kavita says, sarcastic. "She'd love that. More prodding."

"I want to help you."

"You've got your own agenda," Kavita says.

"I do," Clare says. "That doesn't mean we can't work together. Don't we want the same thing?"

The look Kavita shoots Clare is angry, toxic. In her pocket Clare feels her phone vibrate. She unlocks it to a text from Austin Lantz.

Found something for you. Meet at The Cabin in 20?

Clare sighs. *K,* she types.

"Where can I drop you?" she asks Kavita.

"Nowhere. I'll walk."

"You sure? You have my card—"

But Kavita has already exited the car. Clare watches her through the windshield as she crosses the street to head north, then stops, looks around, and turns to continue the other way. Even in a place as familiar to her as Lune Bay, Kavita seems lost.

I n the light of day The Cabin Bar feels less cozy, a thin coat of grime and dust on every surface. The room is empty but for one man on his laptop in the corner. Austin isn't here yet. Clare sits on the same stool as last night. This bartender is older, less friendly than his nighttime counterpart. He slaps a coaster and a menu in front of Clare without so much as a nod.

"I'll have a soda water," Clare says, pushing the menu away. "I'm waiting for someone."

Clare spins on her stool to study the room. She unlocks her phone to call up photographs from Malcolm and Zoe's engagement party. The space in the pictures is hardly recognizable from the one Clare sits in now, the mahogany of the bar gleaming then, the rows of bottles behind it lit up and shining. The article refers to The Cabin Bar as the city's "it" spot—a cozy space that mirrors Lune Bay's relaxed, seaside vibe.

It's been forty minutes since Austin texted her. He's late. The bartender sets her soda water down hard enough to spill some of its contents. As Clare takes her first sip the door opens and Austin enters, striding her way. He is dressed all in black, skinny in his fitted jeans, a leather shoulder bag and a newsboy cap rounding out the ensemble.

"Nice hat," Clare says. "Talk about on-brand."

Austin smiles, then yanks the hat from his head and drops it on the bar, lips pursed. The sort of man, Clare guesses, who cannot take the same jokes he doles out.

"Teetotaling?" Austin points to her drink.

"It's not even noon."

"It's summer."

"It's September," Clare says.

"I guess it is. Technically still summer by the sun."

Austin sets his leather satchel atop the bar and waves to the bartender, who ignores him so intently that Clare can only guess this routine: Austin the unwanted regular, the guy who orders one drink, then proceeds to overstay his welcome. He uses this place as an office, the affable bartender last night said. Finally the bartender pauses in front of him and Austin is able to order a beer. Clare stifles a laugh.

"I was thinking," Austin says, twisting on the barstool. "Maybe you need a tour guide. Someone to show you around Lune Bay."

"I'm not here to sightsee. You said you found something for me."

"Yeah." He rests his hand on the buckle of his bag. "There really is nothing out there on any Clare O'Kearney. I went on a deep dive last night. I pride myself on my research skills. And I've got nothing. Nothing."

"Is that why you texted me?"

"I'm hoping I can get you to drop a few more hints."

Of course Austin is trying to rattle her. In her time doing this work, Clare has learned to always assume that people are withholding, that they have secrets they're trying to keep from you. And Austin seems like a boy playing a part. If she cannot outwit even him, then Clare has no business doing this job. She runs a hand through her hair.

"I met with Detective Germain this morning," she says. "He told me something interesting. He said you once worked as Jack Westman's driver. I found that to be a pretty big omission from our chat last night."

"It's common knowledge," Austin says. "It's not an omission if it's a widely known fact."

"But you didn't tell me."

"I figured you would have done your homework," Austin says. "Gone down the Austin Lantz rabbit hole, if you will. It's all out there for the taking. And you contacted me, remember? So I'd wager you should already know my basic history."

Clare rests a finger on her lips. "Point taken. Anything else I might have missed in my homework?"

"I've got a rich brother. He's very generous with me."

"And yet you're too cheap to order more than one drink."

Austin laughs without a hint of humor.

"I'm back to my alias theory," he says. "Ms. O'Kearney."

"Listen," Clare says. "I think you and I can help each other. I really do."

"I'm all ears."

Clare leans closer. "I guess we've both been omitting a bit. What I didn't tell you last night is that I used to work for Malcolm Hayes. I knew him as Malcolm Boon. After he left Lune

Bay, he took up the cause of looking for missing women. And he hired me. That's how I got started in this work. Obviously I didn't know—"

"Jesus Christ." Austin slaps his hands together. "You're kidding, right? You have to be kidding me. Oh my God."

"I'm not kidding," Clare says, shifting impatiently on the stool.

"This is incredible."

With a flourish Austin opens his satchel and pulls out a silver laptop. He flips it open.

"You're not going to find anything searching for Malcolm Boon," Clare says. "He was good at managing his own alias."

Own alias. Austin catches that slip, eyeing Clare, smiling, his face aglow with the light of the monitor. The tapping at the keyboard makes Clare antsy. She sips her drink again and glances at the bar. A whiskey would dull these nerves, but no. No.

"Can we focus?" Clare asks. "I worked for Malcolm. And you worked for Jack Westman. So maybe, I was thinking. Maybe we could exchange questions. Like you suggested we do last night. Keep going. I go first."

"Fire away," Austin says, closing his laptop and raising his right hand. "The whole truth and nothing but the truth, so help me God."

"When did you work for Jack Westman?"

"Right before he died. I lasted a month."

"Why did you quit?"

"I was too busy with school. He needed someone at his beck and call." Austin narrows his eyes, scrutinizing her. "My question. When's your birthday?"

"I'm an Aries," Clare says. "That's all you get."

"What'd you do before this work?"

"I was a cleaner at a hospital."

"That's quite the career shift," Austin says.

"Just like going from limo driver to investigative journalist, I guess."

His beer arrives. Austin studies Clare with a twinge of longing in his gaze. He likes her. She will use that to any advantage she can.

"I think a lot about that job," Clare says. "The cleaner job. I did it for about five years. People talk about being a fly on the wall. In a hospital, doctors and nurses, orderlies, pastors, whatever, when they walk in the room, everything stops. Patients and their families. Everyone stops talking, stops crying. But if a cleaner comes in, it's like you're not even there. I remember once entering a room to empty the garbage can, and a husband was sitting at the foot of his wife's bed. And he was saying sorry to her in a way that made it clear he was the reason she was in the hospital. 'I'll do better,' he was saying. And I was right there, and he just kept talking. A few hours later I was called into the same room to clean up a spill. But this time, the doctor was there. And it was a whole different picture. The husband all doting, making mention of some accident that clearly didn't happen, nodding at everything the doctor said. And the doctor spoke to the husband and not the wife, like the husband was the patient. I remember making eye contact with the wife as the husband was talking. The look she gave me, I swear. I've thought about that look so many times since."

"Why?" Austin asks.

"Because she knew I'd heard the real story. And her face was blank, but at the same time I could read it exactly. Like her actual expression was written in invisible ink. The sadness, the energy it took to play along."

Instantly Clare sees it, the shift in his expression, a flicker of understanding.

"Sounds like you could relate," he says.

"I think we all can," Clare says, sipping her soda, regrouping. "My turn. Tell me about the Westman business."

"Oh man. I could write a book. I *will* write a book."

"I'll take the crib notes for now. The missing women. Your exposé. 'Connections people haven't made before,' as I believe you said yesterday."

"Wouldn't be much of an exposé if I spilled it all to you, would it?"

"Come on," Clare says, smiling. "Just a crumb."

"The biggest crumb is Donovan Hughes. Jack Westman's business partner."

"I've read about him. He's in jail."

"Yeah. He went down for racketeering and tax fraud about a year after the murder. The prosecution tried to tie the money stuff to the murder, make the jury think that Jack Westman was dead because of the shit they were pulling. There was no direct evidence, but it's not a stretch—"

"Have you ever gone to the prison?" Clare asks.

"Hell, yes. It's a nice drive. It's a regular field trip for me. Donovan's funny. He's like a scholar now, all-serious. He'll sit across from me for the entire visit and say next to nothing. He once told me he's been reading up on law books. Trying to support his appeal. I think he only agrees to see me because he likes a break in the monotony. Not sure he gets many visitors. But he's certainly not answering any of my questions."

"Maybe he just doesn't like you."

This time Austin doesn't laugh at all. He cocks his head at Clare.

"How did you meet Malcolm?" he asks. "How exactly did this little working relationship begin?"

"He hired me."

"But why *you*? I'm guessing he didn't put an ad in the local paper."

Clare can only shake her head. She must give him credit for his astuteness.

"You never sent me that link," Clare says. "The one about the missing women. The niche blog, I think you called it."

"Right," he says, opening his laptop again. "I'll send it right now. Should I use the email on your card?"

"Yes, please."

"Done." Austin drains the last of his beer and looks at her. "Hey, want to hear something crazy? I looked up Detective Somers. I *knew* her name sounded familiar. I knew it. And guess what? She was the detective assigned to one of the missing women cases. Stacey Norton. I guess the last Stacey Norton sighting was in Somers's jurisdiction. Case has been open for about two years. Pretty much gone cold by now. But you probably knew that. Right?"

A knot of bile rises in Clare's throat. Austin's eyes are trained on her. She flashes a smile before pulling her phone from her pocket and lifting the screen to fake an incoming call.

"I've really got to take this," she says.

Austin appears unconvinced. "Sure."

"Hello?" Clare says, standing and walking to the door of the bar.

Once outside, she unlocks the screen and punches in Somers's number. Somers answers on the first ring.

"Clare," she says. "Everything okay?"

"What haven't you told me?" Clare asks.

"What do you mean?"

83

Clare turns around to face the bar's door. The street traffic is loud. She must adjust the volume on her phone and press a finger to her ear to hear Somers clearly.

"You've got some missing woman case tied to the West-mans?"

"So?" Somers says. "I've got cases tied to every corner of the country."

"But you never told me that. You lied to me."

There is a long silence, Clare certain she can hear Somers's deep breaths.

"I wasn't lying," Somers says. "I didn't want to distract you. It's not really relevant."

"Yes, it fucking is," Clare hisses.

"Clare—"

Before she can think better of it, Clare swipes to end the call. Every muscle in her body is tight with rage. It will take her a few moments to gather herself so that she might go back into the bar and address Austin again.

I t is early afternoon. Clare sits on the hotel room bed encircled by papers and photographs from her Malcolm file, the articles she printed in the hotel business center after arriving back here, anything on Donovan Hughes she could find. The article Austin emailed her that mentions the two women ostensibly vanished from Lune Bay. She didn't speak to Austin again after her call with Somers ended. When she'd retreated back inside, Austin had been on the phone too, hovering in a dark corner of the bar, his voice too low for Clare to listen in. She'd paid for their drinks and left without a formal goodbye, texting him only once she was back in her rental car to let him know she'd be in touch soon.

Clare spreads the contents of the file out across the bed, forming a timeline. She places today's date at the end, working backwards until she reaches the date almost a year and a half ago when Zoe disappeared, then the date five years ago when

Jack Westman was shot at Roland's. The key to this story, Clare thinks, is in the gaps, the blank spots in the timeline where the secrets surely lie. First, Malcolm. Gone ten days after Zoe was last seen. But what happened in the three years between Jack Westman's death and Zoe's disappearance? Clare looks through the folder for articles related to that stretch. "Lune Bay Business Park Deal Sours as City Denies Permit to Westman Corp." Bribe investigations implicating developers, city staff, construction companies. The Donovan Hughes trial and conviction for tax fraud.

And then Clare must create space on the timeline for the missing women. Stacey Norton was last seen two years ago. Kendall Bentley, another woman who was last seen in Lune Bay only three months before Stacey disappeared. Austin's article contains an interview with Douglas Bentley, Kendall's father. Clare studies the photograph provided of Kendall. She is young, tall and slim, beautiful. A premed student living at home. The police theory is that Kendall left town with her convict boyfriend when a warrant was issued for his arrest, her father painted as a man unhinged by far-fetched theories. And Stacey was an opioid addict. The police, Austin writes, have no other theory or leads but that. His article mentions that the two women may have crossed paths working summer jobs at a local seafood restaurant: Roland's.

Clare snatches her phone from the bedside table and texts Austin.

Can you send me Douglas Bentley's contact info?

A quick response comes.

What do I get in exchange?

How about I don't spoil your exposé?

He sends a side-eye emoji before sharing the contact information. Clare lies back on the bed and scrolls through the photographs on her phone until she arrives at the one taken yesterday at Malcolm and Zoe's glass house. The family portrait of the Westmans on the beach. The togetherness, the smiles on all but Zoe and Malcolm. But on second glance what strikes Clare the most in this picture is Charlotte, the way her head is angled towards her brother-in-law, the proximity at which they stand.

They seemed tight, Roland had said about Charlotte and Malcolm.

"Where are you?" Clare asks the Malcolm in the photograph.

Driving back to the hotel from The Cabin Bar, Clare had been met with an urge to turn the car around, to point it inland, to disappear herself. She felt rage at Somers, at herself for agreeing to come here. As she stares at the photograph, at this young and brooding depiction of Malcolm, she feels it again, the compulsion. This is about Malcolm. Whatever he became to Clare in those months she worked with him, Clare wants to know his story. She wants to know what happened here. She will work this case until she does. She collects her phone again and presses in Somers's number.

"You hung up on me," Somers says as a greeting.

"You lied to me."

"I didn't. Honestly. You were planning to work this case anyway. Your case is about Malcolm. Yes, I was assigned a case of a woman who went missing from Lune Bay. It landed on my desk because she was last spotted around here. I got it because no one else wanted it. Missing women aren't always a huge priority." Somers clears her throat. "You of all people know that. Anyway, she had some ties to the Westman family. But Lune Bay is a small place from what I could tell. Most people there have some ties to the Westmans."

"Have you ever come to Lune Bay?"

"No. I worked the case from here. I had a detective there as a liaison. A useless one, at that."

"It feels too convenient. It feels like you lied to me."

"Listen," Somers says. "I work hundreds of cases a year. I never got anywhere with this one. I fucking hate the way cops toss out missing women cases. It grinds at me. Eats away at me. I hate that I couldn't figure out what happened to her."

Somers pauses, but Clare says nothing.

"Then you show up with this Malcolm guy, and hey, he was married to a Westman. And you tell me that you need to find him. That's exactly what you said to me, Clare. So I throw some resources behind you, figuring if we're lucky, if I'm lucky, you might dig something up that's relevant to the Stacey Norton case. I know how good you are at this work. I don't have a lot of resources, let me tell you—"

"You put me at risk," Clare says. "When you withhold. When you don't tell me what I need to know, you put me at risk."

"I get why you feel that way," Somers says. "But the Norton case is peripheral. I wasn't withholding. And I couldn't be sure how objective you were."

"What's that supposed to mean?"

Somers sighs in the receiver, choosing her words. "My instinct is that you had feelings for Malcolm. That's why you wanted to find him. Feelings mess with our objectivity, Clare. I wanted to give you a shot, but I wasn't willing to risk the integrity of the Norton case. I didn't want you asking questions on my behalf—"

"Fuck you," Clare says. "Do you really think so little of me?"

"Listen to me, Clare." Somers's voice is a low, angry rumble. "This is not about what I *think* of you. This is about police work, about your work as an investigator. Do you know how many times I've watched cops soil cases because of their own bias? Like I said, my hunch is that things between you and Malcolm are murky. And that solving this case isn't just about testing your mettle. You want him off the hook. So yes, I protected myself from that bias."

Clare can feel the well rise from her chest. Anger, frustration. She cannot bring herself to admit that Somers may be right. She knows she arrived here hoping she might find Malcolm absolved. But now, Clare only wants the truth. She needs to prove she can do this work objectively, thoroughly, professionally. She needs to prove it to Somers, prove it to herself.

"You still there?" Somers asks.

"Yes."

"Listen," Somers says. "I think the Westman story goes way back. My mother used to say that our fate is laid out for us a century before we're born. People might rob a corner store on a whim, or stab someone in a fight, but this stuff? Murder, people vanishing, shady business? This stuff goes further back than any of us can see. A lot of people are tangled up in this web, right? Stacey might have been one of them. I didn't want your bias, I'll admit that. But I also hoped you'd bring some fresh eyes. I didn't want to taint you with my cynical cop shit."

Clare shifts the papers around on the bed. She will make Somers wait for a response. Her gaze lifts to the minibar in the corner of the room. She thinks of the heat down her throat, the warm coating of one of those small bottles. Just one. No, she tells herself. No.

"I need you to do something for me," Clare says.

"Okay," Somers says, suspicious.

"I want to go visit Donovan Hughes in prison. The Roy Mason Correctional Facility, it's called."

"I know it well," Somers says.

"Donovan Hughes was Jack Westman's business partner. Visiting hours end at five, but I've got a stop to make en route and I might be a little late. Can you call ahead?"

"You want me to ask them to roll out the red carpet?"

"I'm sure you'll think of some excuse," Clare says.

Somers laughs. "I guess I will. And hey, I might have something else for you. Something came across my desk earlier today. Can I email it to you?"

"Sure," Clare says.

"Hang on. Sending."

Through the receiver Clare can hear the pressing of buttons, the whoosh of a file being sent. She clicks on her phone to summon the message through. The email arrives and Clare opens the attachment. It is a handwritten note.

Tell C this is where to find me. There is an email address written down too.

"You think that's for me?" Clare asks.

"It could be for someone else whose name starts with C. I've got a few dumb-looking beat cops around here named Clark or Cal. But my gut—and I like to think my gut is pretty smart—it tells me that it's Malcolm reaching out to you. What do you think? Could it be?"

"Maybe," Clare says. "Why not just write my name, though?"

"Has this guy ever made any sense to you?" Somers asks.

"No," Clare answers. "Not really."

"Okay, so. Here's the part where I give you a cop speech. Maybe it's my conscience talking here. You can do whatever you want, and I'm going to shred this piece of paper, and I'm not going to ask you any questions, but you know there's a warrant out for his arrest, right? What side is he on? I want you to remember that he could be dangerous. That makes me really antsy, especially after all this talk about your objectivity. Corresponding with him isn't the best move on your part."

Clare remains silent.

"Wait. You haven't already heard from him, have you?"

It galls Clare to be asked. "No," she says forcefully. "No, Somers. I have not."

"Okay," Somers says. "Sorry. But if you hear from him, you need to go straight to the German guy."

Despite her ire, Clare smiles. "You mean Germain."

"Ha. Germain. Okay, listen. I've got a meeting. You call me anytime, okay? I want you to know that you can. Anytime. No more secrets. Okay?"

"Okay," Clare says.

After she hangs up Clare reads the note over and over again. Has she ever seen Malcolm's handwriting? Jason wouldn't be capable of penmanship so neat. Clare opens a new message on her phone and carefully types in the address from the attachment, the tag a random stream of letters and numbers, nothing to indicate it belongs to Malcolm. This could all be a trick; Jason could be behind it. Nonetheless, she writes.

It's Clare. I was told this was your email address.

She presses send, then clutches her phone and lies back on the bed. Clare closes her eyes and counts her breath. Ten minutes must pass before she feels the phone buzz in her hands.

The incoming email has no sender name, but it is from the address Somers gave her.

Clare,

I'm glad you wrote. Before anything else, I want to say that I'm sorry. It was never my intention to drag you into this or to leave you without a valid explanation. I know where you are. I know you've been digging. I implore you to stop. It could be very dangerous for both of us. Please trust that I can handle this myself. You are good at this work and could continue to do it in whatever capacity you want. Just please, do not search for Zoe or for me. It's not safe and I'm not sure I could bear to see you hurt on my behalf.

You remain on my mind, Clare. I regret how things were left between us.

M

The effort to read the email again, then again, wraps Clare in a wave of nausea. She cannot decrypt her reaction, whether his words have made her angry or sad, or relieved. The formality of his message concerns her. The repetition of her name. Malcolm often repeated her name when they spoke in person too. Clare. She can almost hear him saying it. Another reaction bubbles inside her, deep in her gut. The longing. She lifts the phone and hits reply.

I am not going to stop digging. And don't tell me you're sorry. That word means nothing.

Clare hovers her thumb over the delete button for a moment before continuing to type.

I'm still here, Malcolm. You know where to find me.

C

This time Clare hits send and watches the line edge across the screen as the note leaves her out-box.

T his house on the water is at Lune Bay's south end. Before Clare can lift her hand to knock, a man yanks the door open a crack and peers through at her.

"Fuck off," he says.

"Mr. Bentley." Clare presses the toe of her shoe to the door to prevent him from closing it. "I'm not a reporter."

The man lowers his glasses and squints at the business card Clare offers him.

"I'm working a case that might be related to your daughter, Kendall."

At this mention his shoulders drop, an instant grief response.

"I've been reading about you," Clare continues. "Douglas Bentley. Retired from the army. Decorated. I know your wife died of an aneurysm last year. I know you've been advocating for more resources to be put towards your daughter's case, lobbying the mayor, anyone who will listen. You've been disappointed in the work done by the police. I'm hoping I can help."

"You're too young to be a PI," he says.

"Maybe," Clare replies. "But my track record is pretty spotless. I'm good at what I do."

It still feels disingenuous for Clare to say such a thing. *I'm good at what I do*. A long moment passes, Bentley breathing in and out through his nose, considering. Finally he closes the door to unlatch the chain, then opens it to let Clare in. The inside of his bungalow is not at all what Clare would have expected, the walls warm neutrals, the furniture plush and modern, the space clean and uncluttered. Clare removes her shoes and follows him to the kitchen. It too is gleaming, the entire back wall a giant picture window with a view to the ocean. Clare rests her fingertips on the glass and stares out at the vastness, the blinding blue of it.

"This is some view," she says. "Incredible."

"My wife was an architect. She convinced me to buy this lot in the downturn. Designed the house herself."

"Wow." Clare's gaze is still fixed on the water. "She was good at what she did."

"She loved the ocean. So did Kendall." Douglas coughs. "Do you work alone?"

"Mostly."

"What case are you working?" he asks.

"I'm actually searching for Malcolm Hayes. Do you know him?"

"I know who he is," Douglas says. "How'd you get my address?"

"From Austin Lantz."

"That dumb little fuck. I hate that little twerp, I swear."

"He does seem quite singularly focused," Clare says. "I feel like there's been a failure on his part to read the facts right. His story doesn't paint you in the most favorable light."

"You think? He makes me out to be a fucking nutjob."

"Well," Clare says. "Maybe it's better to be underestimated."

"By whom? No one will talk to me. They won't even let me inside the police detachment anymore."

Clare takes a seat at the breakfast bar. Douglas paces the length of the counter, arms crossed, casting her only the odd sidelong glance. He has the look of a man torn apart by worry, by grief, his clothes baggy on a too-thin frame, his hair a shock of white against the black rims of his glasses. He holds his face in a deep-set frown.

"You do have theories, though," Clare says. "About what happened to your daughter."

"I've got suspicions. And anytime I bring them up, I seem to be pushing the wrong buttons."

"What do you mean by that?"

Douglas yanks at a stool and takes a seat across the counter from Clare. He lifts a saltshaker and fiddles with it, turning it over in his hands, studying it to avoid eye contact.

"That label?" he says. "Conspiracy theorist? I wear it proudly, if you want the truth. My grandfather knew the first guy to push the theory that smoking causes cancer. He was a scientist in this tiny little lab going up against big corporations. He was treated like a pariah. Lost everything. But he knew he was right. And he *was* right, wasn't he?"

Clare props her elbow on the counter and rests her chin in her hand, attentive. She knows not to interrupt Douglas, that letting him speak unencumbered will help him circle closer to the bull's-eye.

"I was in the army. You know that, you read that. I was decorated. Ha. I went overseas five times. I always figured I'd be the one to die and leave my family behind. We considered that carefully, my wife and I. That's why we had one kid. When you're posted in the middle of some faraway desert, every single morning you open your eyes and you say this little prayer. You just want to stay alive. And you do. And you make it home and you seem okay. A few nightmares here and there but no real problems. Got myself a good desk job at the local recruitment office to ride it out." He angles back to the window. "Then you retire. All is well. Then your kid goes missing. Then your wife dies. So what's that expression? I've had a lot of worries in my life, most of which never happened? The bad stuff always blindsides you."

"It does," Clare says. "You're right."

With a sigh Douglas opens a drawer and places a photograph in front of Clare. It's his daughter, Kendall, at her college graduation, flanked by two beaming parents. As she studies the photo, Douglas tells Clare the story. His daughter, Kendall Bentley, didn't come home one night. Her phone was off, texts not going through. They filed a report, but it only hit the news once Douglas convinced a beat reporter to write a piece that was printed in the back pages of the Lune Bay newspaper. And the police? They labeled her a runaway, a young woman under too much pressure at medical school, with addiction issues, a boyfriend in all kinds of trouble with the law. You're not missing if you've left on your own terms, a Lune Bay police officer is quoted as saying in one of the news stories. Clare lifts the picture. Kendall looks the perfect hybrid of her parents, tall like her father, the same soft and pretty face as her mother.

"And you think she was kidnapped?" Clare asks. "Taken against her will?"

"She wouldn't just leave. Do you know anyone who would just leave their family out of nowhere?"

At this Clare feels a stab. *Yes,* she wants to say. If you have no choice, you will leave everything behind, everyone. For a moment they both look out the window, each quieted by their own sadness.

"I never fit in here," Douglas says. "Last spring I showed up to the Veterans Day parade. You know how many of us were marching? Four. People who fight in real wars don't move to Lune Bay. This place is about money."

"Why did you move here, then?" Clare asks.

"Because my wife was born here. I was gone most of the time. So where we raised our daughter was her call."

"I can help you," Clare says. "We can help each other. Can't we? I feel like it might all be connected, right? You obviously believe there's something bigger at play too."

Without answering her, Douglas stands and leaves the kitchen. He gestures for Clare to follow him. Next to the hall closet is a pocket door blended almost seamlessly into the wall. Douglas opens it and hits the light. They descend to a lower apartment, a nanny flat overtaken by rubber bins neatly stacked and labeled with dates. The space that would be the living room is instead set up as an office, a desk at its center with a computer and color-coded files, the largest wall a corkboard adorned with a labyrinth of photographs. Some faces Clare recognizes at once. Kendall Bentley is at the center, a web woven out from there. Clare sees Jack Westman. Zoe, and as an extension of her, Malcolm. Stacey Norton too, the other missing woman, a line drawn from her to Kendall.

"Jesus," Clare says. "Has Austin been down here?"

"Are you kidding me? So he can write a story about how

I'm unhinged? Some crazy dad with a perp wall taking his cues from bad cop shows."

"Right," Clare says.

"We built this flat for Kendall. She moved down here from her bedroom upstairs and six months later she disappeared. So." Douglas removes his glasses and rubs hard at his eyes "I've taken over the space, as you can see."

For a long time, Clare sidesteps along the length of the wall, studying the photographs, the connections Douglas has drawn.

"Who are all these people?"

"Most of them are Kendall's friends. Some from high school, college. Beefs she had. Guys she dated. Dead-end leads."

"I see Stacey Norton."

"Yeah. They worked together for a summer. Maybe two."

"At Roland's?"

"Yeah," Douglas says. "It seems like it should mean something, but Roland is one of the only guys in town who hires students. Most kids have worked there at one time or another."

Clare points to the line linking Kendall to Zoe Westman.

"The Westmans figure pretty prominently. What connects these two?"

"They met at a fund-raiser. Kendall was helping out with the catering. Zoe took an interest in her."

"What do you mean by *interest*?"

"She offered her some side gigs. Bartending at little private events Zoe would throw. Kendall would leave the house in these white dress shirts with a tie, and these tiny fucking miniskirts. Serving cocktails to the biggest assholes Lune Bay has to offer."

"It's pretty clear how you felt about that."

"What am I going to say? I'm just her overprotective father."

"Right," Clare says. "When was this?"

"In the months before she disappeared."

"What were these parties she was working?" Clare asks.

"Cripes," Douglas says, arms crossed. "I think it's pretty common knowledge that Lune Bay was built on handshakes and backroom promises. When the tech boom hit and this area became hot, I think a lot of pockets got lined. It was a different place when my wife was growing up here. More like a small town. Some fishermen around. Some industry. Now it's a suburb for rich people. The kind of rich people who went to Zoe Westman's parties. And my theory is that Kendall got wrapped in something she didn't fully understand. Maybe she overhead something or witnessed something . . . I don't know. Maybe I am a conspiracy theorist, but I feel like this stretches further than Lune Bay's borders. All I know is that my daughter met Zoe Westman and a few months later she was fucking gone."

"Was Malcolm part of this too?"

"Well." Douglas rubs at his chin. "He was married to Zoe. He must have known there was shady stuff going on. I went to him once. Shortly after Kendall disappeared. Tried to appeal to him."

"What did he say?"

"Not much," Douglas says. "He listened to me. Heard me out. Then he told me he couldn't help. Just like everyone else."

Clare keeps her back to Douglas. She recognizes the photograph of Malcolm on this wall. It was taken by a reporter as he left the police station after Zoe's disappearance. She weighs her options. Surely Douglas could be useful to her, might help her cut corners in her efforts. She can build some goodwill with the truth. And so she turns to face Douglas, outlining the basics of her history with Malcolm. He sits back against the desk and listens, his expression never flickering from steady focus.

"Anyway," Clare says, "I'm here. I'm listening. I know you haven't had much help, but I hope to change that. What I can tell you is that in some indirect way, my story is linked to Kendall's. I wish I knew more. I wish I could tell you more. Right now I can't. But I think we can help each other."

"Maybe," he says. "I'm not exactly sure how."

"No one has *me* labeled a conspiracy theorist. There's that. I can dig where you can't."

Douglas offers a small laugh. "Well. Where do we start?"

"Why don't you tell me about Kendall? What was she like?"

"Yeah," he says. "She finished college six years ago. She was only twenty-one. Skipped a few grades along the way. She started medical school way too young. We probably should have encouraged her to take some time off. It was too much for a kid. She dabbled in a bit of modeling. Worked at Roland's in the summers, did some catering. She loved it. She was happier slinging appetizers than she was in medical school. We told her she didn't have to work, but she wanted to. We even told her she could take a leave from school."

His voice cracks. He rubs at his eyes.

"I swear everything took a turn after she met Zoe Westman. She started hanging out with Zoe and her people. These cars would come pick her up. I'd hear her coming home at all hours, even after her classes had started up again. Once, I spotted her in the society page of the Lune Bay paper at some fancy party. I didn't even recognize my own kid in that photo. The whole thing worried me. At one point I even considered installing a hidden camera down here. You know? I figured I'd just spy on her. My wife put a hard stop to that. She said

Kendall was just blowing off steam after a few tough years at medical school. But I didn't like that I couldn't keep track of the comings and goings from my own house. Kendall was technically an adult, but she could be so naive."

Clare's phone buzzes in her pocket. She extracts it to check the message.

It's Charlotte Westman. I need to talk to you.

Clare writes,

Tell me when and where.

Her response comes.

8 pm Pebble Beach

Clare types a response then slides her phone back in her pocket. She turns to the wall of information in front of her. The photographs are all laminated, the lines between them perfectly straight. Douglas Bentley is fastidious, a man who takes great care in his efforts.

"I'm sorry, but I have to go," Clare says. "I need to be somewhere and my timing is tight. Can we connect again tomorrow?"

He sighs, looking suddenly exhausted. "You won't be back."

"Of course I will be. If you'll have me, I mean. We can help each other, can't we? I know we can."

"Right," he says, heading back to the stairway. "Sure."

What petulance, Clare thinks. But at once she softens. This

man, accustomed to working on his own, to being dismissed by the authorities. He is searching for his daughter, grieving his wife. All he wants is to be heard. All Clare wants is to be given the benefit of the doubt. The least she can do is offer Douglas Bentley the same.

C lare stands inside the gate of the Roy Mason Correctional Facility. Beyond her, two tall fences snared with barbed wire stretch between the parking lot and the prison yard. A group of men in jumpsuits hover at the far end of the yard. Though they are at quite a distance, Clare is certain they are watching her, that even with these fences between them she is still plainly in their sights. Only thirty minutes inland from Lune Bay, but this might as well be another planet. *It's a regular field trip for me*, Austin said of his frequent trips here to see Jack Westman's business partner, Donovan Hughes.

Somers must have called ahead, because Clare is waved through despite visiting hours being almost over. In the prison's stark reception area Clare must surrender her bag and empty her pockets, the gun left in the car's glove compartment. She drops everything into a bin, then slides it through a trapdoor in the plexiglass that separates her from the guard. The woman who pats Clare down is humorless and makes no eye contact. Clare follows a male officer as he advances them through three sets of heavy doors, each one buzzing sharply as it opens. When they reach the waiting room, the guard gestures for Clare to take a seat at a table in the center of the room.

"Hughes?"

"Yes," Clare says. "Donovan Hughes."

Clare sits at the tip of the chair, her hands in a tight ball on her lap. After a few minutes the guard returns. The man trailing him wears a beige work shirt and jeans. Donovan Hughes is not much changed from the photographs taken before he was arrested. He may be thinner, his hair grayer, but he stands tall and stoic. He lowers himself to a seat across from Clare slowly to account for the shackles on his ankles and wrists.

"Only my lawyer visits these days," Donovan Hughes says. "Even my wife has stopped coming."

He is soft-spoken in a way Clare was not anticipating. He smiles at her, expectant.

"Mr. Hughes," Clare says. "My name is Clare O'Kearney. I'm a private investigator. I'd offer you a card, but I wasn't allowed to bring anything to this part of the facility. I've been working on a case related to the disappearance of Zoe Westman."

"You don't say." He grins. "Clare. Call me Donovan. Or Don. Whichever you prefer."

"I appreciate your willingness to see me."

Donovan laughs. "Please don't take this the wrong way, but I imagine a rat could come through those doors, literally vermin, and I'd come out here for the visit. Anything for a break in the day." He pauses, scrutinizing her. "You look a lot like Zoe."

"I've been told that before," she says.

"Really. You could be her twin."

"I've never met her. My focus is actually on Malcolm. Zoe's husband. I'm sure you know him."

Donovan looks to the guard in the corner and shrugs at him, as if he were part of their conversation too.

"I knew him."

"Past tense?" Clare asks.

"Well, he's gone, isn't he?"

"Yes," Clare says. "Gone. But not necessarily dead."

"Honestly? I never thought much of him. But I understand why Zoe married him."

"Why'd she marry him?" Clare asks.

Donovan pinches his thumb to his finger and rubs them together in a gesture. Money. Clare knows that Malcolm's parents were rich, that he was the beneficiary of a vast inheritance once he came of age. She leans forward.

"From what I can glean," Clare says, "you and Zoe were quite close. You worked together after her father died. Before you got arrested. She was like a daughter to you, maybe. I know she was trying to keep the business afloat."

"A daughter," Donovan says. "No. She was most definitely *not* like a daughter to me."

He is well-spoken, articulate, and poised, despite the uniform and the setting. Clare notices the guard's eyes upon her. There isn't much time, and she needs to make headway. She will backtrack with Donovan. Find his beginning.

"I've read a bit about your family," Clare says. "Your mother. Lune Bay was her life."

Donovan nods. "She used to say it was called Lune Bay because of the moon. On a clear night it would bounce off the ocean and light up the sky like a muted sun. My mother and Jack Westman's mother were best friends. They moved down the coast together after high school. Got work as secretaries. And by sheer luck, they both married rich." He leans back in his chair. "Both had firstborn sons. Are you following?"

"Yes," Clare says. "You and Jack Westman."

"Exactly. When a downturn hit, our families bought up as much land around here as we could. I hated Jack Westman. God, did I ever. I was bookish. He was a jock and a bully. But we were forced together, and really, it worked out quite well. Our sensibilities around what Lune Bay should be were well aligned. We wanted it to feel both remote and well appointed. Like a village. A close-knit community with all the amenities but none of the crowding. The development needed to be managed, distilled. I think we did very well. Lune Bay grew to be quite the destination. People wanted to live here. If you were brave you could even commute into the bigger cities. Jack and I were good at listening to each other. Certainly after he died, Zoe and I had different visions. My vision died when I was arrested. And while I was winding my way through the courts, she drove the real estate business into the ground. Had her eye on other ventures."

"So maybe you weren't heartbroken when she disappeared," Clare suggests.

"No." Donovan offers Clare a surprisingly jovial smile. "I wasn't."

"What was she doing to drive the business into the ground?"

Donovan pulls his wrists apart until the shackles grow taut. "It's probably better to keep my mouth closed on that," he says. "I'm awaiting an appeal. But tell me, how do you know Malcolm?"

"I'm looking for him. That's all. It's my job."

"Right. But you use his first name only. Malcolm. You didn't say Hayes. You just said Malcolm. You know him."

Donovan's gaze is so direct that Clare feels herself withering under it. This room is hot, the lights buzzing and bright.

"You're right," Clare says. "I do know him. After he left Lune Bay, Malcolm Hayes took up looking for missing women. He was . . . an investigator of sorts. We met, and I started working with him. I won't get into the details beyond that. But I'm charged with looking for him now. I used his first name because I figured you know him."

"I like that you're telling me the truth," Donovan says.

"I've got nothing to hide," Clare says, crossing her arms.

"Do you believe that Malcolm is guilty of murdering his wife?" Donovan asks.

"I don't believe anything yet," Clare says. "I'm just trying to do my job. Speaking to you is part of that."

"I was at Zoe and Malcolm's wedding, you know."

"I'm sure it was quite the event in Lune Bay."

"Oh, it was. I was a guest of honor at Zoe's parents' table. It was a picture book affair. At a winery with views halfway to Japan. Zoe's dress was magnificent. And there was a good feeling in the room. But I found myself spending the whole night watching Malcolm. He was a fascinating case study."

"Why?"

"He *never* smiled. I like to think I'm good at reading people. And I remember wondering to myself: Is this man a sociopath? And then Charlotte caught my eye. Dear Charlotte. I always loved her. What a sweetheart she was. And funny, she was watching Malcolm too. Charlotte seemed onto him as well."

"Onto what?" Clare asks. "Be more specific."

"I spend a lot of time thinking these days. I interact with people I never would have crossed paths with on the outside.

The same men I'd read about in the papers. And they aren't bad. Not all of them, anyway. Maybe some of us here at the Roy Mason are good men who did bad things in the name of someone we love. Maybe some of us were framed, or wrongly convicted. Put in here for things we didn't do. Who decides between bad and good? What's that saying? History is written by the victors?"

"You're losing me," Clare says.

"Malcolm?" he says. "He's not one of the good guys. I don't think he was capable of feeling any real emotion."

A long stretch of silence passes between them. Clare draws a deep breath. She would like to think she has the same ability to detect good from bad, but her history, her experiences with men and even with this line of work, tells her that she's got a long way to go yet. It's too hard to know who means well and who doesn't. Of course, she knows that Donovan may be trying to throw her off. She will not allow it.

"I don't know what you did, Mr. Hughes. I know nothing about you. But a lot of terrible things have happened in Lune Bay in the past five years. Your partner's murder, his daughter's disappearance. Other women missing too. Women with ties to the Westmans. Maybe you didn't kill anyone, but I imagine you're not innocent."

Donovan smiles. "No one is."

"Time's up," the guard says.

"Can we have five more minutes?" Clare pleads with the guard, her hands in prayer position. "Please?"

"You're lucky to be here at all," the guard says. "My shift ended ten minutes ago. You're done."

"I'd like to come back," Clare says, standing. "I'll have more questions. If you'll see me again."

"Anytime," he says. "It's been a pleasure."

The guard takes Donovan by the elbow to support him as he hoists to his feet. Clare watches as he shuffles through the door. Donovan looks back to Clare as the guard bends to remove his shackles. She is grateful for the metal door between them.

The sand is dark and gritty under Clare's shoes. She digs a heel in and drags it to draw a line parallel to the water. Every color on this beach is washed out by the last of the day's light. At the end of the beach is a peninsula with a suspension bridge spanning the bay, the beams of oncoming headlights like yellow eyes pointed at Clare.

Pebble Beach, Charlotte had written. 8pm.

It is 7:57. Clare arrived here directly from the prison. The shore is dotted with gray driftwood but devoid of people. Clare thinks of her mother, dead in her forties without ever having set foot in the ocean. When Clare was little, summers were about their farm, about the harvest. Any trips they took were perfunctory visits to see family members in the city. Their entire life unfolded within a small radius, the ocean a distant dream. How easy it is, Clare knows, to remain tethered to your small corner of the world. She inhales deeply. This day has been too long, too overwhelming. The salt in the air burns her lungs.

"Clare," says a voice behind her.

Clare turns to find Charlotte almost upon her, her approach drowned out by the noise of the ocean. Charlotte sidles up to her so they are shoulder to shoulder, both squared to the horizon.

"I was trying not to startle you," Charlotte says.

"You didn't," Clare says. "I'm glad you texted."

Everything about Charlotte's demeanor has shifted from yesterday morning. She seems relaxed next to Clare, her shoulders loose, hands in her pockets, an entirely different person from the woman Clare encountered at Malcolm and Zoe's home yesterday.

"I was thinking about you last night," Charlotte says. "It kept me up, actually. We got off on the wrong foot."

"A gun at my head is the wrong foot?" Clare says. "You don't say."

"Well. You broke into my dead sister's house."

Dead. Why, Clare wonders, does Charlotte keep insisting that Zoe is dead? It's as if she's goading Clare.

"No more guns, then," Clare says. "We agree on that?"

"No more guns. Kavita talked to me, by the way. She thinks I should trust you."

"I wish you would," Clare says. "I think we want the same thing."

"I just want my life back."

"Yes," Clare says. She pauses for a few beats. "This really is a beautiful spot."

"We used to come here when I was young. My mom would pack us these picnics. She insisted on these gestures of togetherness." Charlotte points to the waves. "I never swam. The water is too cold, and the undertow is fierce. But Zoe and my dad . . ." She pauses, remembering. "They'd swim far out. Zoe would let these huge waves crash into her. I remember my mom yelling at my dad that one of the waves was going to snap her neck. She was so reckless, even back then. So was he."

"My mother used to say the same thing about me," Clare says.

Charlotte shifts so she is facing Clare. "I need her to be dead. Officially declared dead."

"Why?"

"You said yesterday that you can help. Kavita says you'll help."

"I can," Clare says. "But I can't have someone declared dead when there's no proof that they are. Honestly, Charlotte? I find it strange that this is what you want. Your sister dead."

"What do you know about my dad?" Charlotte asks.

"I've done some research. I'm not sure all of your father's business dealings were on the up-and-up."

"Ha. I'll say. But he had this thing about 'taking care of us.' My mom. Zoe and me. Zoe went to college but I never did. I got married and had a kid when I was twenty. My dad loved my daughter. She lived like a princess."

"And then your dad was murdered."

"Yeah. It was like it never fucking occurred to me that he wouldn't be there to take care of me." She laughs. "That the money wouldn't be there. My dad died, then the family business went to shit. My husband left, took our daughter. My mom's heart gave out. My parents' house was repossessed after my dad's business partner was convicted. Zoe was fine. She had Malcolm to take care of her. Then she vanishes. Then Malcolm vanishes too. Jesus. Malcolm was rich, you know that, right?"

"Yes," Clare says. "But I still don't understand why you want Zoe dead."

For a moment Charlotte stares out to the water, kicking at the sand.

"I don't want her dead," she says. "I want her *declared* dead. It's not the same thing. The glass house is in Zoe's name. It's worth millions. I need a place to live. I need to clean up and hire a good lawyer. I need . . . stability. That's all I want. And I'm Zoe's next of kin."

"Isn't Malcolm the next of kin? They never got divorced."

"Next of kin? He's evil. He's a fucking murderer."

The venom in Charlotte's words rattles Clare. A *murderer*. Clare's every instinct wants to push back against this notion, to defend Malcolm against such an accusation. How well Clare knows that she could be wrong about him. After all, what is her life so far but failing to see men for their true colors until it's too late? She thinks of the Westman family photograph, the way Charlotte leaned into Malcolm. Clare crouches to pick up a rock and toss it under a curling wave.

"You believe that Malcolm killed Zoe?"

Charlotte stares forward. Clare waits for an answer, but none comes.

"I don't know what Malcolm did or didn't do," Clare says. "I'm here to find out. He never spoke much about your sister. His wife. I have no grasp on her."

Charlotte looks up to the darkening sky. "Some people are evil. They'll do anything to keep what they have. To get more. I grew up around a lot of people like that on account of my father. But when they're close to you, it's harder to spot. My father was like that. He had two sides to him. One side was a doting family man, and the other was pretty much heartless. He loved his granddaughter, that's for certain. But he crossed a lot of people, and not just in business. I think he took pleasure in it. Lune Bay seems like this paradise, right? But there was money flowing in from everywhere. And my dad was at the coffers. He was king of this place. My mother was a dutiful wife, she stood by him. But she used to yell at him at the dinner table that he was going to get us all killed. She'd ask him, right in front of Zoe and me, how he'd feel if some henchman showed up at our school and shot us in the head."

"Jesus," Clare says.

"I get where she was coming from, though," Charlotte says. "She'd say those things because she wanted Zoe and me to be scared too. To be vigilant. To keep our eyes open, because anything could happen at any time. I don't know if my mother knew the extent of it, but she knew enough to be scared for us."

"That's not a great way to grow up."

"No. It isn't."

Mist from the ocean coats Clare's skin. Since they arrived here, there's been a change in the air, a sharp cooling. Charlotte bites a hangnail from her thumb and spits it to the ground, her face twisted anxiously.

"But Zoe loved it," Charlotte continues. "We'd be walking home from school and some guy would watch us a little too long from across the road, or another guy would drive his Cadillac past us and she'd grab my arm and tuck herself behind me. 'Do you think he's here to get us?' she'd say. But she always had a smile on her face as she said it. Like the idea of being kidnapped for ransom was romantic to her. The idea of our dad going on a killing spree to avenge us. We were tight, Zoe and me. I think she loved me. I know she loved my daughter. But she was hollow. She was drawn to evil. Always looking for something to fill her up. She was like my dad in that way."

In her case file, the stories about Zoe had painted a different

115

picture from the one Charlotte offers now, profiles outlining her successes as a high school student, national wins at debating events, track and field. And in the family photographs printed in news stories, Zoe was always at the center of the frame, her father's hands on her shoulders, Charlotte to the side, often gazing up at her taller sister, her expression mimicking. Clare knows how this feels, her brother, Christopher, a straight-A student and lettered athlete in high school, so that by the time Clare arrived a few years after him, the stage was already set for her to seem the lowly disappointment in comparison.

"You say Zoe was reckless. After your father was killed, was she engaging in the same criminal activities as he was?"

Charlotte throws her head back in laughter. "Engaging? You make it sound so quaint. I have no fucking idea what Zoe was doing after my dad died. Kavita has theories, but I was on a spiral of my own. I lost custody of my kid. I was too distracted to watch her drive the family business over a cliff. She came to me a few days before she disappeared and claimed that Malcolm was going crazy. That she was scared of him, scared of what he might do. But she was giddy when she was telling me. Like she was delivering a speech, planting a seed or something. But hey, your sister tells you something like that, you shouldn't just ignore it. But I did. I didn't act because I'm a terrible person, I guess. And I was busy losing my kid."

Clare cannot bring herself to express sympathy. It was almost exactly a year ago that Clare's pregnancy ended in stillbirth after Jason pushed her down the stairs. Almost a year since Clare lay in that hospital bed after the delivery and began to formulate her plan to leave, to escape Jason. She too has lost a child, the circumstances different from Charlotte's, even if the grief is similar. But Clare will not empathize with this woman whose life has deteriorated in parallel ways to her own. She allows the moment to pass.

"You asked me to meet you here, Charlotte. But I'm not totally sure why."

"Neither am I. I guess I just want this all to end. I want some kind of resolution. And I have no idea how to go about it."

A plane circles overhead, angling its wings to align for descent. Clare looks at her phone. 8:10 p.m. The light is fading fast.

"Kavita and I are going to The Cabin later," Charlotte says. "I hear you've been."

"I was there last night with Austin Lantz," Clare says. "He says you're staying at his place."

"Yeah. I've had a rough month. He's been good to me, actually." Charlotte shifts awkwardly from foot to foot. "You could come. Tonight, I mean. To The Cabin. If you want."

Clare closes her eyes to absorb the wave of exhaustion that rolls in at this prospect. The bar, the drinks. The effort to control herself. But she must go.

"I'd like that." Clare looks side to side, searching up and down the beach. "Are we close to Malcolm and Zoe's house? I can't orient myself."

"If you follow the coast about a mile south." Zoe points. "You'll see it hanging over the edge."

The waves have picked up against the breeze, crashing harder, moving closer. The tide must be coming in.

"You said Malcolm is evil. Do you think that's what brought them together?" Clare asks.

"I never said my sister was evil. I said she was drawn to evil people."

"Like Malcolm," Clare suggests.

"Yeah," Charlotte says before turning to walk back to her car. "Like Malcolm."

The Cabin is busier than last night, the bar lined end to end with bodies hunched over drinks. Clare spots Kavita and Charlotte at a high-top table in a corner, bright cocktails in front of them. She hovers by the door, watching. Kavita rests one hand on top of Charlotte's, and they lean so close that their foreheads nearly touch. So there is something more between them, something more than friendship. Clare straightens, tugging at the bottom of the loose but low-cut black shirt she'd selected in her pit stop to the hotel. When she reaches the table, neither of them smile at her in greeting.

"Is it still okay for me to join you?" Clare asks.

"I guess," Kavita says, retracting her hand. "Charlotte invited you."

"Please," Charlotte says. "I'm glad you're here."

Clare sits and accepts a menu from the passing server. The

silence between them is thick. When the server returns, Clare orders only a soda water.

"You don't drink?" Kavita asks.

"I generally avoid it."

The withering look Kavita gives her shrinks Clare back against her chair. Between these two women, Clare had taken Kavita as the kind and welcoming one, Charlotte hardened and cool. But tonight they appear to have swapped demeanors.

"My father used to own this building," Charlotte says. "The bar too."

"Your father owned the whole town," Kavita says.

"It used to be really nice here," Charlotte says, ignoring her. "Sort of hipster rustic. It's fallen a few rungs since then."

"Where's Austin?" Clare asks Charlotte.

"Oh, I'm sure he'll turn up. He likes to be in on the action."

"You know that Austin isn't a real journalist, right?" Kavita says to Clare. "He's got a rich brother who made millions on some calorie-counting diet app. Billions even, I don't know. Austin lives off his brother's money and fancies himself this genius investigative reporter."

"He did go to journalism school," Charlotte says.

"Whatever," Kavita says. "The guy couldn't catch a squirrel if he was holding a bag of nuts."

Kavita's leg bounces madly under the table, the anger she radiates a cover for her agitation.

"For the love of God, I do not understand why you like coming here," Kavita says. "It's fucking weird."

"It's the only decent bar in town," Charlotte says.

The smell of Kavita's and Charlotte's cocktails makes Clare's throat itch with thirst. She can imagine the sweet coating of the first swallow, the warmth that would come. After returning from the beach to park her car, Clare had opted for a brisk walk from the hotel to this bar, a mile uphill, and as her breaths grew shorter, she grew angry again. Angry at her exhaustion, at Somers, at Malcolm, at Austin and Charlotte; a hazy and dense anger striking anyone who popped into her thoughts. She carried only cash and her phone in her back pocket, her gun tucked under her loose shirt. Now, at this table, she can relate to Kavita, her anger hard to contain too. These women demand her professionalism, but Clare wants to give them her wrath. She doesn't even know why. When the server returns with a pint of club soda, Clare gulps half of it before setting the glass down.

"You two have been through a lot together," Clare says, her tone a touch too sharp.

Kavita lifts her cocktail in mock cheers. "Sisters in PTSD."

"Don't call me your sister," Charlotte says. "It's gross."

"You must hash it out, then," Clare suggests. "What happened the night your dad was killed? Given you were both there. No doubt you've compared details."

The women exchange a glance that Clare cannot decipher.

"Have you ever listened to someone tell a story?" Charlotte asks. "And you're in it? You're a character, you play a part? It's different from how you remember it, but the way they tell the story is so convincing that you figure their version must be right? Has that ever happened to you?"

Yes, Clare thinks. So often, in her marriage, Clare would listen to Jason recount stories of their home life, explaining an absence, a bruise, fending off concerned questions from Clare's brother or from Grace. And though Clare knew he was making it all up, she found herself marveling at the details he invented, the way he could authenticate his rendition, the way he'd pass off Clare's poor memory as a side effect of whatever pill she'd swallowed that day. The way Jason shaped her story for her.

"I know what you mean," Clare says. "But who are you referring to?"

"The cops interviewed Charlotte and Zoe together," Kavita says.

"People talk about your brain freezing," Charlotte says, ignoring Kavita's interjection. "When something traumatic happens. Like your brain has to stop absorbing what's going on. All I remember is my mother blowing out candles on her birthday cake. And my father was about to dig in to his dessert. Then he was dead. I swear."

"You didn't get a look at the shooter."

"No," Charlotte says firmly.

"So who was telling the story for you, then?" Clare asks.

"Zoe," she says.

"I just told you, they were interviewed together," Kavita repeats.

"We were," Charlotte says. "They let us sit together alone in the interrogation room before the interview. Of course, Zoe seemed totally fine. She was always a freak of nature that way. I was numb everywhere, shivering, but she was fine. It was performance art to her. She was going over the details with me. Tell them this, she said. Don't forget to say that. But I literally couldn't remember anything. She just told me what to say. When we were little girls, we'd be horsing around and we'd break something, or someone would get hurt, and it didn't matter how confident I was in how things went down, Zoe would always convince my parents or anyone else that she was the one telling the truth."

If Somers were here, she would call this all into procedural question, two key witnesses left alone in the interrogation room and then interviewed together. A more generous take is to allow that the two main witnesses were sisters and their dad had just been murdered right in front of them. The police paired them up out of sympathy. But it doesn't matter, Somers would say. A witness is a witness. Kavita lowers her head, her shoulders shaking with tears. Charlotte seems annoyed but rubs Kavita's back anyway. Clare is too absorbed by the moment passing between them to notice Austin until he is upon them.

"Look at this trio!" he says, arms open to the table. "Have I won the lottery?"

"Fuck off," Charlotte says.

"Come on, Charlotte." Austin drags over a stool to join them. "You love my company. You, me, and Kavita. We're like *Three's Company* but with a twist."

In their previous meetings, Austin had seemed almost wispy to Clare, small, a pushover. But his air is different tonight. Cold, assured. He tugs his phone from his pocket and lifts it.

"If you take a picture of us," Clare says, "I'll break your phone."

"Whoa," Charlotte says, shooting Clare an admiring glance.

"We're in a public place," Austin says. "No rule against—"

"Austin?" Clare holds her hand across the front of his phone to block the shot. *"Don't."*

The low register in Clare's voice stops him. She glares at him until he sets the phone screen down on the table. Clare will not break her stare until he is suitably unsettled. Both Kavita and Charlotte slide off their stools and disappear to the bathroom. Clare sips her drink, silent.

"You're touchy tonight," Austin says.

"You don't know me," Clare says. "It's been a really long day."

Austin points towards the bathroom door. "It's been something else, watching Charlotte fall from grace," he says. "She was never the smart one, the pretty one. It was hard to be the ugly duckling Westman daughter, I'm sure. But she got her fair share of attention. Married this musician when she was what? Nineteen? Had a kid. For a while she kept this blog about life on the road, life as a musician's wife, carting a kid around on tour. Got herself into some drug trouble. Her husband quit the band and went to law school! Jesus Christ. Talk about a one-eighty. Anyway, after Jack Westman was murdered, Charlotte really dove down the well. Her husband left her. Took their kid as far away from her as he could. I'm pretty sure she's switched teams now." He makes a sexual gesture with his hands. "She and Kavita? That's what I'm thinking."

"I don't think they're trying to hide it," Clare says.

"I think they've got plenty to hide," Austin says.

Clare stands and heads to the bathroom. "Keep that phone in your pocket," she calls back to him.

The women's bathroom has three stalls. In the largest one Clare spots two sets of feet. The door is not latched. Clare presses it open and finds Kavita seated on the toilet leaning over a line she's about to snort. She looks up at Clare as if bored by her arrival.

"You shouldn't be mixing that with alcohol," Clare says.

"Okay, mom," Kavita says.

"Want some?" Charlotte asks. "It's not going to kill you."

The tightness returns to Clare's chest. She listens to Kavita's inhale and can muster the exact sensation that comes next. The euphoric hit, the lightness, the dizziness if you lift your head too fast. She can taste the bitterness in her mouth. She doesn't want to be here, witnessing this. She wants to slap Kavita, Charlotte, both of them. *Get yourselves together*. Clare must grip the stall door to stop herself. Kavita and Charlotte switch places, Charlotte seated and hunched over. Clare exits the stall and the bathroom. Back in the bar Austin is still at their table, a beer in front of him. The lights have lowered, loud music playing for the benefit of a small dance floor at the center of the bar. Austin smirks as she approaches.

"I'm guessing they're not in there reapplying lipstick."

"Hey." Clare lifts herself back onto the stool. "I saw Douglas Bentley today. Thanks for passing on his information."

"He's quite the character, isn't he?"

"He actually seemed pretty levelheaded to me," Clare says. "He claims you're the moron."

Again, Austin smirks, his jaw tense. He doesn't like to be mocked, or questioned. Jason was the same, Clare thinks, an ego too outsize for his actual life accomplishments, an inability to take any kind of joke at his own expense. Clare lifts her glass in cheers and touches his arm in an effort to bring him back onside.

"We can share a cab home if you want," Austin says.

"What?"

"You and me," Austin says. "We could share a cab home."

But Clare isn't listening. When the bathroom door opens, she watches Kavita and Charlotte as they stumble laughing to the dance floor. Austin leans in and recounts his entire past for Clare, the odd jobs taken to put himself through the first years of school before his brother struck rich, speaking free flow on the assumption that Clare is riveted by every word. She nods occasionally, sipping the last of her soda and glancing at Kavita and Charlotte. Clare is so tired. She closes her eyes, but Austin keeps talking. Several minutes must pass before she looks to the dance floor again and notices the women are gone.

"Where'd they go?" she asks Austin.

"I think Charlotte left." He points. "Kavita's over there."

There is a commotion at one end of the bar. Clare's eyes

are pinned on Kavita. Three men surround her. One has her propped up, Kavita unsteady on her feet, swaying to the music, giggling. But Clare sees something so familiar in the vacancy of her expression. She's not herself. The men are laughing and leaning in to each other, one hand up to shield their whispers. Clare feels her heart rate pick up.

"Do you know those guys?" Clare asks.

"The one in the plaid shirt comes here a lot," Austin says. "He's a cop, I think. Wow. Kavita's really wasted."

Clare frowns. "Where did Charlotte go?"

"You think Kavita doesn't know what she's doing," Austin says. "But she does. I promise you, she does. She's a pro at this."

A pro? This interaction feels like déjà vu to Clare, the way Kavita leans into one man until he rights her and guides her to the next, the men passing her around their tight-knit circle like a ball. When Kavita jerks her arm from the man in plaid, Clare notes the force with which he grabs it again. She watches as the man in the plaid shirt takes Kavita and leads her to the front door. Clare stands to follow.

Outside, Clare detects the man's laugh before she spots them. She follows the sound to the alley next to the bar. It is rutted and puddled from the rain, the brick wall of the bar lined with garbage bins. The smell strikes Clare. Kavita is against a wall, the man in plaid's arms lifted to fence her in. Clare can't quite make out the words between them. *Home*, she thinks she hears Kavita say. *Charlotte. Home.*

"Hey," Clare says on approach. "Kavita?"

The man catches his laugh and cranes to look at Clare without lowering his grip on the wall.

"You should probably let her go," Clare says, edging closer.

The smile drops from his face.

"Hey," Clare says, addressing Kavita directly now. "Let's go back inside. I'm going to take you home."

"I'm taking her home," the man says. "We were just about

to leave, weren't we? What's your name again? Kendall. Fuck no, not Kendall. Not even close. That's your friend's name, isn't it? Kavita. Shit!"

The sound of that name stirs something in Clare. Kendall. Clare can picture the photographs on Douglas Bentley's wall, his smiling daughter. Kendall. Clare thinks of her friend Grace back home, the two of them at bars not unlike this one, the pacts they would make. *We only leave with each other*, they would say, snaking their pinkies together to seal the promise. No one else takes us home.

"Kavita?" Clare says. "You're messed up. Come on. Let's go."

The man yanks Kavita across the alley to a back door propped open with an empty beer bottle. Clare tracks them. They pass through a dark hallway, then emerge into the bar. Clare makes eye contact with Austin as he stands up from his stool, smiling. Amused.

Coward, Clare would like to yell at him. *You fucking coward*.

The man has pulled Kavita back to the group at the bar. She sits on a stool and slumps, eyes glassy. But she's looking at Clare. What's that look? Clare wonders. Is that pleading in her eyes? Or anger? Clare can't tell. She approaches the men.

"Listen," Clare says. "I don't want to cause any problems. But this is my friend, and I'm bringing her home."

"No, really," the man says. "What *is* your problem? Because you really are having a hard time minding your own business."

"Let her go. Now."

"Oh, fuck off. We're old friends, Kavita and I. I've known her since she was a kid."

Clare steps forward and takes Kavita by the arm. But Kavita recoils sharply. Before she can react, the man has grabbed Clare and pinned her arm behind her back. Her shoulder screams, the scar tissue from her gunshot wound stretched taut.

"Touch her again and I'll break your arm," the man says.

One of the man's friends is talking now, telling him to let her go. "Come on, man," he says. "Drop it."

His words are garbled, the ringing too loud in Clare's ears. She works to relax her arm to ease the pressure. Across the bar she makes eye contact with Austin again. He's moving her way now, his phone in his hand ready to take pictures. The voices around Clare grow louder, the man's breath hot on her neck.

"Let me go!" she says.

"Fuck you," he replies.

The rage in his tone sets something alight in Clare. She uses her free hand to reach for the gun tucked into her belt. As soon as he spots it, the man drops her arm and takes a stumbling step backwards. There is a collective *whoa* from the crowd. Clare lifts the gun and aims it at the man's head.

"Touch me again," Clare says, motioning to Kavita. "Touch *her*, and I'll kill you."

"Jesus Christ," he says, hands up. "Okay, wow. Lady. Fuck."

Someone turns down the music, leaving only a low hum of voices.

"I'm an off-duty cop," he says. "You're not going to want to shoot."

Clare sidesteps until her back is to the wall, the bar stretched out before her like a tableau, faces frozen in fear. But a few of the men around the room smile, wide-eyed, as though Clare pointing a gun at a stranger is a scene in a movie they're watching and not a danger to them. Clare swallows hard.

"Just leave," she says, her voice low. "Go."

"Fuck you," the man says. "Why don't you shoot me? Go ahead."

Now Austin is close. He hovers behind the man, his phone up, filming.

"Look!" the man says, addressing the crowd behind him without taking his gaze off Clare. "We've got ourselves a vigilante here! Touch her friend in a way she doesn't like and she'll put a bullet in you. Or will she?"

He takes a small step forward. Clare clicks off the gun's safety. He stops. Clare's arms ache. A standoff.

"Fuck you," he says finally.

He crosses the bar in long strides. Clare lowers the gun and keeps it pointed at the ground until he disappears through the front door. Only one friend follows him, the others closing ranks at the bar. Clare feels a deep heat in her cheeks and down the back of her neck. For the life of her she cannot cry now. She cannot. She tucks the gun back into her belt. Kavita's shoulders shake with tears.

Austin rushes over, breathless. "Jesus. Holy shit! I got the whole thing on video."

"Delete it," Clare hisses at him.

"Are you kidding me?"

"We need to take her home," Clare says. "Do you know where Charlotte went?"

"Probably back to my place," Austin says. "Must have been a lover's quarrel."

"You're such an asshole," Clare says.

"You're the one who pulled a gun."

The din of the bar is louder now, some people fixed to their phones, surely recounting the scene they'd just witnessed to whatever contact is on closest tap. Clare's head hurts. She looks to the door, certain the man will return, maybe with his own gun. She has to leave. She needs to get Kavita out of here too. But then the door opens and in walks Patrick Germain, striding her way.

"Her?" he asks the bartender.

The bartender points at Clare. Yes. Her. Germain approaches, and the bar quiets again. This time people lift their phones to film whatever might come next. Clare can barely draw in a breath. She meets Germain's eyes.

"What are you doing here?" she asks, her voice low.

"Give me your gun," he says. "And do it nicely."

For a moment Clare considers her options. She turns and lifts her shirt to allow Germain to withdraw the weapon from her belt. Then she spins to face him.

"You're the beat cop on duty tonight, detective?" she asks.

"Charlotte called me about twenty minutes ago. Asked me to swing this way and check in on Kavita. On my way over I get a radio call about a woman pulling a gun. Just so happened I was already on my way."

"Bullshit," Clare says. "You were following me."

"Jesus Christ." Germain removes the handcuffs from his holster.

"Can we just walk out?" Clare says to him, pleading. "Please? A scene would be bad for me."

"You know I have to arrest you."

"No you don't."

"He was an off-duty cop," Germain says.

"A friend of yours?"

"Don't fight me on this," Germain says, closing in. "Don't make this worse than it needs to be."

Germain tries to get behind her, but Clare turns so her back is to the crowd. She won't give anyone the pleasure of her expression as this unfolds. Germain takes hold of her arms and pinches her wrists behind her back. Clare doesn't fight. He locks handcuffs but leaves them loose enough that Clare knows she could wriggle out. He leans forward until she can feel his breath on her ear.

"We'll go out the back door," he says.

"He was going to hurt her," Clare says through clenched teeth.

"Maybe. But you can't pull a gun in a bar. You're not a cop."

"He was going to hurt her," Clare repeats.

Germain is reading Clare her rights loud enough for anyone within twenty feet to hear.

"Lock her up," one of the man's friends says. He lifts his beer in cheers when Clare looks his way.

Germain leads Clare to the back door to a chorus of boos. When they emerge into the alley Clare rips herself from his grasp, stumbling forward with the effort. But she is able to right herself before she falls. She turns to face Germain, her jaw pulsing with rage.

"You didn't have to do that," she says.

Germain scoffs. "What do you think this is? The wild west? You're in Lune Bay. You don't have free rein. Not here. We won't tolerate it."

"Take the cuffs off," Clare says. "Now."

"I can't do that," Germain says. "You're under arrest."

THURSDAY

The cell door slams, jolting Clare awake. She sits up on the bench, squinting against the sharp fluorescent lights, rubbing her eyes. Her mouth is gritty with thirst. The guard fiddles with the key to lock the holding cell behind him. The newest arrival to the cell, a young woman, stumbles crying to the bench across from Clare and plops down. Her T-shirt reads BRIDE2BE. A ripped and dirty veil hangs from her knotted ponytail.

There are seven women in here now. An hour might have passed since Clare phoned Somers, her voice mail picking up right away, her phone off. The guard had allowed Clare a second call only because Germain said so. She left a message for Douglas Bentley. She could think of no one else.

"Where is Germain?" Clare asks the guard.

"Who knows?"

"Can you call him for me? He said he'd be right back."

"I don't call detectives at three a.m.," the guard answers.

AMY STUART

The wall clock over the officer's desk is frozen at midnight, the time Clare assumed it was when Germain led her to this holding cell at the back of the detachment. An older woman sits in the middle of the far bench, flanked by four younger cell mates. Clare and the drunk bride-to-be are the only two who sit alone.

"Don't stare," the older woman says to Clare. "Stop staring. We don't stare in here."

"Okay. Sorry."

The woman's command is more teacherly than threatening. There are infinite reasons these women might be here. One has a black eye and scratches up and down her arms. They all look disheveled. Clare is sure she does too. The only other time Clare was in a holding cell was when she was much younger, strung out in her hometown. She'd sat alone in that cell, the young guard an acquaintance who'd finished high school a few years ahead of her. That night Clare was so certain of her release, of her father's sway, that it never occurred to her to be scared. What a difference it might have made in my life, Clare thinks now, if I *had* been scared. If someone had scared some sense into me then.

In the corner, the bride huddles with her knees to her chest, her tears marked by black streaks of mascara down her cheeks. She rips the veil from her hair and begins dry heaving, her body lurching forward with the effort. Clare crosses the cell and sits next to her.

"Those dumb bitches left me there," she says between heaves. "Throwing the rock through her window was their idea. Then they ran when the cops showed up."

"That sucks," Clare says. She must bite her tongue. Nobody hurt. No one dead. No one vanished. The ridiculous simplicity of a bachelorette party gone haywire.

136

"Relax," the older woman says, crossing to sit next to Clare. "Your fiancé's gonna come get you."

"No. He's going to *die* of shame. He's a lawyer. Do you know how bad this looks?" She pauses and pats at her outfit. "Those fucker cops took my phone!"

"Seriously," another woman says. "Can you shut up? They'll give you one call. You know? Like in the movies? You'll get to make a call."

The bride looks up earnestly. "Can I ask for one text instead? My fiancé never answers his phone."

Every woman in the cell laughs, sending the bride into a deeper fit of tears. The older woman reaches for Clare's hair. She tugs gently on one of the curls and allows it to bounce back.

"What beautiful hair," she says. "You're very pretty."

"Not in this light," Clare says.

"You look familiar," another woman says.

This statement always jolts Clare. "I get that a lot. One of those faces."

"Are you famous?"

"No. Maybe I look like someone famous?"

"No, wait." The bride wipes her nose with her sleeve. "I saw a video of you getting arrested. One of my friends got a video text of this hot cop arresting a woman in a bar for pulling a gun on some guy who was manhandling his girl-friend." She points at Clare, wide-eyed. "Oh my God! You're that woman!"

"She wasn't his girlfriend," Clare says.

"You pulled a fucking gun on him!" the bride squeals. "And he was a cop! Oh my God, you're so screwed."

One of the women begins a slow clap and the others fol-low. Despite her exhaustion, despite the knot of rage in her belly, Clare smiles. She waves her hand and lowers her head in a mock bow.

"The Robin Hood of wronged ladies," the older woman says. "Keep it up and someone will give you your own TV show."

But Clare isn't smiling anymore. She only realizes now what this means, her image on a video spread far and wide. She imagines Jason watching it, its contents a beacon pointing exactly to where Clare is now. She feels a swell of distress. Clare stands and grips the bars.

"Do any of you know Germain? The cop who dropped me here?"

"The kid detective?" the older woman says. "He used to be a beat cop. Not a very nice one."

Nice, Clare thinks. Germain: *not a very nice one*. She feels only rage at him for bringing her here, for processing her upon arrival at the precinct like any other criminal, fingerprints and a mug shot, for taking her to this cell, for vanishing after that. How many hours has it been since she last saw him? Two? How far has the video of her arrest spread since then? The other women in the cell have returned to minding their own business, a few of them dozing, backs flat on the hard benches. Two have slid to a seated position on the floor. Clare studies them closely, one at a time, until it occurs to her. Ask them.

"Hey," Clare says. "Do any of you know anything about the Westman family?"

The older woman looks up. "Are you a cop?"

"No," Clare says, crossing herself. "I swear to God. But I've been doing some digging on people who've disappeared from Lune Bay. Kendall Bentley was one of them. Stacey Norton?"

The women each look to the older one, who keeps her eyes fixed on Clare.

"Listen," Clare says. "Would I be in here if I was a cop? Would I be pulling a weapon on another cop in a bar?"

"You should know to stay away from the Westman family," the older woman says.

"There isn't much left of them," Clare says.

"Jack might be dead, but his legacy lives on. Lune Bay is a charming little place on the surface." She gestures to the jail cell. "But there's quite the underbelly."

Jack? First name basis? "You knew him?" Clare asks.

The older woman laughs. "Fuck, no. I mean, not personally. Have you ever heard of a whisper network?"

"Yes," Clare says.

"There was a lot of money to be had. If you were a pretty girl willing to . . . bend some rules. Jack Westman wasn't interested in running his business that way. But his daughter certainly was. And she paid very well."

"Running the business what way?" Clare asks.

"I'm sure you can guess the gist of it," the older woman says. "Business is business, right? You need a signature on a permit but someone down at city hall is being difficult. You need some deal to go through. These pencil pushers are all family men. They've got wives and kids. Incriminating photos can go a long way. But sometimes the ladies in these photos would . . . stop turning up."

"You mean disappear," Clare says.

"My take is that most of them just got paid to stay away. To move on. Still, we take care of each other, right? So, the whisper network. Women around here let each other know. Anything with the Westman family is a high-risk venture."

"I heard stories about some kind of cult," one of the younger women says. "They had this cabin in the woods and they'd do these ceremonies. Sacrifices."

"Jesus Christ." The older woman rolls her eyes. "No. That's just some made-up shit to throw you offtrack. It was all pretty bread-and-butter stuff."

"You mentioned Jack Westman's daughter. You mean Zoe?"

"I'm not saying another word." The older woman zips her lips and points to the camera trained on them from the high corner of the cell. "Cops are all in on it too. You're wading into shark-infested waters, my friend."

"I would love to talk to you some more," Clare pleads. "Maybe when we both get out of here?"

The older woman laughs. "Sure thing. I'll invite you over to my condo for some wine and cheese."

The women have all turned away from her now, the older one lying down on the bench and placing her forearm over her eyes. It's over. Clare knows this woman won't say another word.

Clare lies on the bench too and stares at the ceiling, the pipes crossing it coated with moisture. When she closes her eyes some kind of sleep must overcome her, because at once Jason is there, sitting on the bench next to her, the other women in the cell gone.

I'm here, he says to her, his voice gentle. I've come for you.

No, Clare says.

When she snaps awake Germain is standing over her. Clare jolts to sitting. He offers her his hand to stand, but Clare looks at him with such spite that he retracts it.

"You were saying something," he says. "You said 'no.'"

"Can I leave now?"

"You posted bail."

"How? I couldn't get in touch with Somers."

"I posted it for you."

"Whoa," says the older woman. "Friends in high places."

Clare laughs bitterly. "Is that even allowed?"

"It's not your concern," Germain says. "Don't worry about it."

"Oh, I'm not worried," Clare says. "My only *concern* is that you're a huge prick."

At these words the other women gasp and clap. Germain releases a long sigh and gestures to the cell door. Clare stands and follows him out. The older woman shakes her head at Clare as she passes, a warning. Be careful.

"What about me?" the bride yelps.

"Your fiancé's on his way," Germain says.

"Oh God," she says, burying her face in her hands. "Oh no."

Clare offers the group a wave, a grateful smile. Then she follows Germain through the cell door he locks behind him.

From the cell, Clare trails Germain down a windowless hall. They are in the basement of the detachment. Is it morning yet? Clare has lost all sense of time. In the elevator, they stand side by side in silence, Clare catching the subtle scent of Germain's aftershave. She dips her nose to her own armpit and recoils at the stench. The elevator doors open to an atrium six stories high. The light is pink. It is early morning. They walk down a hall open to the atrium below, where Clare can see a skeleton crew of caretakers readying for the day.

A few more turns through clusters of open desks and they arrive at Germain's office. It is nicely decorated, artsy photographs on the wall. Aside from a framed commendation, Clare sees no personal touches, no family photographs or memorabilia. He sits at the desk and turns on his computer. When

Clare takes the seat across from him, he opens a drawer and hands her a bottle of water.

"You're pretty young for an office this nice," Clare says.

"Youngest detective in the detachment's history."

"Your parents must be proud." Clare doesn't mask her sarcasm. "Hey. I'll be needing my phone back."

Germain laughs. "Give me a minute."

He taps at the keyboard until his computer screen comes to life. The events of last night rile her, the trip here in the back of the cruiser, Germain tossing glances back to her at every stoplight, her shoulders smarting from her wrists cuffed behind her back. She thinks of the way he extracted her from the cruiser, her balance off because of the handcuffs. Then a uniformed officer processed her in that too-bright room before leading Clare to the basement cell. Recounting those scenes now fills her with a rage that clenches her jaw.

"How can the arresting officer be the one to post bail?" Clare asks.

"We've got a few workarounds in place here. Besides," Germain says, leaning back in his chair, "I only actually pay it if you break the terms. If, say, you take off."

They watch each other across the desk.

"Where's my gun?" Clare asks finally.

"Yeah. You're not getting that back."

"You didn't have to arrest me."

"You pulled a gun in a bar, Clare. I'll make sure the charges are dropped. But the only way I was getting you out of there was in cuffs."

"There's video of me everywhere. One of the women in the holding cell had seen it."

"Because you pulled a gun in a crowded bar."

"You're not the hero here," Clare says.

"Jesus Christ. Listen, I'll work to get the video wiped. We have ways of making that happen."

"No you don't."

Germain releases a long sigh in an effort to calm himself. He turns to his computer again. Clare watches him with a wave of shame. She knows she is being insolent, that she should instead level up to Germain's coolness, his restraint. She needs to focus again. She pinches the back of her own hand, the sharp pain snapping her alert.

Press reset, she tells herself. Start again.

"I heard from your cop friend," Germain says. "Hollis Somers. She got your message. She's on her way."

"She's coming here?" Clare says. "Like, in person?"

"Yep. Her flight landed an hour ago. She said she was going to rent a car. She should be on her way to the detachment by now."

Somers. Here in Lune Bay. Clare is exhausted, and everything is muddled. The wave of relief she feels at Somers's impending arrival is tempered by the voice in her head: *she lied to you.* The printer behind Germain spits out a handful of papers and he presents them to Clare for signature. *Conditions of Release.*

"A formality," he says.

The pen feels thick and unwieldy between Clare's fingers. She must pause and consider what name to sign, all her identities mashing together. Clare, she writes, scribbling her false last name into a cartoonish swirl. O'Kearney. She slides the papers back to him. Germain opens the top drawer and passes her phone across the desk. Clare powers it on. The battery is low. Did Germain check her phone after he confiscated it last night? She has not deleted the messages from Malcolm, their exchanges. Surely detectives have means of unlocking a home screen, of reading any new messages before marking them unread again. Across the desk Germain leans back in his chair, hands intertwined on his chest. What do you know that you're not telling me? she'd like to ask him. Her phone pings as the messages come in.

The first is from Somers. It reads only:

Jesus, Clare.

The next message is from Malcolm's number. It is a long note that arrived in her in-box last night, shortly after she was arrested. Clare locks the screen and looks up at Germain.

"Am I free to go?" she asks.

"You've got a few minutes until she gets here," he says. "The airport's over an hour away. You want a coffee?"

"No," Clare says. She is being stubborn, she knows. Petulant. But all she wants is a moment to gather herself before Somers arrives. Germain taps at a file folder squared on the center of his desk.

"I've been thinking a lot about what you told me yesterday morning. Zoe Westman's rogue husband hiring you to work as a PI. That's some story, especially in light of last night's events."

Clare says nothing.

"You know," Germain continues, "I feel like I've gained a decent sense of this Malcolm guy since I took over the case. Orphaned when he was fifteen with tons of money left behind, boarding school, college, a PhD, world travel. Must be nice, right? Then he bought himself some rambling ocean-front house in a rich suburb. Ripped it down and had this masterpiece glass box built. Do you know how much the houses up there cost?"

The angled sunlight through Germain's office window is blinding. Clare's eyes ache. Germain opens the folder and spins a large photograph so Clare can see it. It depicts Malcolm and Zoe's wedding, the two of them flanked by the Westmans, the ocean behind them. Clare swallows. Why does this photograph stir anything in her?

"The guy never smiles," Germain says, tapping at the photograph. "This is his wedding day. I mean, come on. You can't smile for your bride?"

Donovan said the exact same thing of Malcolm yesterday. *He never smiled.*

"Some people don't smile in pictures."

Germain eyes her. "Yeah? Anyone I interviewed, every old interview from the case that I've read, has Malcolm Hayes pinned as this quiet guy with a dark side. The kind of guy who can't break a smile at his own wedding. Like, a don't-fuck-with-me kind of dark side. A perfect fit for the Westman family business."

"Yeah," Clare says. "Feels like a lot of bad shit went down with the Westmans. The cold-blooded murder of the patriarch, a couple of women vanishing, including one of the Westman daughters. And yet only one guy's in jail. Donovan Hughes. And for what? Tax fraud? That feels a little thin. Like maybe some people haven't been doing their jobs."

Germain doesn't flinch. "I'm doing my job, Clare. Trust me."

The back of Clare's neck is coated in a cool sweat. She looks down to her phone again.

"Are you hungry?" Germain asks. "We could have breakfast once Detective Somers arrives."

"I'd rather not," Clare says. "I'd rather wait for Somers in the lobby. If I'm free to go."

Germain masks any disappointment in her response with a smile. He stands when Clare does. Clare's phone is warm in her hands. Without another word she ducks out of his office and winds her way back to the elevator.

I n the atrium, Clare finds a row
of chairs close to the entrance.
She sits and sends Somers a text:

I'm out. Waiting for you by the main door.

Clare grips her phone in both hands and looks down to the
screen. There's a metallic taste in her mouth, her teeth coated
with film. She unscrews the cap to the bottled water Germain
gave her in his office and drains it in a few long gulps.

Open the email, she tells herself. *Open Malcolm's email.* But
she doesn't.

The atrium is busy with the comings and goings of a shift
change, fresh-faced officers arriving just as the haggard over-
night crew leaves. A group of uniformed cops stands in a
close huddle adjacent to where Clare sits, laughing at a video
playing on one of their phones. What if it is the video of

her in the bar? The thought fills Clare with dread. This is a regular Thursday morning to them, the air cooler than it was yesterday as September tends to bring, the weekend arriving soon. Clare feels a stab of loneliness. But for whom? For what? Friendship? Camaraderie? She's known so little of that in her life beyond her childhood friend Grace and, perhaps more recently, Somers. Is she lonely for a life she never had? For all the things she believed she'd experience in her life—a happy marriage, a decent job, a family—and then hasn't? Clare's phone pings again. Somers writes:

Twenty mins

Clare's legs tingle. She is still wearing the black shirt she put on last night. Her jeans feel pasted to her legs. A young boy sits with his mother on a nearby bench. He makes eye contact with Clare as he runs a toy car along the seat. When she smiles at him, he stares back for an unnatural stretch, the toy unmoving in his hand. His mother's face is streaked with dry tears, her gaze trained on the double doors at the far end of the atrium. She is waiting for someone to be released. Clare closes her eyes.

From the beginning this case has felt fundamentally different from the first two Clare worked on; she is more assured in her choices, less anxious. But the anger isn't subsiding. In fact, it comes in taller waves now, mixed with sadness and frustration. In the jail cell, Clare had moments of feeling bowled over by it. She thinks of Kavita and Charlotte in the bathroom last night, how mad she'd been at them for snorting lines, for caving to an urge Clare has herself worked so hard to resist. It unsettled her how badly she'd wanted to join them, how little, when faced with it, her own urges have dulled with time.

A laugh from the group of officers startles Clare. She swipes her phone to life. The subject of Malcolm's email is strangely plain: *Pls read*. She clicks it open, then closes it again. Why can't she bring herself to read it? Why does she feel like she wants to cry? You're just tired, she tells herself. Clare can recall a conversation with Malcolm in their time in between their first two cases, as Clare was healing from the gunshot wound. They'd stood on the beach with their feet in the ocean on the first day Clare had felt able to rise from her bed and leave her motel room.

How do you feel? Malcolm asked her.

Okay, she'd replied. Good. Different. Better.

It struck her at the time, that combination of words, that to feel okay, to feel good, was to feel different to her. That the facts of Clare's life up until then meant that her baseline was unhappiness, fearfulness, dependence. She'd glanced at Malcolm, expecting him to concur, but found him frowning.

Don't rest on your laurels, he said.

And though his words had bothered Clare, angered her even, she knew exactly what he meant. It was a warning to heed. Because no matter how confident and well-equipped Clare has felt on this case, she knows she must stay vigilant. That her reckless and angry side will always float just below the surface.

Clare checks the time on her phone. Ten minutes until Somers said she'd be here.

Finally she opens the email.

Clare,

I can't stop you. I understand that much now. All I can do is tell you the truth and hope that it encourages you to stand off.

Zoe Westman is a dangerous person. She is not missing, or
dead. She left on her own volition but allowed it to appear like
she'd vanished so that the police would zero in on me. She
wants revenge for reasons I will not get into here.

I wish I'd given you more reason to trust me in the time we
worked together. I can understand why you don't. But I hope
you will at least hear me out. I believe that Zoe knows about
you. I believe she knows about our working relationship and
that it has set her off. I cannot express to you enough the risk
this brings to both of us. I only care about the risk it brings
to you.

Clare, I have the means to help you move on. I can wire you
money and connect you to people who will help you build a
false identity. You can start over entirely. It is what I should
have offered you the first time we met. I will regret it always
that I didn't. While it pains me to think of never seeing
you again, it pains me even more to think of harm coming
your way.

This email address is encrypted. It is safe to reach me here.
I hope you will. Please do the sensible thing, Clare. For both
of us.

M

Clare reads the message three times, then drops her phone
into her lap and works to control her breathing. Hot tears
spring to her eyes. She looks upward to the atrium's glass
ceiling, the vivid early morning sky. The boy with his mother
watches her intently now, his brow worried, as if he can

AMY STUART

anticipate Clare's breakdown. Is Clare tempted to take Malcolm up on his offer? No. The thought of it crushes her with loneliness. What, Clare wonders, a finger to her eye to wipe at the tears, is this yearning she feels? The concern Malcolm shows, however misguided, leaves her bereft. She could not foresee this sorrow, her own pain at the thought of never seeing Malcolm again. There is a hard ache in her chest. Clare opens the email browser and types quickly:

No, Malcolm. You don't get to do this. I'm really mad at you. Where are you?

The moment she hits send, Clare regrets it. An emotional response, a childish one. Too intimate. She could have taken the time to think logically, to weigh Malcolm's words against the information she's gathered in her time here. Instead, she wrote from her gut. In under a minute, her phone pings with his response.

I know you are. I'm not far.

That's all. Seven words, no sign-off. And yet this response speaks volumes, at once as an apology and a comfort. Clare goes to clear her throat but coughs instead. She wants to weep, from confusion and exhaustion, but when she looks up and sees Somers pressing through the revolving door, she holds her breath to contain it. Somers looks different to her. Sharper somehow, less soft. Clare does not stand. You see a person's true soul when they don't know you're watching them, Clare's mother used to say. Somers scans the room, her face pursed in a way Clare has never seen before. She will not wave at Somers. She will sit here and wait until she is noticed.

152

Malcolm sits on the edge of her bed. *Does it hurt?* He's pointing to her shoulder. Clare looks down to it. The bullet wound is bleeding, soaking through her shirt. *That must hurt*, Malcolm is saying.

Does it? Clare feels numb. She gathers the sheet from the bed to form a ball and presses it against her shoulder. The wound screams with pain. The bleeding won't stop. The sheet has soaked red. Clare feels dizzy, but she must ask. She has to ask him before he leaves again.

What did you do to your wife?

I killed her, Malcolm says. *She's dead.*

Clare wakes with a jolt. She has kicked the sheets from her hotel bed. She sits up, sweaty, thirsty. The alarm clock reads 11:39. It was a dream. Malcolm is not here.

Four hours ago, Somers drove Clare back to the hotel from

153

the detachment. Clare sat in stony silence in the passenger seat of Somers's rental car, unable to parse what was making her uneasy. Clare left Somers at reception, where they'd agreed to go their separate ways until noon. Clare returned to her room, stripped to her underwear, and passed out at once.

The dreams, Clare thinks. They come to her like omens.

In the bathroom, Clare undresses and steps into the shower before the water is even warm. She uses a facecloth to scrub at her skin. She washes her hair, then steps out to towel off and move naked into the hotel room, rummaging through her duffel bag for something clean to wear. Clare has thought so little of her appearance these past months, her figure thinning and expanding according to the rhythm of her days. She dresses, finds her cell phone on the bed and sits to reread the chain of emails with Malcolm. Everything about her dream felt real, Malcolm sitting on the edge of her bed, the motel room dark. I killed her, he'd said with such calm in his voice, a twinge of a smile on his face. Clare hits reply and types,

> If you're close by, like you said you were, then I want to meet.
> I want the whole truth.

Clare throws her cell phone on the bed again and moves to the window. She looks for signs of the ocean through the buildings. Lune Bay feels less like a suburb and more like a village, as Donovan had called it. Clare's phone pings. It's a text message from Austin.

I have it on good word that you've been released. Can we talk today?

Clare rolls her eyes. Before she can type a response, someone knocks. Clare peeks through the spy hole and sees Somers. She unlatches and opens the door, stepping aside to allow Somers to enter. Somers carries two coffees and a paper bag, a satchel over her shoulder. She spins on a heel at the far side of the room to shoot Clare a deadly look.

"You get some sleep, gunslinger?"

"I slept a few hours," Clare says. "I feel better."

"Are you ready to explain yourself? Because I don't like waking up to voice mails from jail. I don't like having to catch the earliest flight out."

"Well," Clare says, "I don't like getting arrested."

Somers hands Clare one of the coffees and a paper bag with a pastry inside. She flops into the corner armchair. Clare sits on the bed and rips a bite off the croissant.

"I had a friend up here send me a copy of your arrest report this morning," Somers says.

"You have friends everywhere," Clare says.

"I do," Somers says. "You'd be smart to remember that. I most certainly do."

Somers is smiling; she means it in jest, but her tone nonetheless irks Clare, the veiled threat of it.

"The woman's name is Kavita Spence," Clare says. "I was at the bar last night with her and Charlotte Westman. Jack's daughter. They were mixing drugs and alcohol. Kavita was completely out of it. There was this meathead with his friends trying to take advantage of her. Apparently he was an off-duty cop."

"He is a cop," Somers says. "He was named in the report."

"Whatever. He was going to hurt her. And he wouldn't back off."

"So you waved your gun around."

"I overreacted."

Somers sips her coffee. "That's one way of putting it."

Clare sighs. "I found them in the back alley behind the bar. And you know what? The guy called Kavita Kendall. Kendall Bentley is one of the women who disappeared from Lune Bay. Just like your girl Stacey Norton. Kendall's father's been searching for her for nearly two years. That's quite the name slip for that cop to make, don't you think?" Clare shakes her head. "I don't know. It triggered me. And now my face is everywhere because of that video."

"We can work on that," Somers says. "Do a bit of scrubbing. Germain is already on it. Your name hasn't been published."

"You can't scrub the internet. It's only a matter of time until my name comes out too."

"Will you please let me try to deal with it?" Somers asks. "Do you trust me?"

Clare is silent. She looks out the window, avoiding Somers's stare.

"You really think I might be in on it?" Somers asks. "That I'm some kind of dirty cop?"

"You lied to me," Clare says.

"I withheld," Somers says. "There's a big difference."

"I don't see it that way," Clare says, her voice rising. "You had information that you didn't give me. You didn't tell me that you'd worked on a case related to Malcolm, to the Westmans. That's not an omission, that's a flat-out lie."

"Listen," Somers says, sitting up and setting her coffee on the hotel room desk. "I get that your instinct is to mistrust. To not believe anything anyone tells you. But in police work there's this thing we call confirmation bias. If you believe someone is guilty or something is true, then you'll look for clues that support your theory. I consider myself incredibly lucky to have met you, Clare. Because you truly are a set of fresh eyes." Somers opens her satchel and lifts herself off the chair to hand Clare a file. "I didn't want to tell you about Stacey because I felt it would bias you. You wouldn't be objective. You couldn't be."

"Maybe you underestimate me," Clare says.

"Quite the opposite. I believe in you so much that I didn't want to spoil it with elements of my own failures." Somers sighs. Her expression softens. She too appears tired. She would have risen in the dark of night to catch her flight. "It burns me to think that I've lost your trust. Because this connection between us? This link between an old case of mine and your guy Malcolm? It was a coincidence. I've worked over a thousand cases in my career. I could find links from Gandhi to Brad Pitt if I want to. I swear. I wanted your fresh eyes. And if I'm going to be honest, it appealed to me that you're not bound by the same rules that I am."

"What do you mean?" Clare asks.

"Cops have a very thick rule book we have to live by. I try to do things by that book. Sometimes that puts me at a real disadvantage. A disadvantage that you don't have." She points to the file handed to Clare. "It's all in there. Everything I've got on Stacey Norton."

Clare opens the file. Clipped to the inside face is a large black-and-white photograph of a young woman. Stacey Norton. She smiles, carefree. She is young, pretty. A twenty-three-year-old aesthetician who moved to Lune Bay to take work in the spa at its most exclusive hotel.

"Kendall Bentley's dad is worth a visit," Clare says, closing the file. "His name is Douglas. Army vet. Like I said, he's been looking for his daughter. He's been pretty diligent. We could go see him."

"I'd like that," Somers says.

For a few minutes they say nothing, Clare making a show of flipping back and forth through the Norton file, sipping her coffee. The knot still sits in her stomach, threatening to rise through her and emerge as tears. She works to keep her face set to neutral, but she can sense from Somers's gaze that she isn't doing a very good job of it.

"You've got to be tired," Somers says. "A crazy few days, barely any sleep."

"Yeah," Clare says quietly. "I'll push through."

"Hey," Somers says. "You've got to learn to show yourself some compassion, you know that? You've been through the wringer."

Clare drops her head. "Can we not do this right now—"

"My guess is you've only told me half the story," Somers interjects. "If that. My guess is some part of you is still hoping for a happy ending with this Malcolm character, even when all signs point to that being wishful thinking. And I think some part of you is even protecting that ex-husband of yours. Glossing over the worst of it. Because you married him, right? So he had to have some redeeming qualities, right? You don't want to make him out to be *that* bad, because what does that say about you?"

"That I'm an idiot."

"No," Somers says. "That's where the compassion comes in. People fool us all the time. We all get fooled. You were young, and you had a lot of shit going on in your life, and he fooled you, and you married him. And you paid way too steep a price for that, didn't you?"

"I really don't want to talk about this," Clare says, a crack in her voice.

"You lost everything. You left everything behind. And here you are on the other side of the country, looking for ways to take blame, for other people to hate. You're this ball of rage. But why? You picked yourself up, and you took this job, and now you're doing good work. Maybe you've found a calling. I believe you're trying to stay clean. Maybe it's not a straight line, but you're trying, right?"

"Stop," Clare says. "Really. I don't need a therapy session right now."

"I'm trying to intervene here, Clare. Because now you're pulling guns on guys in bars."

Clare says nothing. Somers sits on the bed at arm's length from Clare.

"Look at me," she says. "You don't need to take this to your grave. Show yourself some compassion. You were fooled. You deserve more. So let it go." Somers takes Clare's hand and squeezes it. "And, Clare? Just to drive it home: I am not one of the bad guys."

All Clare can do is nod. She can't bear tears right now. She drinks the last of the coffee and stands to use the bathroom, closing the door behind her and bracing herself on the sink.

You were fooled, Somers said. How well Clare knows this to be true.

Douglas Bentley places the sandwich plates down in front of Somers and Clare. Since they arrived at his house he has busied himself in the kitchen, mostly in awkward silence. He seems nervous, his hands shaky, Somers's presence in his home a twist he wasn't expecting. The Stacey Norton file Somers gave Clare rests on the counter next to her sandwich plate.

"I saw your face on the news this morning," he says to Clare.

"Let's not talk about it," Clare says. "It was a misunderstanding."

"Clare told me on the drive here that you made high rank," Somers says to change the subject.

"I did," Douglas says.

"My husband served. Two tours. He retired a sergeant."

"Is he managing well?"

"He is." Somers smiles. "Thank you for asking."

Douglas gives a small *yep* without making eye contact. He sets water glasses down for Somers and Clare, then sits at the counter so the three of them form a triangle. Somers directs a look to Clare that asks the obvious question: What are we doing here? Clare nods as if to say, be patient. Only when Clare bites into the ham sandwich does she realize how ravenous she is. She eats as Somers makes small talk, commenting on the view, on the house, just as Clare had done yesterday. Was that only yesterday? Clare thinks. That feels almost impossible.

"I was hoping we could take Somers downstairs," Clare says, patting the file. "She's got a cold case that has a lot of parallels to your daughter's. A young woman who was also from the Lune Bay area. Maybe if the three of us—"

"I don't like working with cops," Douglas says. "No offense."

"None taken," Somers says. "I'm sure they've given you no reason to trust them. But as Clare says, I've got a case that's been lingering a long time. A young woman with some ties to the Westman family." Somers reaches down and lifts her satchel. "I pulled up whatever I could on your daughter. Seems to me like there's some . . . as Clare said, some parallels."

"You're talking about Stacey Norton," Douglas says.

"I am," Somers says. "Do you know of any others?"

"Women who went missing, you mean? None who were reported. But . . ." Douglas rubs at his temple, his eyes red. "Missing women, especially a certain type, don't exactly rouse the troops, if you know what I mean."

"I know exactly what you mean," Somers says. "We all hear about the flashy cases. The Zoe Westmans who make the front page of the newspaper. That footage of volunteers in formation scouring parks and ravines and beaches. But what if you're dealing with a young woman who just didn't come home one night? Who had the wrong boyfriend or a drug problem or who'd gotten herself mixed up with the wrong crowd." Somers frowns, her voice dropping. "I have daughters too, you know. This stuff feels personal to me. The Norton case? No evidence of foul play, my colleagues would all say. Looks like she's just another runner. Is that what they said about your daughter?"

Douglas nods.

"I'm sorry about that," Somers continues. "I swear, I've always made an effort to take cases like this seriously. But you're right, Mr. Bentley. A lot of cops don't."

A silence passes between them. Clare can see the emotion on Douglas's face, his jaw pulsing in the effort to maintain composure. He lifts their plates and turns his back to wash them in the sink. Somers grimaces at Clare. When he's finished at the sink, Douglas waves for Somers and Clare to follow him to the basement. Downstairs, he stands aside, hands in his pockets, shifting his weight uneasily as Somers studies the photographs and notes lining the wall.

"You've been at this a long time," Somers says.

"It gives me something to do." Douglas points to the top corner of the wall where Malcolm's photo is displayed next to Zoe's. Clare can see a paper with her own name, an enlarged photocopy of her business card. "I put that up there because of what you told me yesterday. Your connection to Malcolm. I don't mean anything by it. I'm just trying to keep things straight."

"Makes sense," Somers says, shooting Clare a look.

Clare retreats to a corner and chews her fingernails as Somers continues to follow the map on Douglas's wall. Above Kendall's photograph is one of Stacey Norton, the few small articles about her disappearance cut out and stapled neatly next to her photo. Clare wants to rip her own name down from the wall. But she is part of this matrix whether she wants to be or not. Malcolm hired her, she worked for him. To see it so plainly on the wall, Clare only one step removed from Zoe, from the Westman family, sends a chill down her spine. Somers pauses next at Jack Westman's photograph. There is a sticky note attached to it. *Autopsy?* Somers taps at it.

"What's this?"

"Jack Westman's autopsy was never released. With public shootings, with something like this, usually the autopsy is released. Neither was the coroner's report. I asked around. Wanted to see if I could get my hands on it."

"Wouldn't it be pretty straightforward?" Clare asks. "Gunshot wound to the head."

"That's what they said about JFK," Douglas says.

Somers allows a small smile. "Conspiracy theorists unite."

A cell phone rings sharply. Somers jolts, then fumbles to extract hers from her satchel and answer the call. She lifts a finger to say *give me a minute*, then disappears up the stairs. Clare and Douglas stand in place, listening to Somers's muffled voice upstairs. *What do you mean?* she is saying. *He's where?* Does Clare hear her say a name? No. She does not hear her say *Jason*. Clare must be imagining things. Douglas approaches the wall and touches his daughter's photograph at its center.

"You know what's made me the maddest?" he says.

Clare shakes her head. "The cops ignoring you?"

"No." Douglas runs a finger along the outline of the photograph. "The cops who suggested she'd killed herself. There was one guy, one detective, this really crusty asshole. Not an empathetic bone in his body. I came to him with some information, and he listened to me like I was a child inventing fairy tales. Like I was amusing to him. And then he leaned forward in his chair and said to me, 'Maybe the problem is that you feel guilty. Maybe you pushed her too hard, and she went over the edge. She was under a lot of pressure.' He was implying to me that Kendall killed herself because her mother and I couldn't lay off her."

Douglas faces Clare. In his grief, he might best understand the loneliness, the isolation that Clare feels. He might be the only person she can trust in all of this.

"I ran away from a really shitty husband," Clare says.

"Oh," Douglas says. "I didn't know that."

"Yeah," Clare says. "Just before Christmas. Nine months ago. Up until two months ago I was sleeping in a different cheap motel every night. I had a gun. I kept it under my pillow. Sometimes I'd toss and turn and my hand would jam itself under the pillow and land on the gun and for a split second I'd think about it. I'd think about putting it to my temple and pulling the trigger. Because I left my life . . ." She pauses and scratches hard at her scalp. "I left everything because I was afraid I was going to die. But after I was gone, it was hard to imagine anything at all. I was still so afraid, but there was this void too. Every day, everything around me changed. I had no footing."

Douglas removes his glasses and wipes away the sweat forming on his brow.

"When I finally did stop in one place," Clare continues, "when I saw this HELP WANTED sign in a window and tried my hand at staying put for a while, that hopeless feeling got even worse. Because I took this job at a restaurant, and right away it set in just how hard it would actually be to build a life from scratch. Everyone else already had their lives, they were settled with their families and their routines. The cooks, the other waitresses. The clientele. People don't like to make room for strangers. And even if they did take a cursory interest in me, I had nothing to give them. I couldn't make small talk or answer any of their basic questions. People want to know where you're from and who your family is and what brings you to their place. I just didn't have it in me to invent an entire backstory, you know?"

"Sure," Douglas says, awkward. "Makes sense."

"And then I hadn't even finished my first week on the job when Malcolm Boon showed up. Malcolm Hayes, as you know him. And I knew exactly why he was there the minute I laid eyes on him. So I ran, of course I did. I literally ran out the back door of the restaurant. I'd trained myself to run for many months, so it was a well-honed instinct. I drove half the night in zigzags before stopping at a motel. I was really scared. The thought of being caught terrified me. But honestly? When I look back on it, on waiting in that motel room with my gun to see if he'd followed me, I can admit that I wanted him to find me. I wanted some kind of reckoning. Because nothing is worse than being invisible."

"Yes. That's why I need to find out. I need to know what happened to her. To Kendall."

"Even if she's . . ."

"Especially if she's dead," he says, his voice steady. "I mean, look at you. You weren't dead. This guy Malcolm found you. And he didn't hurt you."

"No," Clare says. "He didn't. He offered me this job. And it floors me that I took it. And I know that for the rest of my life I'll never be able to truly explain why I did. It was just something in my gut. The relief at something tangible. At having something to do aside from run. Even at having someone in my life who knew my story. He was the first person in months who knew my real name. He was looking for missing women and he wanted a partner. Hey, it takes one to know one, right?

Somewhere near the end of our first case it occurred to me that I was actually good at the job. Great, even. Because if you've spent years honing survival instincts, then you understand how other people do the same. And if you've disappeared, you understand how it happens. Why people run, how they might go missing. How easy it can be, really."

"Why are you telling me all of this?" Douglas asks.

"Because I have this question," Clare says. "Malcolm took on this work of looking for missing women. For something to do, maybe. Because he was driven to find Zoe and needed an outlet for that? I don't know. He never talked about it. Then I got hurt at the end of our first case. Shot in the shoulder."

Clare pulls back the neck of her shirt to reveal the scar. Douglas leans in to examine it.

"Wow," he says. "Five times overseas and I never took a bullet on the job."

"Yeah. Beginner's luck, I guess. Anyway, Malcolm and I spent a few weeks laying low as I recovered. To be honest, I was in a haze. Lots of painkillers. I don't remember much about those weeks, but I learned more about him, some details seeped in. And I think about those details in a new light now. I have reason to question his motives. And last night, I was in a holding cell with these women after I was arrested. And I was thinking: What if my story started here? What if it's all connected to Zoe? Stacey. Kendall, even? What if it's all connected?"

"I'm not following," Douglas says.

Clare points to the photo of Kendall, then to Stacey Norton. "What if he was looking for them the same way he was looking for me?"

"Come on," Douglas says. "You think?"

"Maybe I'm a conspiracy theorist too."

Upstairs Somers's voice rises, clearer.

"I need this from you right away," she says on the call. "As in, yesterday."

Clare blinks, listening. She hates that she wants to cry.

"I need a gun," she says to Douglas. "I can shoot. My dad taught me to shoot. I'd like a gun."

"And?"

"You strike me as the kind of man who knows where to procure one."

"Yeah. I know a place."

"Can you take me?" Clare asks. She sees his hesitation. "Listen. I carry a gun for protection. Like I said, I know how to use one. And mine was taken from me last night when I was arrested."

Douglas considers this, leaning a shoulder into the wall, rubbing at his beard.

"So will you help me?" Clare asks.

Before he can answer, Somers has descended the stairs. She pauses to absorb the air between Clare and Douglas, thicker now than when she'd left to take the call.

"I'm going to need an hour to address some things at home," Somers says. "I may need to go back to the hotel."

"Is everything okay?" Clare asks.

"It will be," Somers says.

"Anything you need to tell me?" Clare asks.

"Nope," Somers says. "Shall we get going?"

"Clare can stay," Douglas says. "We can sift through some things here."

Somers nods, shifting her gaze from Clare to Douglas. Clare plants herself at the desk. She will stay right here.

Though they are less than a mile above the ocean, the trees here are low and crooked, the air dry. The drive from Douglas's house to the sporting goods store had taken only twenty minutes, but Clare was shocked by how quickly the backdrop shifted away from the quaint houses and manicured gardens to a grittier landscape. Lune Bay is its own little world, Clare thought as they pulled into the parking lot. MURPHY'S SPORTS AND HUNTING SUPPLIES, the sign reads. A bell jangles when Douglas tugs the door open.

"No gun stores right in Lune Bay?" Clare asks.

"Never," Douglas says. "The Business Improvement Association would never go for that. Too ignoble."

"Right." Clare smiles. "This is your store of choice?"

"They have a nice range out back. I know the owner. I did a tour with his cousin."

Together they weave through the racks of binoculars and camouflage gear to the back of the store where the gun wall resides. A young man spritzes the glass countertop with a spray bottle, then rubs at it hard with a clump of paper towels. They stand in clear view but it still takes the young man a few beats to snap out of his cleaning trance and look up.

"Douglas! Jesus. Didn't even see you there."

"Hi, Danny," Douglas says. "We're looking to purchase a weapon. One. Possibly two."

"Excellent. Anything specific today?"

"A handgun," Douglas says. "On the compact side. Easy to pack away."

They speak as if Clare isn't there. Danny shuffles down the counter and waves his hand over a selection of smaller guns. He points to one in the corner of the cabinet.

"This one is a very popular model. Inexpensive given what you get. Fits in most pockets. Well, your pockets, maybe. I'm not sure about hers."

"Ha," Douglas says, unamused. "Can we have a look?"

Danny pats at his chest and retrieves a lanyard tucked under his green golf shirt. Clare watches him as he crouches to unlock the cabinet. There is evidence that Danny is far older than he looks at first glance, the way his skin is pinched around his eyes, closer in age to Clare than she might ever have previously guessed. It isn't until he unravels a cloth and sets the first gun down on it that Clare notices the thin band on his left hand. Married. He lines four options up along the counter. Clare picks up the smallest gun. It is heavier than she expected. She must nudge her finger into the trigger loop, cupping the gun so that her thumb can press down and gently roll the cylinder open.

"It's not loaded," Danny says.

169

Clare casts him a look. "Of course it isn't."

"Technically I'm supposed to see your ID before I let you handle the weapons," he says.

Douglas fishes his driver's license from his wallet and slaps it on the counter.

"I know who you are, Mr. Bentley," Danny says. "I was referring to her."

"She's not buying," Douglas says.

"She's holding the gun, though." Finally he looks directly at Clare. "Wait. Have we met?"

"Definitely not," Clare says, eyes to the floor.

"This is my niece," Douglas says. "She's visiting from out of town. Her crazy uncle wants to make sure she stays safe. I know you can appreciate that, Danny."

"Sure." Danny's brow creases as he studies her. "But, hmm. You really look familiar."

Fuck, Clare thinks. The video. Surely a young guy who works in a gun store would have seen it. He's the video's target audience.

"Listen, Danny," Douglas interjects. "We'd like to use the range out back if that's okay with you. Clare had her wallet stolen in a coffee shop yesterday, so all you've got with her is my word that she's not going to put a bullet in my head."

"Okay," Danny says, his focus still on Clare. "There's no one out on the range right now. I'm going say that only you should be handling the guns, Mr. Bentley. But I can give you an extra set of glasses and earmuffs. Just in case you need them. And I'll be busy in here for the next fifteen minutes or so. I won't be checking up on you. Got it?"

"Got it, Dan. We appreciate it."

As Douglas signs the paperwork, Clare keeps her eyes squarely on Danny. She will counter the patter in her chest, the anxiety, by working to put him in his place. It used to be a game for her, this stare, the count to see just how long it would take before her target would start to squirm. Douglas passes the waiver form back and they follow Danny through the rear door. Outside, Clare and Douglas lift their hands in unison to form visors against the sharp sun. It is warmer here than by the ocean. The gun range consists of messy plywood booths and targets at a distance, pocked with bullet holes. Danny sets the guns and safety equipment down in the nearest booth.

"We can handle it from here," Douglas says.

"I'm supposed to give my safety spiel," Danny says.

"I appreciate that, Danny, but unless it's changed from the last thirty times I've heard it, I think you can count on me being safe."

Danny looks slighted. Once he's gone back inside, Douglas hands Clare the smaller of the ear protection muffs and the safety glasses. The muffs give Clare the sensation that she is underwater, the tasks her hands now perform in front of her silenced. The glasses cast a yellow hue over everything. Douglas has set Clare up at one of the stations, the handgun resting on a block. He is saying something. *Read.* Clare retracts the muff from her ear.

"You ready?" Douglas asks.

"Yes," Clare says.

"You need a hand?"

Clare shakes her head and steps into the booth. She holds the handgun on her open palm like an artifact before lifting it into the proper grip. She fits the muff back in place on her ear. The target is about fifty feet away, Clare estimates. *Count,* her father used to say. *Never guess.* In the vast field behind their house he'd measure out specific distances and set up targets for her.

Count.

Clare points the gun and squeezes her left eye closed. She can feel Douglas behind her. There it is, Clare thinks. The trance she remembers so well, the veil that used to descend when she took aim. The focus. She lifts the safety and points to the target's heart. She pulls the trigger and the target jolts. She aims again, this time for the forehead, triangulated from the two dotted eyes. She fires again and holds her position for a moment, breathing through her nose. Finally Clare sets the gun down and removes her muffs.

"Well, he's definitely dead," Douglas says. "You aren't going to shoot the rest of the bullets?"

"My dad used to give me two shots," Clare says. "He didn't like to waste bullets. Especially when the target's already dead."

A small smile creeps over Douglas's face. "I like the sound of your dad. He was a good teacher."

"When it comes to guns, yes."

Next to her, Douglas steps into his booth and gears up. Clare studies his form: elbows too loose, grip on the gun too tight. He fires six shots in quick succession, his grip bouncing with each one. The target buckles and shakes. When it settles, Clare notes the exact pattern she'd have predicted, a scattering of holes around the target's middle. You've only wounded him, Clare wants to say. Made him mad. Now what?

Douglas sets the gun down and examines his handiwork.

"Not exactly accurate," he says. "But consistent?"

"Yes," Clare says. "Definitely consistent."

"How does that one feel?" Douglas points to the gun in her hand.

"Good. Light. Easy to handle."

"You want to empty the rest of your chamber before we head back in? No need to scrimp on bullets. Your dad's not here."

Clare puts her safety equipment back in place and lines up again. As a young girl, she aimed her gun at inanimate objects, tin cans or overripe pumpkins, and thought nothing. But this time, as she squints to the target, she imagines a human in its place. Jason. Clare fires until the chamber is empty, then removes her muffs and glasses.

"You okay?" Douglas asks.

"Fine."

"I'll buy it," Douglas says. "You can pay me back."

Clare nods, grateful. They busy themselves collecting their gear and return to the store, where Danny waits at the counter. As Douglas completes the paperwork, Clare wanders through the racks of hunting vests until she is out of sight. She checks her messages to find one from Austin.

Can we meet?

Clare writes in response,

Where?

He writes with a smiling emoji,

Obviously not The Cabin Bar! My house?

Clare responds,

No.

Oh, come on. Charlotte and Kavita will be here.
I'll send u the address. We can clear the air.

Another smiling emoji. Clare doesn't respond. Her cell phone clock reads 4:03 p.m. This day bleeds into yesterday, so little sleep in between. And yet, she cannot stop moving. She will ask Somers to meet her at her next stop. Clare wanders back to the counter just as Douglas has finished the transaction.

"Ready?" he asks her.

"Ready."

With a nod Douglas takes Clare by the arm and leads her out of the store.

T he retaining wall that separates Roland's parking lot from the rocky beach is coated with mist from the ocean. Clare lays out her sweater and sits on it to wait for Somers. She tugs the elastic from her ponytail loose until her hair releases around her face. The wind catches it and whips it upward. Clare so rarely wears her hair down, unruly as it can be. But right now she'll take any small change that might render her slightly less recognizable.

On the drive back from the sporting goods store, Clare sat in Douglas's passenger seat and loaded the gun, using the box of ammunition he'd bought too. If he minded her performing such a precarious task in the confined space of his car, Douglas said nothing. He only pointed to the weapon as he pulled into the parking lot at Roland's.

"That thing's registered in my name," he said.

"I know," Clare responded.

He needn't elaborate. Clare understands that whatever risks she takes with this gun will implicate him too. As she rose from his car to face the empty parking lot, the ocean beyond it, Clare couldn't bring herself to say anything more. Now the gun is in her bag, and Clare watches the ocean from her perch, gnawing at her fingernails. The froth of the waves disconcerts her. In the farmland where Clare grew up, everything was demarcated, every swath of land and water marked by clear boundaries. The endlessness of this ocean horizon feels inconceivable to Clare.

Roland's won't open for another twenty minutes. Somers pulls up and parks. She emerges from the driver's seat looking down at her phone, her thumbs typing a message. She looks up and waves. Clare stretches her sweater out to provide dry seating for Somers too. Somers sits and squints to look out to the waves.

"What a beautiful spot," she says. "I haven't seen the ocean since my honeymoon. How pathetic is that?"

"I'd never seen the ocean," Clare says. "Until about six weeks ago."

Somers smiles. "You win. Shall we?"

"Wait," Clare says. "Before we go in. Do you need to tell me something?"

"Nothing that can't wait."

"What was the issue you had to deal with?" Clare asks. "Back at Bentley's house?"

"Nothing, Clare. Really. We should get inside before the restaurant opens. We can talk about this later."

"I thought I heard you say Jason's name," Clare says. "When you took that call at Douglas's house. I thought I heard you say *Jason*."

Somers is silent. She tracks a flock of gulls that flies over the crashing waves, diving and rising in chaotic unison.

"Is it about the calls?" Clare asks. "The ones you were getting?"

"Well," Somers says. "I got a call from that contact of mine in a detachment not far from your hometown. I'd asked him to keep track of this Jason of yours. Once a day, twice. I did some real grunt work on a case for this guy a few years ago, before he relocated east. So he owed me."

"And?" Clare says.

"He claims Jason hasn't shown up to work in a few days."

"Sometimes that happens." Clare's voice wavers. "He goes on a bender that outlasts the weekend by a few days. A week if it's a bad one."

"Right," Somers says. "Sure. Yeah. But he doesn't seem to be at home either."

"So what?" Clare says. "Why are you telling me this?"

"Because they can't find him."

"But it was a woman calling you, right?" Clare's words are sharp, desperate.

"Yeah. Hey, I haven't totally pieced this together. That's why I wanted to set it aside for now."

"Okay, but do you think he's here? Or headed here?"

"Do you?"

What kind of question is that? Clare wants to scream. She thinks of Malcolm's email. *I believe that Zoe knows about you.* It feels too possible that everything is connected. Clare buries her face in her hands.

"I'm sorry," Somers says, patting Clare's leg. "Listen. I've told you, I'm on this. I'm working on it. I'm not interested in putting you at risk. I've got a lot of options here. Lots of tricks up my sleeve. Let's just stay on course for now. Go inside, speak to this Roland guy, move forward. Okay?"

"Okay."

They stand and Clare ties her sweater around her waist. Roland's is empty, but the door is unlocked. He is again perched behind the bar. He waves them over. Clare phoned earlier to tell him she was coming with Somers, and if it bothered him, if he had anything to hide from them, his reaction gave her no indication.

"I hear there's a new detective in town," he says, shaking Somers's outstretched hand. "Seems like our cold cases are warming up again."

"I hear you're famous for your seafood." Somers plucks a menu from the bar and scans it.

"It's as local as you can get." He looks to Clare. "My eyes around town tell me you've been busy."

"I have been," Clare says. "Just trying to do my job."

His bemused look tells Clare that he has likely seen the video, but she will not bring it up.

"Hey," Somers says. "Can I get a plate of this shrimp pasta? Maybe Clare will have the same?"

"Sure," Clare says.

Roland takes their menus and punches their order into the computer behind him. Somers walks to the empty booth, Roland and Clare trailing her.

"Scene of the crime?" she asks.

"It is," he says. "Honestly, after five years, it's still a little tough for me to stand here."

"Do people sit and eat here?" Somers asks. "By choice?"

"You'd be shocked," Roland says. "When the shooting happened, I was sure the business was toast. I figured we'd never weather the publicity. That I'd end up shuttering and selling to a developer even though I'd promised my father that would only happen over my dead body. But it actually became a bit of a tourist thing. This macabre attraction. For a while the booth was booked six months in advance. People are weird."

Somers slides into the booth and rests her forearms on the table, looking up at them.

"Tell me something, Roland? Do you think the cops did a good job on this case?"

"If they'd done a good job, they'd have figured out who killed Jack," Roland says. "Forty eyewitnesses. Only four ways out of Lune Bay. It's an absolute disgrace that they didn't catch the guy."

"Sit," Somers says, patting the tabletop.

Both Clare and Roland slide in, the three of them fanned in a semicircle just as Jack Westman would have been with his wife and daughters. From her vantage, Clare can see the hostess station, the door, the trajectory the shooter would have taken. Somers removes a file from her bag and opens it to extract photographs of Kendall Bentley and Stacey Norton. She slides them over to Roland.

"Are either of these young women familiar to you?" Somers asks.

"Sure," he says. "They both worked here. Kendall and Stacey. Both fell on pretty hard times, I think."

"They both went missing," Clare says.

"That's right. I believe they worked here for a few summers. Patio season. The tall one, Kendall, she was in medical school. The other one—"

"Her name is Stacey," Somers says sharply.

"Yes. She wanted to open a beauty salon, I think. Honestly, we'd have fifteen of these girls every summer. You should see our patio on a busy night."

AMY STUART

Two staff enter the room from the kitchen, a server and a bartender. They stop short and look to Roland, who waves them onward. Clare watches the bartender as he takes his place and begins counting the bottles lined up behind the bar. She feels a dryness in her mouth. Suddenly, Clare is sweating. She wants a drink.

"Can you point me to the bathroom?" Clare asks.

"To the back right and downstairs," Roland tells her.

Clare weaves through the tables to the stairs that lead to the basement. In the early days of their relationship, Clare can remember signaling Jason at the bar to join her in the nook under the stairs. Those scenes return to her now, Jason pressing her back into the wall, how brazen they'd be when they were drunk. Clare studies her reflection in the mirror as she washes her hands. She cannot tamp down the anger. She is tired. She lets out a long sigh, then presses the bathroom door open.

On her way up, Clare slows to study the photographs that line the stairwell, some autographed by famous patrons, others marking celebrations like the restaurant's fortieth anniversary. Clare can pick Roland out in one of the earliest photographs, barely a teenager. He sits propped on a stool at the bar between his parents, smiling, raising a can of soda to the camera. Clare takes the last of the steps and has nearly turned the corner back into the restaurant when she stops dead and descends two stairs again.

No, she thinks, staring at the picture. It can't be.

There are about a dozen people in the photograph. It is taken on the rocks out front of the restaurant. To the far right is a slightly younger Roland, smiling broadly. Some in the photograph wear the white of a cook's uniform, others are dressed smartly, as servers would be. Three women stand, their arms interlocked, on one large rock: Kavita, Stacey, and Kendall. And next to Roland is Austin Lantz. How is this possible? Clare thinks. She unhooks the photograph from the wall.

"Fuck," she says aloud. "Get a grip, Clare. Get a fucking grip."

But her hands are shaking when she plucks her cell phone from her back pocket to take a picture of the photograph. She breathes deeply to collect herself before rounding the corner to return to Roland and Somers in the booth.

"What's that?" Roland gestures to the frame Clare holds to her chest.

"It was on the wall." Clare sets it down on the table and rests a fingertip on the glass overtop Austin's image. Somers watches her, wide-eyed. Clare withdraws her hand before Roland can see it shaking. "Who's that?"

"The kid next to me?" Roland leans over and squints. "Can't remember his name. He was a busboy for while. That's the worst job, next to maybe dishwasher. They never last long."

"How old is this picture?" Clare asks.

Roland lifts the frame to study it closely. "Let's see. Marco's in it. He was head chef for a few years. Best we ever had. Quit after the shooting. He claimed it gave him the shakes to walk through the dining room to the kitchen. 'Then use the frigging back door!' I'd tell him. But he couldn't hack it."

"So this was taken before the shooting?"

"Yeah. Must have been." Ronald narrows his eyes at Clare. "Why? You know that kid?"

"You *don't* know him?" Clare asks.

If he is acting, if he is pretending not to know Austin, erasing any connection that might exist between them, Clare can't tell. Her skin prickles with sweat. It is not just the back and forth of this exchange that unnerves Clare; it is the idea that Austin has omitted this fact too. The fact that he worked at Roland's. His house is supposed to be her next stop. Clare rubs at her temples.

"Wait," Roland says. "The cooks used to call him Texas, I think. No way that's his actual name."

"Austin?"

"Yes!" Roland snaps his fingers. "Austin, Texas. Right."

"Austin has been covering this case for years," Clare says. "As a journalist. And he was Jack Westman's driver for a while. Surely you've come across him since he left his job here?"

Roland raises his hands in defeat. "I'm not playing dumb, I promise you. Do you know how many reporters I've had in here since the shooting? Cops? Weirdos? Daughters of old friends who write crime blogs and want the inside scoop? Actors? Novelists?" He jabs a finger at Clare. "I told you that. I had a novelist in here the other day. You can draw whatever lines you want, but I'm not going to say I remember some kid I barely remember."

"But look." Somers taps at the photograph. "Three women in this picture, two of whom we've just discussed. Two of whom are missing. That's a lot of coincidence for one picture, I'd say."

Roland shrugs. "You two are the detectives."

"You're right," Somers says. "And right now, I'm getting the urge to start really digging. Like, getting my shovel out."

The bartender has paused, frozen in place, listening.

"Hey now," Roland says. "My father used to say that half this town worked on our patio at some point over the years. We'd hire rich kids, his friends' kids, summer jobs when the patio is hot, winter jobs so they could pretend they're paying for their own jaunts to Europe. You know how much turnover I have? Hundreds of girls have worked here in my tenure. So did they meet here? Probably. Who knows? You knew they worked here. There's no revelation."

"Seeing them all together like this," Clare says. "It really does feel like a revelation."

"It's a lot to take in." Somers points to Stacey's photo. "This case has been on my desk for a long time. I hate unsolved cases, particularly ones involving young women. So if you remember anything that might be related to them, I'd appreciate you telling me. Telling us."

Roland releases a long exhale. "I don't know anything about Stacey. She wasn't from Lune Bay. Kendall? She just wanted to party. She wasn't interested in being a doctor. Her father might have come a bit unglued. He's been around here a few times, now that I think of it. His kid probably just took off to get out from under him."

"Right," Somers says.

The door opens and a family enters, scanning the restaurant and then smiling at Roland when they spot him.

"Listen," Roland says. "We're about to open. I've got to get to work. But you're welcome back anytime."

Somers closes the file. Clare collects the frame and returns to the stairwell to rehang it. She sets the back of her hand to her too-warm cheek. It's totally plausible, Clare thinks, that Roland's is simply the epicenter of Lune Bay, a place for young people to break into the workforce. She straightens the frame on the wall and leans in close. A coincidence. But there is something in the way Austin stands next to Roland, one man in a sharp suit and the younger one in a uniform dirtied by the toils of his work. It seems to Clare that they are edged just slightly closer together than everyone else in the photo, the way friends might be. Clare shifts her gaze between the two smiling men. It might all be a coincidence, Clare thinks, or it could be pieces of this puzzle falling into place.

The taxi pulls away and Clare stands in front of a modern white oceanfront house, all stucco and glass. Tight quarters, Austin called it. This is not tight quarters. Clare hears movement inside before the large steel door clicks open. Austin wears shorts and a T-shirt, bare feet. Behind him the house is all white on the inside too, the moon lighting a path on the ocean out the far window.

"Clare O'Kearney," he says. "I'm glad you came."

"Is this your house?" Clare asks.

"I called to see about posting bail, but someone beat me to it. And yes, it's my house."

He steps aside to allow Clare in. She follows him to the living room. He gestures for her to take a seat on the same oversize couch he does. Clare chooses a small chair across from him instead. Only once she's seated does she notice the figure on the deck, a woman lying outstretched on a lounge chair, wrapped in a blanket. Kavita.

"What's she doing here?" Clare asks.

"She goes where Charlotte goes," Austin says. "She's been crashing here too. And after last night, she needed a soft landing."

"Whoever said chivalry was dead?" Clare waves grandly at the space, the ocean out the window. "This is some pad for a freelance journalist."

Austin smiles. "Like I told you. My brother. Extremely rich."

"I googled your rich brother," Clare says. "I couldn't find much about him. I couldn't find him at all, actually."

"He's my half-brother, detective. We have different last names. His father is from Brazil. We look nothing alike. Hey, I'll give you his business card. You can call him directly and set up a time to interrogate him." Austin pulls his phone from his pocket and calls up a photograph to show her. "See?"

Clare leans to examine the photo. Austin and his brother stand arm in arm on a beach, both in wet suits, surfboards propped next to them, his brother taller, olive-skinned, more filled out. Far better-looking, Clare thinks. When Austin stands and moves past her, Clare hangs back.

"I'm going to say hi to Kavita," she calls to him. "Is that okay?"

"Why wouldn't it be?" he hollers back before disappearing into the kitchen.

Clare strains to pull the sliding door open. Kavita doesn't move, doesn't acknowledge her at all. Only when Clare takes a seat in the lounger next to hers does Kavita glance over and lift the wineglass she holds in cheers. Beyond the deck is a rocky shore. The ocean is calm tonight, the waves lapping instead of crashing, the moon a perfect crescent over the water.

"Are you okay?" Clare asks.

"Fine. You?"

"I'm fine. It's been a long day. Where's Charlotte?"

"Downstairs. Sleeping."

"Are you safe here?"

Kavita rolls her eyes. "Austin is totally harmless. He's an idiot, but he wouldn't hurt me."

They sit in silence for a moment. Clare stands and moves to the railing. About a quarter mile to the south, a glass house appears cantilevered over the water. The main floor lights are on. It glows yellow against the cliff it hangs from. Clare points to it.

"Is that Zoe and Malcolm's house?"

"Yep," Kavita says.

"The lights are on."

"Charlotte has them on timers. They come on about seven and go off at midnight."

Clare leans over the railing and studies the house. There is no movement inside it, no sign of life, but from this vantage you could watch entire scenes play out should anyone be home. Malcolm and Zoe's lives unfolding for you like a film.

"Why don't you and Charlotte stay there?" Clare asks.

"She refuses," Kavita says. "I don't blame her."

Clare returns to the lounger and sits again, drawing in a deep breath. There is something different about the ocean air. It's fuller, heavier, easier to inhale. Next to her, Kavita's eyes are closed, wisps of her dark hair lifted by the breeze.

"Did you know that guy from last night?" Clare asks. "He said he knew you."

"Yeah. Kind of. He's a cop. I've seen him around a few times."

"Around?"

Kavita adjusts her position on the lounger and wraps the blanket tighter.

"He was a minor fixture when I worked at Roland's. One of the regulars. Loved to harass the waitresses."

"Roland allowed that?"

"Let's just say that Roland benefited from having some of Lune Bay's finest on his side." Kavita sips her wine again. "Do you want a drink?"

"No thanks," Clare says. "I was at Roland's just now, actually. I saw a picture of you on the wall. With Austin. And Kendall Bentley and Stacey Norton too. You knew them?"

"I'm not really in the mood for an inquisition, Clare. I've had a rough day."

"Fair enough." Clare swings her legs so she too is laid out on her lounger. "But listen to me, Kavita. I'm trying to get to the bottom of things here. Of the Westman family's dealings. I know you're trying to move on, and you may not want to talk about it. But I think you can help me. And I'd like to think that helping me might ultimately help you. Charlotte too. If we found some real answers, I think it could help Charlotte."

Kavita chews on her lip, considering.

"Zoe Westman, for example," Clare continues. "She took over her father's business after he died. And I don't think it was all aboveboard. Do you know anything about that?"

"I don't want to talk to the cops about this," Kavita says. "Germain or anyone else."

"Okay."

Why no cops? Clare wants to ask. But she thinks of the scene last night, Kavita incapacitated and passed around by that circle of men. *He's a cop.* Kavita doesn't want to speak to the police. Of course she doesn't. Clare bends her knees and hugs them to her chest to ward off a chill from the cool air.

"Zoe came to me once," Kavita says. "Maybe a year after her dad died. I was still working at Roland's. I was a mess. Could barely drag myself out of bed. I'd dropped out of school by then, and Zoe knew it. She told me there was a politician coming to town. This environmentalist senator whose big passion was preserving oceanfront land. Roland owned the plot next to the restaurant. It was ripe for development, and the Westman group was right in there, but then there was some debate about whether it should be turned into protected parkland instead. And this senator was coming to town to survey the scene. He was this wool sweater, family-man grandfather type, but rumor had it, he had a thing for younger women. Zoe asked me if I'd be interested in showing him around Lune Bay. Playing the friendly hostess." Kavita laughs. "*Hostess* is an interesting euphemism. I knew exactly what she meant."

"What did she mean?" Clare asks.

"Everyone at Roland's knew. Zoe would befriend waitresses, and after a while, they'd quit. Stacey and Kendall were two such examples. I ran into Stacey once, about six months after she quit. She was all dressed up. Really fancy clothes. She looked beautiful, but kind of strung out too. She told me I should take Zoe up on any offer she made me. That I could make more money than I ever dreamed. Then she disappeared. Kendall did too. Both kind of under the radar. Like by the time anyone realized we hadn't heard from them, they'd already been gone for a while."

"Kendall's father has been looking for her. He filed a missing persons report years ago."

"I know he did."

"So did you take Zoe up on her offer?"

Kavita grimaces. "God, no. But after that, working at Roland's became kind of untenable. I can't even put my finger on it. It was like Roland knew I'd said no to Zoe. I mean, the senator came to town and a week later he announced that he supported the development. I'm sure Zoe found some hostess to wrangle him. Roland got to sell the land, and condos went up. But after that, I seemed to get the worst shifts on the schedule, or none at all. And truth be told, I was slipping by then anyway."

Slipping. Clare knows exactly what Kavita means. She too can remember the slip, those moments where you catch yourself just before taking whatever drug is on order in that moment; and those very words come to you: I'm slipping. But for Clare, it was easy enough to convince herself that she could stop. That she *would* stop, just not right at that particular moment. She can picture Kavita bent over to snort a line in The Cabin Bar bathroom last night.

"You could get help, you know," Clare says.

"Help for what?"

"The drugs."

"Did you ever get help?" Kavita asks.

"I'm sorry?"

Kavita taps at the bend of her arm. "Scars," she says. "You've got plenty of them. I spotted them last night."

Even though she wears a sweater, Clare instinctively crosses her arms. The scars are indeed there: Tiny pinpricks of white tissue in the crooks of her elbows. Track marks that have faded but will never disappear. Clare's been good, clean. But it will always live within her, she knows, these scars a reminder, her signal to keep her distance from any path that might lead her astray.

"What about Charlotte?" Clare asks. "She's got a daughter. She won't regain any custody if she keeps using."

"She's never getting her daughter back," Kavita says. "The

kid is ten. She lives on the far coast with her father and his new family. Charlotte's got this dream scenario where she gets custody again, but give me a break. She's a stranger to that little girl."

"That's tough," Clare says. "I get why she's angry."

"Charlotte isn't a bad person. She's just damaged."

"You two are close." Clare shifts on the lounger. "Like, *close*."

Kavita laughs. "Oh my God. Look at you, dancing around it like some kind of prude."

"I don't want to pry."

"There's no secret," Kavita says. "I've never been into guys. Some people have phases, but I never did. By the time I was nine, I knew I liked girls. Maybe it's just a phase for Charlotte. Lord knows she's had her share of phases."

"Did she have any other relationships after her husband left?"

"She told me once about a guy she dated. I can't remember his name. Maybe she never told me his name. She said they kept the relationship a secret. And I guess he eventually dropped her."

A wind knocks over an empty planter at the edge of the deck. Clare twists and scans the house. She can see Austin in the kitchen, leaning against the counter, scrolling on his phone. Kavita takes another sip of her drink. When Clare's phone dings, she digs it from her jeans to find an unread email from a numbered address, a large file attached. Clare goes to swipe it away as junk until she notices the file name. *JW @ Rolands*. And then a date. The date, Clare recognizes at once, of Jack Westman's death. A video file. Clare clicks to open it.

Her phone says,

Cannot read this file type.

"Fuck."

"What's up?" Kavita asks.

"Nothing. Hey, are you hungry?"

"A little."

"Why don't I see what I can rummage up inside?"

Clare stands. She inhales the salt air again, eyes back to her phone.

It can't be, she thinks. This file. It can't be what she thinks it is.

D espite the ocean out the window, the airiness, this house is stark and cold. Clare closes the sliding door behind her and focuses on her phone again, working to open the video. No luck.

"Come here!" Austin calls from the kitchen.

Clare obeys, entering and taking a seat on one of the counter stools across from him. Austin fiddles with a corkscrew.

"Is there a video of the shooting?" Clare asks him.

"What?" Austin says, yanking the cork free from the bottle. "Jack Westman's shooting?"

"Yes," Clare says, her cheeks hot.

"God. No. I don't think so. A reporter can only dream."

"Are you sure?"

Austin's eyes narrow. "Why are you asking?"

"Douglas mentioned it," she says, a lie. "But we know he's a conspiracy theorist, so . . ."

When Austin offers her a glass of wine, Clare waves it away. She must weigh her options. She could share the video with Austin now; surely he'd have the tools on hand to open the file. But Clare doesn't know what the video will depict. She can't be guaranteed it has anything to do with Jack Westman. She must keep it to herself.

"You have quite the view of the Westman house," she says.

He grins. "Isn't that something? A real selling point for this lowly reporter."

"Not sure an oceanfront mansion qualifies you as 'lowly.'"

There is scorn in Clare's voice, and Austin detects it. She swipes her phone to retrieve her photos, then holds it aloft so Austin can see the photograph she'd taken at Roland's. He squints at it, still smiling, unbothered.

"I can explain that," he says.

"You never told me you worked at Roland's."

"You never asked."

"I think I did. Either way, I'm asking now."

"Okay, okay," Austin says. "I was a busboy. Literally the worst job imaginable. One day I was cleaning glasses at the end of a shift and I got to talking to Jack Westman about cars. He was sitting at the bar. Closing time didn't apply to him. He hired me on the spot to be his driver. I figured driving was a much better job than hauling dirty dishes. Soon enough, I was driving him to these warehouses, and these guys would come out and they'd all be talking in a circle. I'd be sitting there dead sure that the whole scene was going to turn into a Tarantino movie. I'd catch a stray bullet and my brain would end up all over the headrest. I got anxious. I wasn't sleeping well. As luck would have it, my brother made his first ten million around the same time. And he's generous. So I quit."

"You were telling me your life story at the bar yesterday," Clare says. "That's a pretty key detail to leave out."

"Have you ever left anything out of a story, Clare?" Austin laughs. "I think you have. I know you have, actually."

Something in his tone tugs at Clare. Her stomach flips. Austin tries to nudge the wineglass her way again. Clare accepts it, then pushes it aside. She cannot drink it. She won't cave tonight.

"I offered to take you home last night," Austin says. "Share a cab. I like to think I'm a decent-looking guy. I thought we had something, you know? It might have been nice."

"Jesus, Austin."

"I'm just saying. It feels one-sided, this relationship. Unrequited."

"Fuck you."

"Ouch!" Austin sips his wine, the glass oversize for his grip. "You needn't be so harsh, Clare."

"You filmed what happened last night with Kavita and sent the video out."

"Of course I did. This is the viral age, Clare. That shit was gold."

"You screwed me," Clare says.

"How? I made you famous."

"You know my work relies on anonymity. You took that from me."

"Oh, come on."

When Austin reaches to pinch a strand of her hair, Clare recoils sharply.

"Here's the thing," Austin says. "I got home last night and turned off my phone. I never turn off my phone. But the notifications from the video post were insane. I was getting so many that my phone was literally too hot to touch. I jerked awake in the middle of the night, and I was all sweaty and thirsty. I hate that. I was in my bathroom chugging water, thinking about Kavita down the hall. I know she and Charlotte have this thing, this lesbian dabble or something, but she's right down the hall and I know she'd be too hopped up to remember anything."

How Clare wants to punch Austin now, to throttle him.

"You better not have touched her," she hisses.

"Relax," he says. "I wouldn't do that. My mother raised me right. But what I did do was fire up my laptop and get to work." Austin plucks his phone from the counter and swipes at its screen. "There's this reverse search you can do. You know, where you take a photo of someone, or in your case a screenshot from a video, and you drop it into a search engine? And any other lookalike pictures out there on the internet will pop up."

Clare feels the blood drain from her face. Austin angles his phone to allow Clare to see the screen.

"Clare O'Callaghan," he says. "Look at this! Missing since December from some farm town way east of here. You went for a jog and just vanished into thin air? Crazy. There were search parties, a husband who seemed wracked by it all. Jason O'Callaghan. Look at this. You were in the news for a while there. The really local news, at least." He swipes at more photographs. "Then there's a blank spot over the winter and spring. I'm guessing you were lying low? That was smart. And then you show up a few months ago in some mountain town where another woman has gone missing. But wait! In that story, you're Clare O'Dey? And now you're Clare O'Kearney?" He turns the phone again to swipe through more photographs.

"The *O* name thing is cute, I've got to say. Kind of like a calling card, right? But, Clare O . . . can I call you that? Clare O? You've definitely left a bit of a crumb trail in your travels."

It takes everything in Clare not to lunge for his phone and smash it to the floor. As if detecting her instinct, Austin holds his phone high, a smirk across his face. Your gun, Clare thinks. You could pull your gun. Fire a bullet into his forehead. The rage she feels at his crooked smile is enough to compel her to do so, to end this. But she can't. Instead she inhales deeply and holds her breath until her heartbeat steadies. Then she lays her hands flat on the cool stone of the kitchen island and looks Austin squarely in the eyes.

"What do you want?" she asks.

"Yours is a good story," he says. "I could tell it for you."

Clare must change her tack. She summons the tears that have been threatening to spill over. She allows her eyes to fill and her cheeks to streak. Austin looks stricken. He darts across the kitchen to collect a box of tissues for her. Clare smiles at him through the tears. She sees the look in his eyes. Though the tears are easy enough to come by, though Clare's fear feels real, it still seems too easy.

"I really need you to back off on this," she says, her voice cracked.

"Can I ask why?"

"Can I tell you another time?" Clare whispers. "How about I promise to tell you another time."

"Okay," he says. "I didn't mean—"

"It's fine." Clare reaches out and allows her hand to linger on his arm. "I get it. You're just doing your job. And I promise you I'll give you the whole story, Austin. I just need a little more time."

Austin nods, solemn. It irks Clare that she must use her

charms to gain the upper hand, that Austin's weakness is so predictable. Still, she needs him on her side. She cannot risk the details of her life emerging now. Her phone burns in her pocket. The video. Clare knows that Somers is the only person she dares trust with it. She will text her as soon as she can and ask Somers to meet her in the hotel lobby tomorrow morning. But right now, Clare will stay here with Austin until he finishes his wine, steering the conversation as far away from herself as she can.

FRIDAY

Clare lies flat on the bed, no memory of the dream that woke her. She's in her hotel room. It's Friday morning. She lifts her phone from where it charges on the bedside table. 7:52 a.m. She arrived back here around midnight, setting her gun in the drawer, then peeling her clothes off to tumble into the bed. Her mouth is dry, her head screams. In the bathroom Clare chugs three glasses of water and leans forward to meet her own stare in the mirror. *You're just tired*, she mouths to her reflection. She turns on the shower and jumps in.

Back in the room, wrapped in a towel, Clare checks her phone again. There is a text from Somers.

I'm in the lobby. Where are you?

Quickly Clare dresses and brushes her teeth. Her stomach is pulled tight with hunger. The hotel hallway is empty but for an abandoned cleaning cart at the far end. Clare stares at

201

her reflection again in the tinted mirrors of the elevator. In the lobby she finds Somers seated at a cluster of lounge chairs. She stands as Clare nears.

"Sorry," Clare says. "My alarm didn't go off."

"You don't look that hot," Somers says. "Where'd you go last night?"

"Nowhere. I'm just tired."

"Okay. So what's up? Why the late-night texts?"

"Something's come up," Clare says. "At least, I think it's something. It's a video file. It won't open on my phone. I figured we can use your laptop. Is there somewhere more private we can go?"

"Give me a second," Somers says, all-business.

Somers proceeds to the front desk and flips open her badge to the clerk. Clare slumps in the chair and tracks the business travelers who come and go, their wheeled carry-ons clicking along the marble floor. Despite the coolness of the lobby, Clare's back and neck are coated with sweat. Somers returns, waving a key, and directs Clare to follow her down a hallway at the rear of the lobby. She unlocks a small boardroom and hits the lights. Clare and Somers fan out to opposite sides of the conference table. Somers unpacks her laptop.

"While I love a good mystery," Somers says, "can we cut to it?"

Clare digs her phone from her pocket and unlocks it to access her email. "I'm going to email you the file," she says. "It's large. I received it yesterday from an encrypted email address. No sender name."

"Okay," Somers drawls, hitting at the keys of her laptop. "What is it?"

"Like I said, I couldn't open the file on my phone. But I think it depicts Jack Westman's murder."

Somers gapes at Clare. "Someone emailed this to you?"

"Yes," Clare says. "Last night."

"How do you know that's what it is?" Somers asks. "If you haven't watched it."

"I don't know. The file name implies it. I might be wrong. But I have a hunch."

Somers's baffled stare is broken only by the ding of an arrived email.

"Okay." Somers taps at her laptop again. "I've got it. Let me try to open it."

They roll their office chairs closer until their elbows touch. Somers allows the first few seconds of the video to play. The camera circles the table. Clare recognizes Roland's, the booth. The shot stops on Colleen Westman. Somers hits the pause button.

"Jesus." Somers slaps the table. "You were right."

"I knew it."

"Okay, listen. This is what we do. We watch it once through. Once. Then we share what we saw. What we noticed. Then we watch it again and hash it out."

"Why?" Clare asks.

"Because we both know what we're going to see next. A guy comes in and shoots another guy. We don't know who took this video, or who's seen it, or what else is in it. I've seen the case file and I know for a fact that the cops haven't declared a video as evidence. If any of them have seen this, they buried it. So we watch, and we see what we notice. Fresh eyes. Okay?"

"Okay," Clare says.

"It's not going to be pretty," Somers says. "You up for it?"

"Just play it."

Somers aligns the mouse to restart the video. Clare feels like she might vomit. The video window opens on the screen. At the bottom, Clare notes the running time at just under two minutes.

"Ready?" Somers says.

She presses play.

Again, Colleen Westman. The video is shot from the same vantage where Clare sat yesterday at Roland's. The booth. To Colleen's left is Jack Westman, to her right, Zoe. Charlotte must be filming, Clare thinks. Desserts sit untouched in front of them. Among the three of them, only Colleen is smiling.

"How old are we today, Mom?" the filming voice says. Yes. Charlotte's voice.

"Oh, forty-five," Colleen says with a dismissive wave. "Not a day older, I swear."

Charlotte laughs. "Then I won't ask how old you were when you had me," she says.

It unsettles Clare to see Zoe Westman animated like this. Alive, talking. How many people have told Clare that she looks like Zoe? And as the camera zooms close, Clare sees it too. It *is* remarkable, she thinks, their hair and pale skin tone, but even something in the mannerisms. The smile. *You remind me of someone*, Malcolm had said to her at the end of their first case. Clare leans closer to the screen.

The camera shifts to take in the room. Clare spots Kavita standing at the hostess table, tapping at a touch screen. And though there is a crowd, Clare can clearly see Roland behind the bar. He is deep in conversation with a patron, laughing, a bar towel draped over his shoulder. The camera circles back to Colleen. Then Clare hears it.

"Whoa there, friend. Can we help you?"

This is Jack Westman's voice. The camera is still trained on the three at the table. Jack, Zoe, Colleen. Then there is a yelp and the camera jerks to the shooter. He comes into fuzzy view before the first shot is fired. Another. Then another. "What did you do?" someone yells. Zoe is screaming, and the camera waves about, focused on nothing. There is a brief flash of Jack Westman slumped against his wife, his temple marked with a red circle that looks dabbed on with paint. Finally the focus settles on the ceiling. Charlotte must have dropped the camera. "What did you do?" A woman screams again. "What did you do?" Then: "Get him!" From there the sounds are mixed together, too many voices at once. The video ends.

Clare and Somers shift back in their chairs.

"Less gory than I was expecting," Somers says. "Anything in particular you noticed?"

"That was Zoe in the video. So Charlotte must have been filming. One of the witnesses I spoke to, Kavita Spence, the hostess—you can see her in the video. She had conflicting memories with Roland about what door the guy used. I don't know why she'd lie."

"She probably isn't lying," Somers says. "Not intentionally, anyway. Memory is garbage. It's the worst possible witness. Especially with something like this. Your mind will play tricks on you. She can't describe his face properly even though she probably looked right at the guy. She thinks he came in one way when he actually came in another. Her brain inserts that element so she can process what she witnessed."

"Can you zoom in on the shooter and take a screenshot?" Clare asks.

Somers toggles the video to land on the frame that best depicts the shooter. Though it is grainy, it is clear that the shooter is wearing eyeglasses, the hood of a jacket pulled tight to conceal the color of his hair. But his face is visible enough. If you knew him, you'd recognize him.

"He probably wore glasses to mess with facial recognition," Somers says. "This guy knew what he was doing. Do you recognize him?"

"No," Clare says.

"He's probably a hired gun. I'll get copies of this image printed at the front desk. Anything else?"

"One thing," Clare says. "Jack. Did you notice something about him?"

"He seemed pretty calm," Somers says. "But I guess he didn't know what was coming. He's just out for dinner with his family."

"I know," Clare says. "But . . . hmm. Can we replay it?"

This time Clare edges over to the laptop and cues the video up herself. They watch the first minute again. Then again.

"What do you see?" Clare asks Somers.

"He seems distracted?" Somers guesses. "But also kind of out of it. Drunk, maybe."

"Yes," Clare says. "He does."

"He keeps looking at the door."

Clare clicks at the video to zero in on the section with Jack clearly in the frame. It seems plain: His smile is put on, and he is looking to the restaurant's entrance. As if waiting. Next to him, Zoe and Colleen laugh and lean into each other, hamming for the camera. Clare presses pause. In the frozen frame you can see Jack clearly. His eyes are glassy. His coloring is off. He looks ashen.

"I'm not exactly sure what I'm supposed to see," Somers says. "He's thin. Doesn't look all that great. Kind of sickly. But the guy was old."

"No." Clare touches the screen. "Look. Look at his expression."

"I'm not sure," Somers says. "But he seems scared."

In the paused image Jack has edged away from his wife in the booth. He is waiting, watching.

"Actually, it's pretty clear," Somers says. "I see it. He knew."

"Yes," Clare says. "He knew it was coming."

The road hugs the cliffside over the ocean, then curls and climbs. Clare checks the dashboard clock. The drive to the prison is thirty minutes from these final outskirts of Lune Bay. Clare pulls her rental car over at the top of the switchback and steps out to a brisk wind. The sky is gray. Black cliffs rise from the frothy sea and stretch for miles northward.

It takes Clare's breath away, the beauty of it. This craggy end of the earth. From here, she will drive inland to see Donovan Hughes again. An hour ago she left Somers in the hotel conference room to work at decoding the video file and its source. Clare found her rental car in the depths of the hotel parking lot and started out of Lune Bay, stopping only at a drive-thru to satiate her aching hunger. Now she walks to the stone guardrail and peers over. It's a precipitous drop to the ocean below.

Clare returns to the car and sits on its hood, eyes still out to the water. In the hotel parking lot, Clare found herself scanning the backseat of the car and even the trunk before getting in. She feels antsy, paranoid. And then the fear makes her angry. It is easy enough to keep going, to focus on the case, when she is with Somers, when Somers is reassuring her. But alone, Clare can't help looking over her shoulder.

In her marriage, Clare developed a kind of sixth sense, a means to navigate Jason's moods, his next steps. She could anticipate him. And here, alone at this lookout point, Clare feels it more distinctly than she has since those early weeks after she left. His presence. Jason, right behind her.

Where are you? she thinks. Are you here?

Clare unlocks her phone and inputs a number she's known by heart for two decades. Before it can ring, Clare hangs up, gnawing at her lip. She should get in the car and go. Instead she phones the number again. After two rings, the line clicks.

"Hello?" comes a familiar voice.

The anguished jab in her chest takes Clare's aback.

"Hello?" the voice says again.

"Grace?"

There is a pause, an unnatural silence.

"Grace?" Clare says again. "It's me. It's Clare."

"Clare," Grace says. "I saw the blocked number. I hoped it was you. Where are you? What's that noise?"

"It's the ocean," Clare says. "I'm outside. Are you okay? It sounds like you're crying."

"Clare," Grace says again. "I'm so sorry. I'm sorry."

The phone is hot on Clare's ear. She listens to Grace's long breaths.

"I'm so sorry," Grace repeats. "About everything."

"Hey," Clare says. "What are you talking about? Did something happen?"

"He convinced me, you know? That you were the bad one. What can I say? I was grieving. I lost a lot in a short time, with Brian leaving, with you gone, and with a new baby, I wasn't coping. And then I ran into you, and you seemed totally okay, and I just . . . I reacted."

The scene is still clear to Clare, encountering her dear friend Grace by chance in the city of her last case, Grace's shock at seeing Clare over eight months after she'd disappeared. How many times since that day has Clare replayed their conversation, the bitterness Grace displayed? Of all the things that have broken Clare's heart in the last few months, nothing did so more than the notion that, in her absence, Jason had managed to turn the few people Clare loves against her.

"I'm sorry," Grace says again.

"It's okay," Clare says. "I'm sorry too. I am, honestly."

"I didn't know if you'd see my message."

"What message?" Clare asks.

"I emailed you. I didn't know how else to reach you."

"I haven't checked my old email address in months. Not since I left."

"So where are you?" Grace asks. "The ocean? What ocean?"

Clare's silence is answer enough. She thinks of the video Austin took, her arrest in the bar. How far might it have spread by now? Clare's palms are sweating. Something hangs in the air. Something has happened. But she doesn't understand what.

"Grace," Clare says, steady. "You need to tell me what's going on."

"A woman came around a few days ago. She was looking for you. She said you two were old friends."

Clare swallows, closing her eyes.

"I didn't know her," Grace continues. "I told her I'd know

any old friend of yours. She gave me this story about going to high school with us for a few months while her dad was posted at the army base. She said she remembered me too, that she was here taking a trip down memory lane, but honestly, you know we wouldn't just forget someone who moved here for a few months. And kids from the army base were never posted to our school. Anyway, the whole things just seemed—"

"What did she look like?" Clare asks.

"Curly hair. She looked like you, actually."

Clare's ears are ringing.

"Did she give you her name?"

"No. For the life of me, I don't know why I didn't ask her for it."

"What else?"

"I'm glad you called," Grace says, a desperate lilt in her voice. "I'm just glad to know that you're still out there, that you're okay. After I saw you—"

"Did you tell Jason that you saw me?"

Grace doesn't answer.

"Okay. I'll take that as a yes. And this woman. Was she alone?"

"Clare," Grace says. "I've been thinking a lot about the ways I let you down, the things I didn't see, or the things I did see and just let go because it was . . . because I didn't know what to do. But there was something about this woman, it just didn't sit right, and after she left I pulled out our high school yearbooks and looked at every page. I'm telling you, I scanned every single page of all four books and this woman was not there." Grace's voice cracks. "I just got this feeling. I'm so glad you called."

"Was she alone?" Clare asks again.

"Yes. At least, I think so. The sun was bouncing off her windshield. I couldn't see anyone else in her car. I know she got into the driver's seat."

"Listen," Clare says. "I'm going to send you an email with a photograph. Right now. I'm emailing it to you from my phone."

Clare minimizes the call and types out Grace's email address. She presses send, her heart flipping in her chest.

"It's sent."

To think it takes only a split second for a message of such weight, for a photo so crisp and clear, to travel the thousands of miles between Clare and Grace. In the pause, Clare hears the ding of the message arriving to whatever device Grace is using. Grace snivels and lets out a small gasp.

"That's her!" Grace says. "That's definitely her."

An imaginary vise tightens around Clare's neck. Zoe.

"Clare?" Grace says.

For a moment Clare teeters. She places a hand on the hood of the car to steady herself. It always amazed Clare how the earth continued to spin even in the moments of her most acute pain. Death. Departure. Terror. No matter how bad things get, everything else moves forward. The world always seemed so vast to her. It never seemed small. Until now.

"Clare?" Grace says again. "What can I do?"

"Did she say anything else to you?"

"She asked me where your brother was living now. Where Jason was living. I thought, How would she even know Jason? But it seemed like she did."

"Did you tell her?"

Grace's silence is again answer enough.

"Clare?" Grace says. "I'm sorry. I don't know what I've

done. The baby was crying and I was flustered. What have I done?"

"It's okay," Clare says finally. "I have to go."

Before Grace can protest, Clare has ended the call. Her number is blocked, she knows, the email encrypted. Grace will not be able to call her back.

I n rote motions, Clare makes her way through the prison reception's processing area: her ID, the sign in, all her possessions in a bin. The printed screenshot of the shooter that Somers gave her is folded flat in her back pocket. Clare heaves a sigh of relief when the guard patting her down doesn't detect it. She is directed to sit in the waiting room's row of chairs. Clare closes her eyes and tunes out the chatter among the other visitors. She can call up Grace's voice perfectly, and then the image of Jack Westman slumped against his wife, a small hole in his head.

The guard hollers for the visiting group to gather. They move through the long series of halls and checkpoints. This time, Donovan Hughes is waiting for Clare when the buzzer at the final set of doors signals their arrival to the visitation room. He tracks her with a faint smile as she approaches the table.

"I hoped you would return, Ms. Clare O'Kearney," he says, frowning. "You look awfully pale."

"It's been a long day."

"It's barely noon. Is there anything I can do to help?"

"I'm hoping you'll share more than you did last time I was here."

"I thought I was rather generous with my storytelling last time," Donovan says. "And I'm not entirely sure why you'd presume it's my job to help you."

There is no time for this, Clare thinks. She has questions to ask. Her toe taps impatiently under the table.

"It must eat away at you to go down for the crimes that you did."

"You mean the crimes that I *didn't* do."

No. This won't work. Start over, Clare tells herself. Get a grip. Keep it curt, professional.

"Right," Clare says. "I'm sorry. I'm a little overwhelmed. I didn't mean to get off on the wrong foot."

"Yes. Thank you. We ended on a good note last time, didn't we? Even if you wouldn't tell me much about yourself."

"I was here in a professional capacity."

Donovan laughs. "Yes you were. Private investigator. And here you are again. Professionally."

"If I've learned anything in the past few days," Clare says, "it's that the Westman family has a lot of collateral damage. People who've disappeared into thin air, others who've gone to jail, maybe for things they didn't do. Others murdered, even."

"Only Jack was murdered," Donovan says. "And I wouldn't call him collateral damage."

"That's unkind."

He eyes Clare closely. "I put in a few requests around here.

Tapped into my lines to the outside, as they say. I found a few people kind enough to ask around about you. Turns out no one knows a Clare O'Kearney, PI. You're not exactly in the Yellow Pages. You're quite the ghost, it seems."

Clare's hands feel numb. She grips them together and thinks of the photos on Austin's phone last night, her history so easily traced all the way back to Jason. The sound of Grace's voice today, distant yet so familiar. *She looked like you*, Grace said of Zoe. The last time Clare was here, Donovan revealed his acuity at making connections. He very well could have found someone on the outside to trace the same path that Austin did. Clare is not anonymous anymore. Anyone could have her life story tucked up their sleeve.

"I'm new to this job," Clare says. "I don't advertise."

"You told me that you worked with Malcolm."

"I did."

"You said"—Donovan leans back in his chair—"that after he left here, he started looking for missing women. That he became an 'investigator of sorts'—I believe those were your exact words."

"Yes."

Behind them a chair squeals against the floor. Clare turns to watch a woman in tears stand and back away from the prisoner she is visiting. Clare's brain is fogged. In the stretch since she was last here, she knows that Donovan has likely been dissecting every word they'd exchanged. He has nothing but time to ruminate, while Clare, exhausted and overwhelmed, can't recall the subtle details of their exchange.

"Malcolm was not a selfless person, from what I could glean," Donovan says. "I told you that. He was rather glacial. So here's the trouble I'm having. I can't quite reconcile why he would choose to search for missing women. To put himself at risk in that way. Why not just go into hiding? Abscond to the other side of the world? He certainly had the money. Enough to buy a tropical island and live out his days as a ghost, breaking open coconuts under a tree."

"He's not that type," Clare says.

"You know him well enough to declare his type?"

"Women go missing," Clare says. "His wife went missing. I assume he meant to help."

"Then you assume he wasn't behind his wife's disappearance."

Zoe is not dead, Clare wants to scream. Zoe is alive, tracking me. She pulls her chair closer to the table.

"Do you know Kendall Bentley?" she asks. "Or Stacey Norton? Two young women. Both of them worked at Roland's. Both went missing. Everyone around here presumes they left of their own volition, but Kendall's father certainly doesn't think that's the case. Malcolm was connected to these women, however indirectly. From what I can gather, both of these women knew Zoe and might have been working for her in some capacity."

"Some capacity?" Donovan laughs. "Why skirt around it, Clare?"

"Okay. Fine. She was using them. Selling them, I guess? Trafficking them. To men. Businesspeople. Maybe even to cops. She was using these women to entrap men."

"Or to reward them," Donovan offers.

"Did you know about this?"

"I have two daughters, Clare. I had no interest in Zoe's business practices."

"That doesn't answer my question."

For a long moment Donovan studies her.

"Is that why you're here, Clare? To grill me on this? Because

I'm already in jail. They can't jail me twice, can they? And we might have three minutes left."

He is right, Clare knows. She must prioritize. She lays her palms flat on the table.

"I have something I want to show you," Clare says. "It's a photograph. I'll take it out of my pocket now and you can look at it quickly." She angles her head to the guard. "Before he intervenes."

"I'm intrigued," Donovan says.

Clare waits until the guard is focused on a family preparing to leave. She slides the folded paper from her back pocket and sets it down in front of Donovan.

"That's the shooter," she says.

"Where did you get this?"

"It's not important," she says. "Do you recognize him?"

"I do." Donovan looks up at Clare. "His name is Grayson Morris. He was an acquaintance of Malcolm's."

Clare grips the table to steady herself, an action that Donovan notices.

"You're sure?" Clare asks.

"Hughes," the guard calls to them. "Time's up. Let's go."

"Thirty seconds," Donovan replies. "Pretty please."

"How do you know him, though?" Clare asks. "If he was Malcolm's friend."

The desperation in Clare's voice is plain. A cry might come. Donovan smiles at her gently and shakes his head, wistful.

"There was always rumor of a video. So it *was* Grayson. What a strange turn of events." He cranes to check the guard again, then leans in to a mock whisper. "Charlotte was in love with him. With Grayson. They were an item. The other day you suggested that Zoe and I were close, but we weren't. Those young women you mentioned? Well. Zoe could be quite vile in how she conducted herself. She had no scruples to speak of. But Charlotte was such a sweetheart. I loved her daughter, Shelley, like she was my own grandchild. But Charlotte had terrible taste in men."

Clare taps the photo, incredulous. "So Charlotte and this guy were a thing?"

"It was brief, I'm pretty sure. He was not right for her. Got her mixed up in all the wrong things. He insisted they keep it a secret, like she embarrassed him or something. I only know because I came across them once while walking my dog on the beach. I introduced myself and he gave me his name. I never forget a name. After that, Charlotte confided in me a bit about their relationship. Their troubles. I think it helped her to have someone to talk to. Anyway, I believe he left Lune Bay around the time of the murder. I suppose now we know why."

The room is empty but for them. Clare folds the photograph and returns it to her pocket. The guard approaches.

"Thank you," Clare says. "You've been helpful. I appreciate it."

Donovan stands and opens his arms to Clare.

"I can't hug you," he says.

"No, you can't."

"I certainly wish I could. Forgive me for saying this, but you're gorgeous. I've enjoyed looking across at you."

Clare says nothing. The guard hovers almost shyly, an indication of Donovan's status here.

"Thank you, Clare. There's been something cathartic about this. I feel almost at peace."

"Hughes," the guard says. "I've been generous. Now let's go."

"Okay, fine," Donovan says, retreating. "Let's go."

With a heavy clink the door swings closed. Donovan Hughes disappears.

Before she is even outside the prison's doors Clare has unlocked her phone to search the name: Grayson Morris. When the results are not specific enough, she adds a place name. Lune Bay. Nothing of note. Clare opens her text messages and types one to Somers. She gives her Grayson's name and tells her that Donovan Hughes identified him as the shooter.

At her car, Clare collects a water bottle from the trunk and gulps it down. The sun is high in the sky, the air too warm in the absence of the ocean. Clare leans against the car door and unlocks her phone again, this time noting the red circle on the call icon. Five missed calls. Unknown number.

Clare feels it. Someone is watching her. She spins in a full circle to search the parking lot. No one else is here other than a guard stationed adjacent to the prison entrance. She shields her eyes from the sun and circles slowly again, looking to the prison yard, to the woods beyond it, her pulse in her ears. Missed calls? Clare gets in the car and grips the steering wheel until her knuckles are white. When her phone rings she jumps, fumbling it into the passenger footwell. She bends to collect it and swipes to accept the call.

"Hello?"

"Clare."

She will not say his name. She cannot afford to be wrong.

"Clare?" he says again into the silence. "It's Malcolm."

Yes. She knows it. The depth and tone of his voice. Tears of relief spring to her eyes.

"What the hell, Malcolm. Where are you?"

"I'm in Lune Bay," he says. "If I email you directions, will you meet me?"

Clare closes her eyes and wills herself to breathe.

"Yes," she says.

She can't be sure who hangs up first. Clare grips her phone until the email with the map link comes through. It directs her to a picnic area on the ocean five miles north of downtown Lune Bay. Clare starts the car. She cannot decipher what courses through her, whether it is rage, relief. Anticipation.

Beyond the prison gate, she takes a left and drives on autopilot, cued by the pings of her phone. She comes over a rise and the ocean appears in front of her, and then a signal to turn right. SEASTONE CONSERVATION AREA a sign reads in faded paint. A single car is parked in the lot. Clare collects her gun from the glove compartment and then steps out of the car, both hands gripping her weapon. She kicks the driver door closed.

"Malcolm?" she calls.

No one. No answer. A path marked by a faded map stems off the parking lot. BEACH UNSUPERVISED the sign reads. USE AT YOUR OWN RISK. Clare follows the path until it widens to a pebbled beach. The sky is low and cloudy here, the sun gone, the waves kicked up. Clare scans left to right.

"I'm here," a voice behind her says.

Clare spins. There he is, sitting on a wooden bench where the beach meets the trees, watching her with sad eyes. Clare is surprised at the look of him, his hair longer by a touch, his skin tanned. Malcolm stands. She'd forgotten his shape, his height, the scar on his forearm in full view with the white T-shirt he wears.

When Malcolm steps forward, Clare tightens her grip on her gun. She thinks of the scene weeks ago, months now even, when Malcolm first burst through the door of her motel room, knocking the gun from her hands and tying her to the chair. He'd come for her, and in that moment Clare had felt so certain that she would die. Now, she walks backwards until she edges close to the incoming waves, out of his reach. He matches his steps to hers, holding the distance between them.

"What is this, Malcolm? What are you doing here?"

"Clare—"

"Have you been here all along?" she hollers at him. "In Lune Bay? Watching me? Stalking me?"

"No," Malcolm says.

"I don't believe you."

"Clare," Malcolm says. "Please. I just got here. I can't—"

"Shut up!" Clare yells.

Clare casts a quick glance up and down the empty beach. She lifts the gun and points it to Malcolm's chest. She stares down the barrel, perfecting her aim, right at his heart. Malcolm lifts his hands in the air, but nonetheless, he steps forward. Clare hates the way she feels as she watches him. She hates the magnitude of the relief, how badly she wants to step forward too, to move closer to him.

"Please, Clare. I just want to talk to you. Please put the gun down."

"Talk to me?" she says. "You left!"

"I know I did. I can explain. It's not safe for you here, do you understand that? I need you to leave Lune Bay. Now. I want you to leave with me."

"*With* you?" Clare laughs bitterly. "Oh my God. Fuck you."

All Clare can do is hold the gun in place, grip it to force a steadiness to her hand. In her life she's so rarely been graced with certainty about anything, but Clare knows if she fires, she will not miss. The bullet will pierce his heart.

"Shoot, then," Malcolm says, louder. "Why don't you shoot me, Clare? If that's how this ends."

"How *what* ends?" Clare yells.

He takes a small step closer. Clare holds her stance.

"If you give me the chance, Clare, I will tell you everything."

"Fuck you," Clare says again. "You had your chance. You had weeks' worth of chances. You told me nothing."

"I was trying to keep you safe."

"You abandoned me!" Clare shouts, at once ashamed for saying it.

"Abandoned?" Malcolm scoffs. "I was trying to protect you. I told you that."

"But you're here now? What's changed? Is it any safer? No."

"I told you to stop looking for me!" Malcolm yells too. "I told you to back down. Christ, Clare. Put the goddamn gun down. I'm not going to hurt you."

A long moment passes, Clare considering. Finally she lowers her gun, her gaze locked on Malcolm's.

"I want to get you out of here," he says. "Get you to safety. Once I know you're safe, I can come back to Lune Bay and turn myself in. Speak to Germain. But only once I know you're safe."

AMY STUART

"Turn yourself in for what?" Clare asks.

"Give me the chance to explain," Malcolm says. "We can sit. Talk. Let's go somewhere."

"Zoe's alive, you know."

"I know," Malcolm says, edging even closer. "I told you that. This is all a game to her, Clare. That's what you don't get. There isn't some big reveal. This is all just a game."

"It's not a game," Clare says. "There's so much that *you* don't get. Everything's changed, Malcolm. This isn't about you."

Malcolm rubs at his forehead. He looks right at Clare, then strides to close the space between them. Clare allows it. It startles her to see him up close, the circles under his eyes, the worry on his face. He lifts his hand, as if to reach out and touch Clare, but thinks better of it and retracts.

"You want to hear something completely nuts?" Clare says. "Zoe and Jason might be together."

Malcolm's face twists with genuine shock. "No," he says. "That's impossible."

"Nothing is impossible anymore. Do you see that? That's what I mean. You don't understand. I've been here working, figuring this all out. This isn't about you anymore, Malcolm. I'm not doing this for you, or because of you, anymore. This is about me now."

"Let me get you out of here," he says. "Please. I can bring you somewhere safe."

"I'm not leaving, Malcolm. Do you get that? I'm not leaving."

"You can't stay. Listen—"

"No," Clare says. "You listen. Do you know how many days I've been running, Malcolm? Because I've counted. Since I left Jason, I've counted in days." Her voice rises. "Do you know what that's like? To count your life in days? It's been over two hundred and fifty days of running. And I'm done. I'm done, Malcolm. I'm not leaving. I'm going to see this through, no matter what. I need this to end."

Clare's phone rings in her pocket. She looks down at the gun as if she'd forgotten it was in her hand. Clare tucks it back into her belt, then extracts her phone from her pocket to silence the call.

"That's Somers," she says. "I was supposed to meet her at the hotel ten minutes ago."

"You can't leave, Clare. We need to talk."

"You don't get to tell me what to do anymore, Malcolm. If you want to talk, we can talk. Later. I have things to do. Do you understand that?"

When her phone rings again, Clare lifts a finger to stop Malcolm from saying more. She swipes to retrieve the call. Somers.

"Sorry," Clare says. "I got held up. I'm fifteen minutes out."

"It sounds like you're outside. Is that the ocean I hear?"

"I stopped for gas," Clare says. "I'm on my way."

Clare can't bear the way Malcolm is watching her as she speaks.

"Okay," Somers says. "You sound a little off."

"Fifteen minutes," Clare says, ending the call.

Behind Malcolm, Clare spots a couple on the path. They wave at her in friendly greeting. Clare watches them start up the beach arm in arm, the wind kicking up the woman's hair, the man laughing at something she's said to him. Clare takes a step forward and brings her face close to Malcolm's.

"Listen to me," she says, her voice low. "I'm not leaving. I don't know what you hoped would happen here. That you'd show up and whisk me away like some knight in shining armor?"

"Clare—"

"This needs to end, Malcolm. I have a job to do. So you go ahead and turn yourself in. Or don't. Stay with me and help me do my job. But I'm not leaving."

"Okay," he says, frowning. "Okay."

"Text me in an hour," she says. "Tell me where to meet you."

Malcolm nods. Clare takes a wide berth around him and walks away. Her heart beats too fast in her chest. She feels angry, exhilarated. When she reaches the foot of the path to the parking lot, Clare glances over her shoulder. Malcolm has walked forward into the water. He stands so that the waves wrap him to the knees. He need only take a few more steps for the ocean to absorb him whole.

Clare sits in the passenger seat of Somers's car. They weave through the one-way streets of Lune Bay's small downtown. If Somers is bothered by the lack of conversation, she reveals nothing, fiddling instead with the radio knobs and making occasional commentary on the scenery, the ocean that flits in and out of view. Clare's eyes are fixed out the window. It is Malcolm who occupies her thoughts now. The sight of him, the pleading tone in his voice. *It's not safe for you here.* Why does Clare feel numb to his pleas? She knows Malcolm could be right. Danger is circling, closing in on her. Zoe. Jason. She feels it in the air. So why is her reaction to Malcolm anger and not fear?

"You okay?" Somers asks.

"Fine. Lots on my mind. Lots to think about."

"You've got that right," Somers says.

In her message en route from the jail, Clare gave Somers

the name of the shooter, Grayson Morris, but did not reveal that Donovan Hughes linked him to Malcolm. Despite everything, Clare is still protecting him. She knows she should tell Somers about their encounter this morning. But she can't. Not now. Not yet.

They pull up outside an older brick building. The sign reads COUNTY GOVERNMENT OFFICES. Somers kills the engine and shifts in her seat, unbuckling herself so she can face Clare head-on.

"How do you want to play this?" Somers asks.

"Play what?" Clare asks flatly.

Somers heaves a long sigh. "Are you with me here? You're in the clouds."

Clare cannot look at Somers. She remains turned to the window, silent.

"I sent the video to forensics," Somers says. "I copied Germain. Included the guy's name you gave me too. We're dropping this stuff in Germain's lap. I did a quick search on any Grayson Morris names and couldn't find much of note. A couple of hits, but I'll need access to the wider database to really mine the options. Your jailbird friend Hughes might have it wrong, who knows?"

"You knew all along," Clare says.

"Knew what?" Somers asks, impatient.

"You knew that everything here was connected. You sent me here knowing that. Knowing that these missing women were connected to the Westmans. Knowing . . ."

Clare trails off. Somers reaches over and jabs a finger into Clare's leg.

"Look at me," she says. "Look at me."

"What?"

"You're mad," Somers says. "I get it. You've got a lot to be mad about. You don't even have a specific target for your anger, do you? You're just mad at the world right now and I'm in your sights. But let me tell you something. For the last time, I am not your enemy here. I'm not the person to turn on. You've been telling yourself the wrong story, Clare. Because I don't know how many times I have to tell you, I am not the bad guy. I know I didn't tell you about the Norton case, and I'm sorry about that. But trust me, I'm the one who's got your back."

Clare bites at her lip. The car is too warm. It feels impossible to make sense of the day so far, the video of a man knowing he was about to get shot, Donovan naming the shooter, Malcolm here. These scenes that feel unreal, dreamlike, even though they unfolded barely hours ago. Somers is right: Clare can't pinpoint where to direct her rage. She takes a few deep breaths to compose herself before speaking.

"I had this realization this morning," Clare says. "I was driving back from the prison and I had an epiphany. Is that the right word for it? *Epiphany*?"

"Yeah," Somers says. "The aha moment."

"Right." Clare pauses to quell the tremble in her voice. "The thing is, my whole life I've been a pawn. A chess piece in someone else's game. My dad was obsessed with teaching me how to shoot. He didn't want a daughter in pink, a doll-playing daughter. He wanted a sharpshooter. Then my mom got cancer, and my brother and my dad were absolved somehow of anything to do with her illness and death. I was a teenager, but she was my problem. Then I met Jason, and by then I just—I felt like my role was to play along. You know? To just participate in other people's games. It was easier. So that's what I did. I did what other people told me to do. I went along with plans. Jason proposed and I said yes because honestly? I just couldn't conceive of an alternative. And we got married, and it was horrific, but I couldn't break away. Eventually I did. Because when he hurt me and I lost the baby? That was the first thing in my life I felt happened to *me*. It was my loss, and mine alone. So it spurred me to leave."

"Yes," Somers interjects. "It would."

"But then I met Malcolm," Clare continues. "And I wonder now: Did I let myself become a pawn in his game? Old habits die hard, you know. But, Somers? You? I figured somehow you'd be better, that you were actually my friend, that you were trying to help me, but now maybe I'm just a pawn in your game too. You need me to do this work for you. You're too visible as a cop. And I fit right in, no matter the danger to me."

At this Somers shakes her head.

"You need me to do your dirty work. You're using me."

"Come on, Clare."

"Really?" Clare says. "Am I wrong?"

"Come on," Somers says again. "All investigation is dirty work. All of it. I'm not using you. I need your skills. I hired you because you're good at this work and I wanted you to see that. Like you say, my hands are tied as a cop. I have a long list of rules and procedures I'm bound to follow. I walk a thin line that you don't need to walk. Yes, I need you. You could argue that I'm using your skills to my advantage. But I found room in my tiny little cop budget and a workaround with my superiors so I could pay you. I gave you a shot at your own case. Have you ever considered that I might be doing you a favor?"

"A favor that suits you."

"Ha!" Somers laughs before her expression snaps back to focus. "I'm not going to apologize to you. You say you've always been a pawn. Let me ask you something, Clare. Do you have free will? Does your brain function on its own?"

Clare crosses her arms, silent.

"Well. You know what? I'm a black woman and I've been a cop for fifteen years. You have no idea the shit I've dealt with in my life. The crap people throw my way. Half my colleagues can't make small talk with me without regularly jamming their foot in their mouth. I won't bore you with the stories, because there are thousands of them and there's just no way you'd understand. You couldn't. Just like I can't understand what it's like for you to have endured the kind of marriage you had, to have lost your mother so young, to have dealt with addiction like you have, and losing a baby? That's a form of grief that could do anyone in. It could. But I'm going to tell you what I tell my kids every day: don't exhaust yourself focusing on the various ways other people have failed you. Shit will come at you that you can't control, and no one else is going to change their ways on your behalf. And if you operate that way? Looking to others? You might end up blind to the people who actually care about you. So scrub out anyone who causes you harm and move forward. But telling yourself that things are the way they are because you've been a *pawn*? Fine. Fate has not been good to you. But that way of thinking isn't getting you anywhere. You need to jump off the hamster wheel, Clare. You've got to take control."

Clare blinks fast and looks up. Her cheeks feel flushed. She cannot make eye contact, but when Somers reaches to squeeze her hand, Clare does not withdraw. She releases a sharp laugh to mask the tears.

"Okay?" Somers says.

"Okay."

"We ready to regroup?"

"Yes." Clare rubs her eyes and gestures to the building. "What are we doing here? Seeing the coroner?"

"Jack Westman's autopsy was never publicly released. You remember when Douglas Bentley mentioned that? Well, he was right. That's pretty standard when no one is charged. I could request access from the police file, but that can take a while. And I have this feeling that your friend Germain might not be terribly amenable to sharing it. So I figure we'll go right to the source."

"And the coroner will just give it to you?" Clare asks.

"I have some tricks to make sure he does," Somers says.

Again they sit in silence. Clare cannot give in to how tired she feels. Part of the exhaustion comes from trying to keep everything straight, to keep track of what she's told Somers and what she hasn't. Perhaps, Clare thinks, full disclosure is just easier. She takes hold of Somers's arm.

"I need to tell you two things before we go inside," she says.

"Uh-oh."

"I called my friend Grace this morning. My friend from home. I grew up with her. She and my ex, Jason, kind of became friends after I left. Long story short, he convinced her that I was bad news." Clare coughs. "That I was just some junkie who ran off on all my family and friends because I couldn't hack my life. Anyway. I called her after I left the hotel this morning. And she told me that a woman came to her door a while ago, asking about me. So I had this gut feeling, like this terrible gut feeling, and I emailed Grace a picture of Zoe Westman. It was her. Apparently, Zoe Westman showed up at her house asking about me."

Somers presses her fingers to her temples with a groan.

"This is not computing," she says. "I don't get it. How is that possible? She must be wrong."

"She's not wrong," Clare says. "She wouldn't make that mistake."

"Eyewitnesses are notoriously unreliable. You know that. They can see things that aren't really there."

"Not this time," Clare says.

"What in the bloody hell, then?" Somers says. "So Zoe Westman is alive and she's searching for *you*? I do not get it."

"There's nothing else you know that you haven't told me?" Clare asks. "About Jason? About Malcolm? Because like I said, this is all connected. It is. It must be. And I feel like I'm in the middle of it."

"I don't know anything I haven't already told you," Somers says. "Like I said, I've got my best people on it. And now I'm confused as hell. What's the second thing you need to tell me? Do I even want to know?"

"I saw Malcolm Hayes this morning," Clare says. "He's here."

"Jesus Christ. Are you kidding me?"

"We've been emailing back and forth. That note you got that was directed to me? It was from him."

"Okay," Somers says. "Remember that conversation we just had about lying to each other?"

"I know," Clare says. "I saw him less than an hour ago. I was going to tell you. I just needed—"

"He just rides back into town after taking off, what? Eighteen months ago?"

"He thinks I'm in danger. That's why he came back. Or so he says."

"Or he's putting you in danger, Clare. Maybe you're exactly where he wants you."

"He says he's willing to talk to Germain. To turn himself in. After he knows I'm safe."

"I'll believe that when I see it," Somers says. "You don't know what he's going to do."

"You're right," Clare says. "I don't. He said this is all a game to Zoe. So this is what I'm thinking. I think that he's telling the truth. That Zoe has been alive this whole time, and she disappeared because she'd gotten herself embroiled in some bad business dealings. It was a game to her. She knew they'd pin her disappearance on him, because they always do. It's always the husband, right? And then she found out about me. I don't know how. And I became part of her game too. Why? I don't know, but I have to find out."

"So, she went to find Jason. She found out about you." Something dawns on her. "She was the one making the calls to me."

"Maybe," Clare says. "I think so."

"And now they're here together?" Somers squeezes her eyes closed. "Jason and Zoe Westman? I don't get it. What for?"

A cry finally escapes Clare. It comes to her suddenly and clearly, her sprint through the woods behind her and Jason's home. Running. Running to the car she'd hidden deep in the grove of trees. The note she'd left for Jason to say she was out for a jog, hoping it would buy her enough time, that before he realized, she'd be too far gone for him to catch her scent. She can recall the precise crunch of the snow under her feet. But the strange thing is, the memory of that escape no longer plays in first person for Clare. Instead, it unfolds in her mind as if she's watching it from above, a spectator instead of the woman running.

"Listen," Somers says. "If they show up here, we'll bring them in. I can drum up some reason to round them up. Give you a head start. Simple as that."

"Nothing about this is simple," Clare says. "I want this to end."

"This?"

"Everything. Malcolm. Jack Westman. Zoe. I'm done running, Somers. I'm done. That's why I'm still here. I need to see this through. I need to find my way to the other side so I can stop running."

"Okay," Somers says, quiet.

"And I want Jason dead."

"Jesus. Don't tell me that. Let's go with, I want Jason arrested."

"I want this to end," Clare says again.

Somers removes a notebook from the center console, all-business. "Let's just do this right, get to work. I'll call my guy who's been tracking the signal on Jason's cell phone. I'll read him the riot act about the importance of it. We'll figure out where he is, track him. They're working on the video, we're doing everything we can. For now, we deal with this coroner."

"Okay," Clare says. "Let's go."

The county offices are modern and clean. Clare follows Somers through the reception area to the desk. A young man looks up from his phone and offers them a wide smile. Behind him is a poster of a cartoon rabbit outlining proper hand-washing technique. Whatever dark notion of a coroner's office Clare had formed over years of watching detective shows with her mother, this does not match it.

"What can I help you with?" the young man asks.

Somers pulls her badge from her pocket. "Detective Hollis Somers. Is Dr. Flanagan here?"

"He just arrived back from his lunch, actually. You can go right in."

They circle the desk and the receptionist buzzes open the heavy set of double doors. On the other side is a long, sterile hallway. Somers cranes to read the name plates on each door until she comes to the one marked DR. SAMUEL FLANAGAN. CHIEF CORONER. She knocks and enters before getting any response. A man in his fifties looks up from a laptop. This office is large and square, the picture window behind him giving way to the green of a park.

"Officer Somers," he says, standing to offer his hand.

"Detective," Somers corrects him, glancing at Clare.

"Right. My mistake. And this is?"

"Clare O'Kearney. She's working with me on a case. It's related to the Westman family. The Lune Bay Westmans. That family."

Dr. Flanagan nods with no shift in his expression. "Of course. And you need something from me?"

"I need Jack Westman's autopsy report."

Dr. Flanagan laughs heartily, then waves at Clare and Somers to sit in the chairs across from him. "Something tells me you don't have a warrant for that. Or you'd have gone directly to the detective assigned to the case."

"I don't have a warrant," Somers says. She taps the top of his desk. "Listen, I appreciate that you have a job to do. And I know that coroners and cops aren't always in simpatico. But the system works better when we get along, doesn't it?"

"I'd say it does," he says.

"Let's just assume I did my research. Clare, you've heard of the term 'dirty cop'?"

"Sure," Clare says.

"Well, a dirty cop's lesser known cousin is the dirty coroner. You know, the one who fudges results here and there. Adds or leaves out a key detail in their report. Maybe forgets to write down a piece of evidence the prosecution needs to seal the case. A grimy nugget about a bad death that a rich family wants buried with their beloved. Coroners who act as judge and jury. Ever heard of such a thing?"

The smile on Flanagan's face turns hostile.

"I'd like to think that you coroners have your hunches about which cops are dirty," Somers continues. "And cops? We have the same hunches about you. About which coroners are bribe prone, and which ones are more committed to . . . what? To the purity of justice? There's one thing we likely agree on: our work is complicated and we don't need other people breathing down our backs. Am I right?"

Despite her fatigue, her aching chest, a swell of admiration fills Clare. It is a form of genius, Clare thinks, the way Somers disarms him. Now she can extract exactly what she needs.

"Which report did you say you needed?" Flanagan asks.

"Jack Westman," Somers says, referring to her notes. "I believe his birth name is John."

The coroner's capacity to keep his composure is admirable, his ability to distill his anger to only a small shudder of his jaw muscles. He stands and disappears through a door to the left of his desk.

"You're good at that," Clare says.

"There's a golden rule," Somers says. "Always arrive to an interaction like this prepared. Don't let them take the wheel. Always retain control."

"You've got dirt on him?"

"His reputation precedes him," Somers says. "Nothing particularly terrible. He's not setting serial killers free or anything. Lune Bay isn't exactly a murder hot spot. But let's just say that some sudden deaths have been brushed off as natural causes. Some of the richer people around here tend to die with more dignity than they ought." Somers laughs. "It's not funny. But hey, he retires next year. He doesn't know what I know. It's an easy upper hand."

What effortless confidence, Clare thinks, studying Somers sidelong. It might be a function of how long she's been doing this job, or it might just be her, built-in. Either way, Clare wishes she could find that kind of ease in anything she does. After a few minutes Dr. Flanagan returns, a file in one hand and a handful of foil-wrapped candies in the other. He sits and sets the file down, dropping a candy in front of each of them. Somers unwraps hers and pops it in her mouth.

"This better not be laced with arsenic," she says.

Dr. Flanagan opens the file. "If I were going to kill you, I'd use something untraceable, Detective Somers. Give me some credit."

Somers's laugh is genuine, booming. A pressure valve has been released between them. Flanagan has accepted his defeat. He pores over the open file as he unwraps his own candy.

"I'm just scanning the summary report," he says.

"Did you conduct the autopsy?"

"I did," he says. "Five years ago."

"You probably conduct a lot of them," Clare adds. She is grateful that Somers doesn't flinch at the obvious question.

"Indeed I do," Flanagan says. He looks up at Clare, staring a second too long, smiling at her. "Right. Says here: gunshot wound to the head. Three shots, one fatal."

He spins the top page to show it to Clare and Somers. The words come at Clare in a blur.

Gunshot wound, left templar lobe. Fatal.

Patient dead on arrival. Early stages rigor mortis.

"Sometimes there are details about a case you don't forget," Flanagan says, the candy knocking against his teeth. "This case was certainly one of those."

Somers uncrosses and recrosses her legs. Clare knows her well enough now to see this as a sign of her frustration. The coroner's wistfulness is getting on her nerves.

"Can you be more specific?" Clare asks.

"The first step is to examine the obvious trauma. Here, the deceased was struck with multiple bullets. Three. We accepted that the bullet to his temple was the fatal one, but he may well have died from the piercing of another organ. When death is so sudden it's not necessarily possible to—"

"What's this?" Somers interrupts, pointing to a word on the page. *Metastases*.

Clare leans forward to follow the path of Somers's finger. *Evidence of advanced metastases*. Lungs, liver. Multiple. Source unknown.

"Well," the coroner says. "He had cancer."

"Yeah," Somers says. "I think we understand that much."

The years Clare spent in close range to her mother's cancer had taught her the basic vocabulary of the disease: tumors and their spread, metastases like weeds popping up unwelcome throughout her body.

"Advanced," Clare says. "Multiple. Lots of cancer, basically. He was dying?"

"We're all dying," Dr. Flanagan says. "Just at different rates."

Somers pushes out a hard breath, all efforts to conceal her impatience fallen away.

"Listen," she says. "Your calendar might be clear today, but Clare and I have places to be. I really do appreciate your lessons on the meaning of life, but—"

If Dr. Flanagan is wounded, his smile doesn't show it. He leans back in his chair.

"My guess is the liver was the site of origin, but his cancer was so advanced that it wasn't easy to pinpoint. And since he was already dead from another cause . . . well, there isn't much value in digging through his innards to find out where the cancer started."

"Did he know he was dying?" Clare asks.

"The symptoms at this stage would have been intense," Flanagan says.

"Like he had months left?" Somers asks.

"Not months. Weeks. There was some early-stage jaundice too. Fluid in his abdomen. Not terribly overt, but enough. Hard to believe he wouldn't have noticed."

"Or his wife wouldn't have known," Somers says.

"But," Flanagan continues, "the coroner's office was never presented with corroborating records from his medical team. Nothing to indicate there'd been a previous diagnosis. That doesn't mean he didn't know, but it sure is odd, now that I think about it."

"Now that you think you about it." Somers shakes her head.

Clare remembers her mother in the final months of her own illness, the way the disease invaded every nook of her body until even the most mundane tasks required a surge of pain medication. It feels impossible that someone at the same stage of disease would not have known they were dying.

"I've seen stranger things," Dr. Flanagan says. "Women in the final trimester of pregnancy with no record of it in their files. People with advanced cancers, or hearts calcified with decay before the fatal infarction. You think it would have been impossible not to recognize that something was terribly wrong. At the very least, he must have known. And his family could have suspected something. But we don't know what he knew. And his family very well could have been in the dark."

"Or they knew and kept it hidden," Somers adds.

"Yes," Dr. Flanagan says. "That's possible too."

"Anything else? Anything in the blood?"

Dr. Flanagan flips over the page and scans the findings. "Some opioid, a sedative, but not at palliative levels. His blood alcohol was slightly elevated, which makes sense, given he was drinking wine at dinner before he died. Nothing beyond that."

"Fine. Good. Listen," Somers says again. "I'm going to take a picture of this report with my phone. I know that's against the rules, but you know well that some rules are made to be broken, right? So I'll take the picture, then you file this report away again, and I promise you that this picture will never see the light of day. This conversation never happened."

"I'd appreciate that," Flanagan says.

Somers aligns her phone with the page and takes the photograph. She and Clare stand and shake the doctor's hand.

"We're grateful for your time and expertise, Dr. Flanagan," Somers says, a hint of sarcasm in her voice.

His expression is almost sad when they turn to leave. Clare must jog the hallway to keep up with Somers as she walks past the reception area and through the door to the outside world. Somers stops at the bottom of the steps and fishes through her bag for her sunglasses.

"I know I've already said this," Clare says. "But you're really good at that."

"You played your part too," Somers says. "You know. The quiet, cute, good cop. The little questions you innocently threw in here and there."

"I'm not sure 'cute' is a real thing in detective-speak. And I'm pretty sure it's meaningless. Unhelpful."

"Ha," Somers says. "You'd be surprised. When you come across a lot of men like Flanagan, you know—men with egos incrementally larger than their brains?—cute helps a lot. At one point he was looking at you like he would have handed over his scalpel and the key to the morgue if you batted your lashes and asked him for them."

They reach Somers's car. In the passenger seat Clare feels hot with anger. Her entire life Clare resented those around her for whom things seemed to come easily, Grace first and foremost, and Somers now, exacerbated by the implication that Clare's best weapon is her looks. No, Clare thinks now. Settle down. She buckles her seat belt.

"Do you think Jack Westman knew he was dying?" Clare asks.

"He must have."

"Do you think it matters if he did?"

"Everything matters," Somers says. "Every little secret matters."

Somers turns the key in the ignition. They pull out of the spot and drive up the hill. When they pass a park, Clare can see the ocean overtop of it.

"I think we should go see Germain," Somers says. "It's time I met him."

"Sounds good," Clare says, even if her tone does not match the conciliatory nature of her words.

The police detachment is open and airy. Clare barely remembers its layout from yesterday morning, all the upper floors open to the atrium, where Clare and Somers wait. Just like the coroner's office, this space seems too well appointed to be a government building. Looking up, Clare spots Germain standing at the third-floor elevator. They make eye contact before Somers sees him too. Even from a hundred feet away Clare can read his look, the sly smile. He descends in the glass elevator facing outward, his hands in his pockets, his eyes never leaving Clare. So confident, she thinks. So self-assured. Somers is looking at her phone and only spots him when he arrives at the desk and stretches out his hand to greet her.

"Detective Somers," he says. "It's a thrill to meet you. Thank you so much for your work on this case."

"What case?" Somers says. "We've got a few of them on the go, don't we?"

"Sure, maybe," Germain says. "I see it as one. One big present tied together with a bow."

"I don't," Somers says.

The front desk clerk follows their volleys intently, chin propped on her hands.

"We don't have much time," Clare says in an effort to insert herself. "Can we take a few minutes in your office?"

"Sure," he says. "I've got a soda maker."

"He's very domestic," the clerk chimes in.

The clerk recedes into her chair under Somers's withering look. They follow Germain to the elevator and wait for its arrival in an awkward silence. On their way up, they stand shoulder to shoulder, Clare between them.

"Not a terribly busy place," Somers says.

"Well, it's Friday. Start of the weekend."

"That's when chaos reigns in most detachments."

Somers is toying with him, working to gain the upper hand. Clare can feel Germain stiffen next to her. The elevator doors open and they follow him along the third-floor hall and through the cubicles to his spacious office. Both Clare and Somers take the chairs across from his desk and watch as he prepares them two sodas from a machine that sits on the bar fridge. Somers looks to Clare and rolls her eyes, tapping on the notebook in her hand as if to say, *I don't have time for this shit.* Germain hands them the drinks and sits.

"The video was . . . an interesting twist," he says. "Quite the break in the case. You said you received it in an email?"

"She did," Somers answers for Clare. "I've had my guys working on the encryption. Seeing what they can dig up about the sender. But the file was bounced around a lot before it arrived in her in-box. It'll be next to impossible to triangulate."

Germain holds quiet, watching them. "It looks like Charlotte Westman was filming," he says. "I've sent an officer out to pick her up for questioning. But I doubt she was our sender."

"I doubt it too," Clare says.

"You have ideas about who sent it, then?"

"No," Clare says, a lie.

"What did you find on this Grayson guy?" Somers asks Germain.

Germain opens the file on his desk. "It's not a common name. I can see about eighty records in total. There's a decently long record for a Grayson Morris who grew up in Newport, which is three hundred miles north of here. He'd be about forty by now. I've got his school records. Two arrests, one for assault, one for drug charges, both a decade old. Nothing since. No record of him anywhere since. And he didn't serve time for either of the—"

"Malcolm grew up in Newport," Clare interrupts.

"Did he?" Somers says. "Well, well, well."

"His parents were from Lune Bay," Clare says. "But they moved when he was young so his father could start his business. He lived in Newport until his family died. He finished at boarding school, then went to college to study forensic psychology. Only came back after he met Zoe."

Both Somers and Germain nod in approval.

"Is Newport a big place?" Somers asks.

"No," Germain says. "Ten thousand, give or take."

"So odds are, two guys roughly the same age would know each other. You have a mug shot?"

Germain unclips a photo from the file and extends it across the desk. Somers reaches for it before Clare can, an act that

Germain seems to notice because he looks to Clare for her reaction. Somers is in control. Of course she is.

"Hard to tell if this is the same guy," Somers says. "Shooter had the hoodie on. Glasses, which he probably knew would screw with facial recognition."

"Plus, these mug shots are ten years old," Germain says. "Still, his mug shot is in the system. Presumably the facial matching scan would have caught something if the resemblance was in any way clear."

"His mug shot would be in the *local* system," Somers corrects. "Not the federal database. Not for misdemeanors. A scan wouldn't find it."

"Right," Germain says, folding his arms across his desk. "We'll have to run our own manual search, then."

The tension between them is thick. Germain clicks his pen and writes something in the file. He looks small behind the desk, too young for this job. Still, what does Somers have to gain by pushing him offside?

"I'm going to float a theory," Somers says. "How long have you been a detective?"

"Eleven months," Germain says.

Somers smiles. "Still counting in months. I like that. And your time on this case?"

"Six," Germain says. "Six . . . months."

"Right. So this case was dead cold when it landed on your lap. You got both the Jack Westman murder file and the Zoe Westman disappearance, right? And Malcolm Hayes going vamoose. That's on your plate too?"

She waits for Germain to nod.

"You've got this architectural masterpiece of a detachment here, don't you?" Somers continues. "Half-empty, but lots of beautiful nooks and crannies. Just now, Clare and I were down the street digging up Jack Westman's autopsy, which was easy enough to do, because your coroner is dirty as a pig in shit. Lune Bay has seen about five murders in a decade, most of them open-and-shut cases, domestics or robberies gone wrong, but the most high-profile murder of all isn't solved. Jack Westman. This business magnate who was in deep with all kinds of city councilmen, politicians, builders, landowners, businesspeople. Hell, I'm sure he was friendly with the local priest."

"Not all unsolved murders can be blamed on dirty cops," Germain says. "If that's what you're insinuating."

"I hope not," Somers says. "I know I've got a few of unsolved ones on my desk. But a live-action video of a murder turning up five years later, not to mention an autopsy with some decently revealing tidbits that were never brought to bear. Am I wrong to say that it all feels a little swept under?"

"I can't speak to the efforts of my predecessors," Germain says. "What I know is since she arrived"—he gestures to Clare—"things have taken a turn for the better. Lots of action. An arrest, even. I mean you, Clare. You were the arrest, weren't you?"

At this Clare sits erect. She needs this to stop, this back and forth that excludes her, casts her aside, speaks of her as if she isn't here. Speaks of her as if she is to blame. She slaps a hand on Germain's desk, quieting them both.

"Listen," Clare says, her voice strong, steady. "We all want the same thing. You both have unsolved cases on your hands. That arrest of mine will go away, just like you said it would, because you and I are working together, Germain. Because you need me. I know Austin Lantz loves a hot local story. Imagine the headline: Rookie private investigator swoops into town and solves the Westman murder in about a week. Ends up with a video of the shooting in her in-box."

Clare pauses to absorb the look of wonder Somers gives her. She has taken control. No longer the pawn.

"What I need from you," Clare continues, "is the ground-work. The stuff I don't have access to. The records, the facial matching. Any more digging you can do on Grayson Morris. I need you to call that officer you sent and tell him to leave Charlotte to me. I'll talk to her."

"I can't do that," Germain says. "You're not on this case in any official capacity."

"So what? What good have your *official* officers done here, Germain? Just give me a few hours. Charlotte trusts me. I think she does, at least. There's a chance I'll get somewhere with her. Can you honestly say the same?"

Somers wears only the slightest smile, and when Clare looks her way, she lifts her eyebrows at her as if to say, keep going.

"Can we agree?" Clare says. "You use whatever resources this beautiful building affords you to track things down, and I'll deal with Charlotte? You have my word that I'll report back whatever I find."

At this Clare stands. She makes her way to the door and exits the office before Somers can even rise from her own chair.

The front door is unlocked, Charlotte's message said. I'm outside on the back deck.

In the late afternoon light, Austin's house is even more striking, the ocean like a painting out the long run of windows. Clare steps inside. She can see Charlotte on the deck, curled under a blanket on the same lounger that Kavita had been on last night.

Even from inside the house, Clare can hear the ocean. She knocks on the glass door to alert Charlotte of her presence before sliding it open. The ocean is kicked up today, angry waves bending and crashing into tall rocks. Clare drags the other lounger to within arm's length of Charlotte. The circles under Charlotte's eyes are a deep purple. She is otherwise pale, dressed in track pants and a sweater, pilled and moth-eaten.

"You're making your way around," Charlotte says. "So I hear, anyway."

"Where are Kavita and Austin?"

"Asleep. They're night owls."

"Are you all right?"

"You're not here to check up on my well-being, Clare. Can we cut to the chase?"

"Okay," Clare says. "If I ask you something directly, will you tell me the truth?"

Charlotte shrugs. "That depends."

"You filmed it," Clare says. "When your father was shot at Roland's, you were filming."

"That's not a question."

"I have the video. It arrived in my in-box when I was here last night, actually. From an encrypted email address. Did you send it to me?"

On the lounge chair Charlotte pulls her knees to her chest, her stare fixed on the ocean, silent. Her eyes are glassy with tears.

"Charlotte," Clare says. "I don't know what you've done. I think you probably got caught up in something, and I'd like to help you figure this out. You filmed your father's death, but the video never saw the light of day, and there must be a good reason for that, right?" Clare reaches into her pocket and hands Charlotte the photograph of Grayson Morris. "I think he might have something to do with it."

For a long time Charlotte holds the photo aloft and studies it. She pulls it in up close and then extends it away, squinting at it from different vantages. Finally she sets the photograph down on her lap and returns her gaze to the sea. Clare snatches the picture when it flutters in a breeze and nearly lifts away.

"Grayson Morris," Clare says. "He shot your father. My theory is that he was hired to do so. You were in a relationship with him."

Charlotte will not look at Clare.

"Like I said," Clare continues. "My guess is that you didn't hire him to kill your father. But somehow, you got caught up in it all, right? The cops just want to arrest the guy who pulled the trigger, Charlotte. As long as they can throw the killer behind bars. But now they know you were filming. Germain has the video. You're going to face an inquisition. Maybe it's time to tell the truth."

Finally Charlotte shifts so she is facing Clare. "Do you know why I sit out here?" She laughs and runs a fingertip under her lashes to wipe away the forming tears. "It's not for the view. I swear Austin has this place bugged. Pinhole cameras, recorders. He just seems like that kind of guy. Kavita thinks I'm paranoid, but I'm convinced he's spying on me."

"You don't need to be here," Clare says. "You could find somewhere else to stay."

"Where else can I go?" Charlotte asks. "I was evicted at the end of last month. I had the shittiest apartment in all of Lune Bay but they still managed to evict me. Fucking Charlotte Westman, daughter of the King of Lune Bay, and I can't cobble together cheap rent."

"You could leave Lune Bay altogether," Clare offers. "Start over."

"Right. You're all about that, aren't you? Get up and run away as soon as things in your life go awry?"

The sting of her words takes Clare aback. What has Austin told her? Indeed Clare can no longer assume her past is her own secret. She feels rage at that prospect. Clare thinks of Somers hours ago at the coroner's office, the tricks she'd used to steer the conversation, to right the course when the coroner tried to veer them offtrack.

Don't let them take the wheel, Somers said. *Always retain control.*

"You have a choice," Clare says. "I'm sure every media forensics team within five hundred miles is dissecting the video as we speak. I've seen your father's autopsy report. Germain was going to have you picked up for questioning, but I was able to call him off. I bought us a few hours. So here's what I'm going to suggest to you, Charlotte. You tell me everything. And we sort it out together, and figure out what version you're going to give to the police. At this point you owe them the truth, but even the truth is subjective, right? I can protect you."

Charlotte scoffs. "Protect me? You're not a cop."

"No," Clare says. "Lucky you too. Because if I were a cop, I'd have no choice but to arrest you for obstruction of justice. That's what they'll do, Charlotte. You filmed that video, then buried it."

From under the blanket Charlotte withdraws a pack of cigarettes and a lighter. She curls into herself to shield the cigarette from the wind as she lights it. The first waft of smoke hits Clare. That smell, so sharp and particular, forever a reminder of Jason, the way he too would lift his chin to blow the smoke upward even when a breeze promised to carry it Clare's way. Clare feels an anxious flutter in her chest. Just like that, Jason appears in her mind's eye. Like he's here, like he's in the air.

Breathe, Clare tells herself. Breathe.

"Your dad was dying," Clare says. "According to the autopsy record, he had advanced cancer. Weeks to live, maybe. And when I watched the video, I noticed one thing. Well, I noticed a lot of things, but one in particular. There's this moment right before the shooter comes in. The camera pans to your father.

He's looking at the door. Waiting for someone to come in. Like he knew. Like he was expecting your boyfriend Grayson to show up."

"You don't know what you saw," Charlotte says. "Because it wasn't that."

"Did *you* know what was coming?"

"No," Charlotte says.

"But you knew it was Grayson when you saw him."

"No."

"What bullshit," Clare says. "Come on, Charlotte."

It's always a dead giveaway, the way a person's shoulders drop the moment they are caught in a lie. Clare remembers that feeling too well from her own life, lying to Grace or her brother, Christopher, about whether she'd been using, lying to Jason about why she was a little late arriving home from work. Lying to avoid conflict or accusations, to keep herself safe. She sees that same tension in Charlotte now, the way she exhales the last of her cigarette with a protracted sigh, debating what to say next.

"I'm not repeating this story to Germain," Charlotte says. "Do you understand? It'll be your word against mine."

"Okay."

"You'd better not be recording me."

Clare stands and lifts her shirt to confirm the absence of a wire. Then she collects her phone from her pocket and powers it off, setting it on the table between them.

"My dad did have cancer," Charlotte begins. "He figured he did, so he had me drive him to a clinic fifty miles away. Paid for all the tests and reports in cash to keep it off his medical records."

"How long was this before he died?" Clare asks.

"Two weeks? I don't know. It's all jumbled up."

"Okay," Clare says. "How did he react to the diagnosis?"

"He was stone cold." Charlotte chokes on a cry. "On the drive back to Lune Bay, he told me he'd known for months that something was wrong. He couldn't piss properly, he was losing weight, his stomach hurt, you name it. 'I'm not dying of cancer,' he told me in the car. He turned on me. 'I can't die,' he said. 'You and your sister will drive everything I've ever built into the ground.' I didn't understand why he was lumping me in. Zoe? Sure. She was working with him by then and it was obvious that she was pretty reckless. Taking risky ventures. Branching out in unsavory ways. I was just trying to keep my shit together. I had a custody battle to fight. I was trying to play the good mother and stop myself from popping pills. And then one day my dad is in the passenger seat of my car, riddled with cancer and accusing me of wanting to prey on his death."

The sob finally escapes Charlotte. Clare touches her arm and waits for her to gather herself and continue.

"There was an insurance policy," she says. "Right after he was diagnosed, he put it in my name. He wanted me to use it for Shelley. My daughter. That was the deal. Zoe would get the company, or what was left of it, and I'd get the insurance policy. He made me promise to keep the cancer thing to myself. I wasn't allowed to tell my mother. Zoe didn't know. At least, I think she didn't."

"But you never did get an insurance payout?"

"That's the crazy part." Charlotte's laugh is shrill. "If he'd just died of cancer, I would have gotten the money. Over three million dollars. But when the cause of death is a bullet to the head, claim investigators don't let go of the cash so easily. Especially when the beneficiary has been changed only a few weeks earlier. And then the murder goes unsolved. So I get nothing. All his assets are frozen and eventually seized. His business partner goes to prison. Zoe takes whatever's left and runs it right into the ground, just like he predicted she would. Some part of me wonders if my dad did it all on purpose. To screw with us. He always said we didn't know how to fend for ourselves."

"That's a hard thing to hear from your father," Clare says.

"He was a bad man," Charlotte says. "He said to me, 'There's not a fucking chance I'm dying of cancer.' You know what he meant by that? That he wasn't going to wither away in some hospital bed. He wanted his death on the front page of the newspaper. Can you imagine?"

Clare thinks of the video, of Jack Westman's anticipatory gaze turned to the door. Charlotte leans to pick her phone from the deck floor next to her lounger. She unlocks it and scans the photographs for a long stretch, back through months and years, until finally she slows the scroll and zeroes in on one portrait. She hands the phone to Clare. The picture depicts three people with the ocean behind them, Charlotte at the center, her daughter, Shelley, next to her, pressed into her hip, the little girl's hair whipped up by the breeze. A man stands on the other side with his arm around Charlotte. It is easy enough to identify him even though he doesn't wear glasses: Grayson Morris.

"He grew up with Malcolm," Charlotte says.

"In Newport," Clare adds.

"Yeah. I don't think they were best friends, but they knew each other. Grayson knew who Malcolm was."

A pit of dread forms in Clare's stomach. She can feel herself wanting to lead Charlotte, to suggest other possibilities that point away from Malcolm. Charlotte takes the last drag of her cigarette, then mashes out the butt on the wooden arm of the lounger. She can tell by Charlotte's expression that the dam is cracking, that she can no longer keep these secrets to herself.

"Grayson came to Lune Bay looking for a fresh start," Charlotte says. "Maybe to take advantage of his connection to Malcolm. We're all guilty of that, right? Mining our connections. Grayson and I met at The Cabin. What can I say? We hit it off. He was attentive. We agreed to keep things under wraps. Just between the two of us until I could settle my custody case. Shelley knew him as my friend. She loved him. But Malcolm wasn't stupid. He caught on. He hated that I was dating him. He said that I couldn't possibly know the true Grayson. That he was bad news. Malcolm would come over and pace around my house, opening cupboards and drawers, looking for shit, drugs or whatever. He'd say that there was no way Grayson actually loved me, that he was only using me, that he just wanted a piece of the family name. That I was a fool to believe there was anything good or real in the relationship. Jesus, Malcolm. He could be so fucking cruel."

"I don't know that he's cruel," Clare says. She sees the look Charlotte gives her. Clare must redirect. "The other day you called Malcolm a murderer, Charlotte. Do you remember that?"

Charlotte nods.

"But you don't think he killed Zoe. So—"

"I think he killed my father."

"I don't understand," Clare says.

"My father told Malcolm. About the cancer. The one guy he thought he could trust. And a week later, Grayson walked into a restaurant and shot my father in the head." Charlotte releases a sob. "It's almost like Malcolm killed two birds with one stone, right? My father gets his blaze of glory ending, and Grayson is out of the picture."

No, Clare thinks. What kind of person would plan their own murder in lieu of a natural death? Clare must bite her tongue to stop herself from challenging Charlotte's account, an account where Malcolm is the killer.

"Did you send me the video?" Clare asks again.

"No," Charlotte says. "I don't have the video. I never did."

"What do you mean you never did?" Clare asks. "You were the one who filmed it."

"Remember the other night at The Cabin? When I asked you if you ever felt like someone else was telling your story for you?"

"I do. You told me that Zoe was the one to tell yours."

"Yeah." Charlotte lifts a hand to her mouth, her shoulders heaving. "On our way to the police detachment, right after we'd watched our father take a bullet to his skull, Zoe took my phone. 'We're deleting the video,' she said to me. 'It never existed.' It was Grayson, for fuck sake. He walked into a bar and shot my father right in front of my eyes. So yeah, I let her delete it. I thought she was protecting Malcolm. Maybe she knew his plan."

Clare feels sickened by her own skepticism, how hard her brain is working to keep Malcolm in the clear.

"Did you ever ask Malcolm outright?"

Charlotte laughs. "Once, I did. After the fact. He played dumb. Of course he did."

"But you think Zoe knew?"

"I let Zoe do all the talking in the police interview. I just sat there like a little coward, because I didn't know what else to do. But fuck, of course she sent a copy of the video to herself before she deleted it. Of course she did. That's Zoe for you. Always thinking ahead. She has to control everything. She needed it to use against me, or maybe against Malcolm. She gets whatever she wants." Charlotte looks directly at Clare, her eyes wild. "And she'll kill anyone who stands in her way."

This open-air fish shack is on the water at the outskirts of Lune Bay. The only patrons are two men nursing beers at opposite ends of the tiki bar. Malcolm sits alone on the patio, the dark ocean behind him, the moon propped high in the sky. When he sees Clare, he stands and tips back the baseball cap he wears, as if she wouldn't have recognized him if he hadn't.

Clare knows that her fatal flaw is her recklessness. To not feel trepidation where others might. *Maybe you're exactly where he wants you*, Somers warned her. Perhaps she should not have come, but Clare knows that was never an option. All she wants now are answers, resolutions. Endings. In the hours since Malcolm summoned her to the beach, Clare has stumbled her way through a bewildering mix of anger, longing, conviction. She stops short at the patio's edge.

"Sit," Malcolm says, nudging the chair across from him away from the table with his foot.

"You're not exactly incognito," Clare says.

"It doesn't matter anymore," he says. "Like you said earlier, Clare. This needs to end."

"Is that whiskey?" she asks.

"It is."

"I'll have one too, then."

Malcolm gives her a look.

"I can handle it," she says.

Malcolm gestures a peace sign to the bartender—make it two more. They watch in silence as the bartender pours. Malcolm stands to collect the tumblers from the end of the bar and sets one in front of Clare. Her lips tingle as she tips the glass. She focuses on the scar that runs the length of his arm. The scar she's studied so many times but has never touched. She points to it.

"You never told me how you got that scar."

"Charlotte," he says. "We were in her kitchen. It was a while after Jack Westman died. She was angry with me. She reacted in a heated moment. Life was hard for Charlotte after her father died. It was an accident. She didn't mean to nick me."

"That doesn't look like an accident," Clare says. "Or a nick. What happened?"

"It's hard to remember. She was angry about everything back then."

He is skirting the truth. Malcolm takes off the baseball cap and runs a hand through his hair to shake it out. Despite herself, Clare feels a clench deep in her gut. She shifts to face the ocean. Clouds are moving in overhead.

"You look good," Malcolm says. "Really good."

"Don't say that."

"I mean it. You look healthy. You didn't give me the chance to tell you that earlier."

"Because you ambushed me."

Malcolm will not take the bait. "Speaking of scars," he says. "How's your wound?"

Clare tugs at the neck of her T-shirt and bares the skin of her shoulder. She adjusts her bra strap to give Malcolm a clear view. The circle that marks where the bullet pierced her is still pink and smooth but no longer painful to the touch. Not a wound but a scar. Malcolm frowns.

"This is rather anticlimactic," Clare says, her whiskey already finished.

"What is?"

"Well, I feel kind of ripped off. Like I was robbed of the gotcha moment. Because I've been looking for you, you're the person I'm supposed to be searching for. Then you just show up? Walk into a bar like some kind of punch line."

"You gave me no choice," Malcolm says. "I warned you to stop, Clare. And you didn't."

"You could have just warned me and been done with it. Coming here puts you at risk too."

"Maybe," Malcolm says. "Maybe it came down to seeing you again, or not seeing you again. Which one could I live with?"

It bothers Clare, the way her heart thuds in her chest, the way the whiskey takes hold. Now that he's in front of her, Clare is keenly aware of how hard she's been trying to conjure him in his absence. Trying to remember what a room felt like when Malcolm was in it.

"There's a video of Jack Westman's shooting, you know. Charlotte Westman was filming when her father was shot. The video never saw the light of day, or at least the cops never saw it." Clare snaps her fingers. "But then, boom! It gets emailed to *me*. Do you know anything about that?"

Clare detects some shift in his expression. A flicker of disbelief.

"Do you know who sent it?" Clare asks again.

Nothing.

Clare unfolds the photograph of Grayson and lays it out for Malcolm. She watches him study it just as Charlotte had done, his expression sad, resigned.

"The shooter was your friend," Clare says. "That's quite the plot twist."

"I knew nothing about it."

"Then who the hell did?" Clare lifts the empty tumbler and drops it with a clank on the glass tabletop. "Somers and I went to the coroner today and read Jack Westman's autopsy report. The guy was chock-full of cancer when he died. But I have a feeling you knew that. Did he hire you to plot his own death?"

"Oh my God." Malcolm throws his head back in exasperation. "Do you actually believe that could be true? Do you think that little of me, Clare? That I would help plot my father-in-law's murder?"

Malcolm falls silent when the bartender approaches. He sets down their drinks and hovers a moment too long, gauging the tension. After he walks away, Malcolm edges his chair as close to Clare's as he can. He leans until their foreheads nearly touch and drops his voice to a whisper.

"Listen to me, Clare. I will tell you anything you want to know. I swear to you, I'm here to help you, not to hurt you. I did not kill Jack Westman or plot to have him killed. I never hurt Zoe. Ever. If anything, I let her get away with far too much for too long. I've screwed up a lot of things in my life, but these things—they are not on me. I'm not the bad guy. Do you understand that?"

Clare says nothing. *I'm not the bad guy.* Somers has uttered much the same to Clare, Donovan Hughes too. How easy it is to deny culpability when the truth remains shrouded. And Somers and Malcolm are the two people Clare wants so badly to believe, to trust, the ones she wants desperately to have the right instincts about.

"I deserve the whole truth," she says.

"I know you do," Malcolm says.

"So tell me, then. What happened here? What happened to Jack Westman?"

"It should have been open-and-shut," Malcolm says. "As far as I knew at the time, he was murdered in cold blood while celebrating his wife's birthday. I wasn't there because Shelley, Charlotte's daughter, she was sick and I offered to stay back with her so Charlotte could go to dinner. I got a call around ten from Charlotte, frantic. They were on their way to the police detachment. She told me her father had just been shot in the head in the middle of a crowded restaurant. The shooter made a clean getaway."

"And you knew nothing about it?"

Malcolm raises a hand. "I swear I didn't."

"And Charlotte didn't say anything about who shot her father?"

"The only version I had for the longest time was the one she and Zoe gave me. And their stories jived. A man walked in while they were eating dessert, fired three bullets at Jack, and ran. There was chaos after that. Both said they couldn't identify the shooter. Their stories jived with everyone else's too. Grayson vanished from Lune Bay around the same time, but that was par for the course with him."

"It never occurred to you that there was a connection?" Clare asks.

"No," says Malcolm squarely. "I wish it had, but it didn't. I knew Grayson was good for nothing. But I didn't peg him as a cold-blooded killer. Then, Charlotte started to . . . unhinge. She accused me of plotting her father's death, of trying to get Grayson out of her life. She told me about her dad's cancer, how he wanted to die on his own terms. I had no idea what she was talking about." Malcolm gestures to the scar on his arm. "She was out of her mind when she did this to me. That's when she accused me of hiring Grayson to shoot her father. It was only then that it clicked. That I understood. Grayson was the shooter and Charlotte knew all along."

"But Zoe hired him."

"I believe she did. Yes."

"To kill her father," Clare says, incredulous.

"You don't know Zoe, Clare. What she's capable of."

"But you should have known, Malcolm. You were married to her."

Malcolm sips at his whiskey, watching Clare overtop his glass. He's considering what to say next.

"When Zoe and I moved back to Lune Bay, Jack took me under his wing. You know, the son he never had. And I was susceptible to it. I had no family of my own, and he was gifted at making you feel like you were at the center of the universe. I knew his business dealings were shady. That he was lining pockets down at city hall. My cop friend, Colin Rourke, was wrapped up in it too. Donovan Hughes, Jack's business partner, was handling the dirty money. More than a few cops were in on it. Zoe loved that I was involved."

"Involved?" Clare asks.

"Involved, yes. I don't know what to else to call it. Zoe and

I traveled the world when we first got married. I made connections. Once we were back here, I was able to bring in some foreign money, some investors. Lune Bay was this shining real estate star. You can't lose with oceanfront, Jack would always say. And he was gifted at turning a dime. But lots of the deals seemed to happen behind the scenes. I'd hear promises in restaurant meetings that never showed up on official documents. Roland Song was right in there. Jack paid off some of his business debts, helped the restaurant weather some slow times. And in exchange, Roland offered him a place to do his dirty work right out in the open. I literally watched envelopes of cash get passed around. I asked questions, but honestly? I didn't push very hard. And that was my mistake—looking the other way because I liked Jack's attention. He could be fatherly when he needed something from you. But I never knew the extent of his criminal dealings. He kept the worst of it from me. He saved that for Zoe."

"The worst of it. You mean the women. There were young women involved in these 'behind the scenes' deals, Malcolm. Kendall Bentley, Stacey Norton."

Malcolm nods "See? You've put the pieces together. Jesus. I knew you would."

"You knew about them?" Clare's voice shakes with rage.

"No. Not until long after," Malcolm says. "I knew bribes were happening. Fraud. But I didn't know about the women. The trafficking. After Jack died, Zoe really started amping it up. She wanted an empire. That's the word she'd use. I could see the young women around, some way too young. They worked at Roland's, or at The Cabin. And I see now that I was turning a blind eye. I regret that. A few years after Jack's murder, a man showed up on my doorstep clutching a photo of his daughter."

"Kendall Bentley's father," Clare says. "He told me that he went to you."

"Yeah. And I played dumb with him because I didn't know how else to handle it. But my ignorance ended then. I knew what Zoe was doing. Who she was hurting in the process. She was finding young, vulnerable women and taking them under her wing, then selling them to the highest bidder, using them to close business deals, rewarding cops or lawyers or coroners who looked the other way. Kendall disappeared. Others had too. I couldn't believe what was happening. My wife, for God sake. I even brought it up with Colin Rourke, and he said he'd look into it. But turns out, he was in on it. A lot of cops were in on it. By then, Zoe was mostly living at her parents' house. We barely spoke or saw each other. But after Kendall's father came to me, that was it. I couldn't abide by it anymore. I confronted Zoe. I told her I was going to blow her whole sick business wide open."

"Then what?" Clare asks.

Malcolm scratches at his head and drains the last of his whiskey, waving to the bar for yet another one.

"She told me that she'd never loved me. That I'd been a fallback plan. You know, because of my family money. She could feign love, but I don't think she ever really felt it. And in that moment, I saw the worst of her. She said she should have handled me a long time ago. That was the word she used. *Handled*."

"A threat?" Clare asks.

"Very much so. A final warning. She told me there was a video of the shooting. She said that she knew I'd hired Grayson to kill her father. That she'd take the video to the police. That Charlotte would corroborate. And I understood then exactly how far she'd gone."

"That she had her father killed."

"Of course she did." Malcolm laughs, shrill, eyes to the sky. "I was fucking blind. Numb. Ashamed that I'd married her, to be honest. Jack told her about the cancer. And Zoe, ever the good daughter, gave him what he wanted: a quick death. They were both just insane enough to orchestrate such a thing. It suited Zoe to have him gone. It installed her as the head of the business. She actually instructed Charlotte to film him while his wife was blowing out her candles. She told her own sister, who knew nothing about it, to film their father's death. Then Grayson came in and shot him. And then Zoe? She took the video and tucked it away. To frame me, if necessary. She knew Charlotte was fragile. She was fueling her own sister's drug habit."

"Why?"

Malcolm shrugs. "To keep her pliant. To keep her out of the business. It's the perfect crime, if you think about it. Zoe's father was gone. She was the kingpin. She had us all exactly where she wanted us. I'm telling you, Clare. Zoe is a deadly combination. She's evil, a soulless kind of evil, and she's brilliant too."

A misting rain has started to fall, but neither of them make a move to head inside.

"What about Colleen Westman? She must have known something."

"She was the good wife," Malcolm answers. "Whatever she knew of the family business, she'd rather die than turn on her own family. I supposed it killed her in the end."

Clare drains her second drink. She feels overheated, her tongue singed by the sharpness of the whiskey. Malcolm has fallen silent, but he watches Clare. What's his expression meant to convey? Sadness? Anger? Regret? There is no way to be sure that Malcolm is telling her the truth. It comes down to simply making the choice. To believe him, or not. To trust him, or not. Trust is a gamble.

"Even if everything you say is true," Clare says, "do you see how messed up this is, Malcolm? You participated in this. You are not absolved."

"I know I'm not," he says, rubbing hard at his forehead. "That's what haunts me, Clare. That's why I left. Zoe was trying to frame me for her disappearance, but it wasn't just that. I didn't just leave because of that. I needed to find out what happened to these women. Once I was gone, once I started digging, I really understood the magnitude of what Zoe had been doing. She was trafficking young women in networks that stretched far beyond Lune Bay. And if these young women wanted out, their only option was to disappear. They knew they couldn't stay here. They were under threat. If they wanted to live, they had to run—"

Clare has heard enough. She feels anxious, unsteady, chilled from the mist.

"Why did you let Jason hire you?" Clare asks, her voice low.

"I needed a front to be able to ask questions," he says. "I needed to set myself up as a pseudo investigator. I put up a website. And honestly? I wanted to take on a few legitimate cases. The work was absorbing. Then Jason called me."

"And he hired you. And you found me."

"Yes," Malcolm says, his face sad. "I did."

"And then you hired me for no reason I can discern except that I looked like your wife. The wife you claim is evil."

"Clare—"

"You said that Zoe knows about me, that she'll come after me. How do you know that?"

"She emailed me a photo of you, Clare. Not one from the

paper. It was a photograph I'd never seen before. Like she knew exactly who you were. Where you are."

"When was this?"

Malcolm withdraws his phone from his pocket and unlocks it. He scans his email and hands his phone to Clare. The photograph is a portrait of Clare from the shoulders up taken last summer, her hair down, her face rounded by pregnancy. She is not smiling. The sight of it wraps Clare in a wave of nausea.

"Malcolm. Jason took this photo. How would Zoe have it?"

"I tried to warn you, Clare. You didn't listen to me. But it doesn't matter. All that matters is that Zoe knows you're onto her. That's what's driving her. She knows you're onto her. That, and . . ."

"And what?" Clare snaps.

"She knows that I fucking fell in love with you, Clare. Jesus Christ!"

Clare freezes. The anger in his tone breaks something inside her.

"Clare," he says, a whisper. "I'm sorry."

"No. Stop talking. Just stop."

Malcolm sets his hand down atop hers. Clare withdraws, as if he's burned her. She jumps to her feet. The bartender gapes at Clare as she weaves through the patio tables and climbs over the rope to the beach. She walks fifty paces on an angle to the water's edge, the bar out of sight. She wants room to breathe. She wants Malcolm gone. But what Clare wants too, she knows, is for him to follow her.

This beach is empty, dark, the froth of the waves lit only by the clouded moon. Clare removes her gun from the back of her jeans and grips it squarely. Malcolm's figure appears and approaches her. Clare stands still. Malcolm closes in, taking shape, stopping only when he is right upon her.

"Clare," he says. "Please."

Clare pushes the gun barrel right into the muscle overtop his heart.

"Why should I believe anything you say?" she asks.

"Clare."

She presses the gun harder into his ribs. He doesn't back away.

"It always been about you, Clare," Malcolm says. "That's all I need you to know. I should never have left your side. I should have told you everything from the start. I should have stayed with you and faced things down. If you want this to end, Clare, you need to trust me. I'm not lying to you. I'm not."

Clare feels pushed, pulled. Finally, she lowers the gun and backs up. Malcolm moves forward in lockstep.

"I'll do whatever you tell me to do," he says.

Clare shakes her head. She looks down at his outstretched hand. When she places hers into it, Malcolm tugs her in until he can wrap his arms fully around her. He kisses her forehead. *I'm sorry.* With her ear to his shoulder, Clare can't be sure that he's spoken the words aloud. She untucks his shirt and lifts her hand to touch the bare skin of his back.

When she looks up, Malcolm kisses her. She responds by pressing herself against him, teetering, their feet sinking in the sand. Malcolm edges her legs open with his knee, his hands to her face, and he kisses her so deeply that Clare must turn away briefly to catch a breath. Her body is right up against his now. She feels a heat rise through her.

SATURDAY

The blanket is tangled in their legs. Clare lies on her back, Malcolm propped on one elbow next to her. The lamp next to the bed offers enough light that Clare can see the texture of Malcolm's face, the lines that cross his forehead, the stubble of his beard.

"I've never looked at you this closely," she says.

"I'm not sure that's a compliment," he says.

They haven't slept. The sliver of light that cuts through the closed curtains tells Clare it's morning. Malcolm's motel room was only a block from the fish shack. Clare allowed him to lead her here, to hold her hand and guide her in the rain to the safety of this room.

They said nothing to each other in that short distance. Then Malcolm fumbled to open the motel room door. He closed it behind them, locked it. Aside from a gym bag in the corner, from the briefcase Clare has seen him carry, there were no signs that Malcolm's been in this room for very long.

Now, this morning, Malcolm places a hand on her back. Clare arches. She takes hold of him and pulls him in against her, kissing him. She cannot make sense of this warmth. Even in the early days with Jason, when they were insatiable, there was always a coldness between them, an air of detachment. This affection from Malcolm feels almost too much to bear. Clare pulls away from the kiss and rests her head on his chest.

"Are you okay?" he asks.

Clare doesn't answer. A car horn blasts out the window. She reaches for the glass of water on the bedside table and sips it. Malcolm props himself against the headboard. Clare brings herself to sit too, wrapped in a bedsheet.

"What is it?" Malcolm says. "Are you okay?"

There's a knock on the door. They both jolt.

Clare reads the fear on Malcolm's face, a mirror of her own. She stands up, collects her clothes from the floor, and scrambles into them. Malcolm plucks his jeans from the chair in the corner and pulls them on. He looks at Clare and touches a finger to his lips. *Quiet.* He retrieves a gun from the drawer of his bedside table, then moves to the door and squints through the peephole. He turns back to Clare.

Charlotte, he mouths.

"Malcolm?" comes her voice on the other side of the door. "Malcolm? It's Charlotte. Let me in."

Malcolm opens the door with the chain still in place. He holds his gun behind him so that Charlotte can't see it.

"Charlotte," he says, his voice soft. "What are you doing here?"

"I followed Clare last night," Charlotte says. "Then I followed you both here. I left, then came back. Can you let me in?"

"Are you alone?"

"Jesus. It's five a.m. I'm alone."

Malcolm twists to look back at Clare. He shakes his head, but Clare nods at him. *Let her in.* Malcolm closes the door and slides the chain unlocked, opening it enough for Charlotte to step into the room. The space feels instantly smaller with Charlotte there. She looks around, taking in the unkempt bed, the too-warm air.

"You said you worked for him," Charlotte says to Clare.

"What are you doing here, Charlotte?" Malcolm asks.

But Charlotte ignores him, still addressing Clare. "I followed you after you left Austin's house last night. I had this feeling. The way you were defending Malcolm. You spoke about him in the present tense. Like he was here."

Suddenly Charlotte is crying, her face buried in her hands. "I haven't seen you in almost two years, Malcolm. You left me here."

"Left you? You accused me of killing your father, Charlotte. I had no choice but to leave."

Charlotte looks at Clare, blank, lost.

"Zoe is here," Malcolm says. "I believe she's in Lune Bay."

"I think she's with my husband," Clare says. "My ex-husband, Jason. I think they're together."

"No," Charlotte says. "No."

At this, Clare and Malcolm exchange a look.

"Malcolm," Charlotte says. "I need to speak to you. There are things I need to tell you. Before this blows up. I need to talk to you privately."

"We can speak here," he says.

Charlotte is shaking. She clasps her hands together to mask it.

"Five minutes without her," she says, gesturing to Clare. "I'm your family. You owe me that much."

Again Malcolm looks at Clare. She nods.

"Okay," he says.

Charlotte steps back out of the room. Malcolm goes to Clare and pulls her in to kiss her forehead. The act feels so intimate that Clare feels herself stiffen against it.

"I'll be right outside," he says.

When he closes the door behind him, Clare returns to the bed. She sits down again, then stands, pacing, her pulse too quick, her brain unable to compute fast enough. She watches the alarm on the bedside table, anxious. Two minutes. Three. Five. There is another knock.

Clare? She hears through the door. It's Charlotte, again.

Clare stands to open the door. But as soon as she twists the door handle, she thinks better of it. No. What are you doing? Get your gun. Check the peephole. But the door is already open. Charlotte. Her expression is blank, ghostly.

"What do you need?" Clare asks.

"I'm sorry," Charlotte says flatly. "I'm sorry."

Beyond Charlotte is a car, its headlights on. A woman is in the driver's seat. A woman: Zoe.

No. Clare tries to slam the door but Charlotte stumbles into the room as if someone has pushed her from behind, knocking Clare off balance. The motel room door slams closed. He is here. Before Clare can scream he's taken hold of her from behind, a hand gripped to her mouth. He has her in a bear hug. Clare presses backwards into his hold and lifts her legs in a flail. His gun goes off. There is a scream. Charlotte is on the floor next to the bed, holding her stomach, a look of terror on her face. Bleeding.

Clare opens her mouth, but only a gasp escapes. She writhes

and jerks against his hold. Then something hits her. She feels it, the crack against her skull, a stab of warmth on the back of her head. Clare falls forward to the bed, crawling on all fours and then collapsing to her stomach. She looks up and tries to focus. No.

And then, nothing. The room blurs and fades to black.

C lare blinks and pats at the back of her head. Warmth. She looks down at her fingertips, red with her own blood.

Strange, she thinks. I feel no pain.

The room takes shape. She sits in a large bathtub empty of water, clothes on. The bathtub is in the center of the room. This bathroom: airy, too big, everything white, an open shower. The window over the vanity looks out to a sharp blue sky. Too bright. Clare shifts her position and cranes to check behind her. The bathroom door is closed.

Yes, Clare thinks. This place. Of course. I know where I am. This is Malcolm and Zoe's house.

The pain comes, her skull throbbing. Clare leans back against the tub and closes her eyes to stave off the dizzy spell. She remembers. She was trying to scramble away. It was a strike to the head.

Voices. Clare cannot decipher how many she can hear outside the bathroom door. She works to pull herself up so she is sitting on the edge of the bathtub. Two voices. A man and a woman. The man's voice is so acutely familiar that it brings a stabbing pain to Clare's chest. Jason. He's here. Of course he's here. And Zoe. They are here together.

Malcolm, Clare thinks. *Where is Malcolm?*

A small laugh escapes her. This is what you get, Clare thinks. After everything that's happened, everything you've done, this is how it ends.

The bathroom door cracks open. Clare stands, still in the bathtub. She must steady herself.

"Clare," he says, pressing through the half-open door. "Clare?"

Jason. In front of her. Clare squeezes her eyes closed and then pops them open to regain her focus. He is smiling too kindly. He holds a gun loose in one hand. Clare sees the streak of blood across its barrel. Her blood. Or Malcolm's?

"Are you hurt?" he asks. "I didn't mean to hurt you."

He looks different. He's grown a beard, put on some weight. Something else too—a deadness in his gaze. Jason steps forward and reaches out to take her by the arm. When Clare recoils, he frowns playfully.

"Don't do that, Clare. You've got nowhere to go. This is finally over. I'm here."

It comes back to Clare now. This morning, dawn. Malcolm. The motel.

Where's Malcolm? Clare wants to ask. But that familiar instinct stops her. She knows the rage Malcolm's name might stir in Jason.

"Where's Charlotte?" she asks instead.

"Oh wow," Jason says, ignoring the question, reaching for her hair. "You're still bleeding."

"Don't touch me," Clare says, a hiss.

"Come on," he says. "This doesn't have to end badly, does it? You can behave."

"Who else is here?" Clare asks. "Who's here with you?"

But she need not ask. She knows. The blood drips from her hair and travels in a stream down her spine. It takes all her effort not to sway. Clare closes her eyes again. She must find a way out.

"You owe me the truth," Jason says. "Don't I deserve the truth?"

The truth? Clare cannot speak. They will not let her out of here alive. She needs to focus. Focus. But she is dizzy. Her thoughts churn too quickly. The truth. He smiles at her. Anger roils in her instead of fear.

"Let me get you something for the bleeding," he says.

When Jason steps out and closes the bathroom door behind him, Clare stands frozen, listening. She hears him say something. To whom? She hears a door open and close. Clare grips the sides of the tub and steps out onto the tiled floor. She opens the door. The sunlight in the master bedroom shocks her, the wall of glass. Clare squints against the light in her eyes. She moves to the bed to sit, gather herself. She needs to think.

The motel room. Dawn. Jason struck her unconscious in the motel room. And then? There'd been a drive, Clare in the backseat with Jason, in and out of consciousness. Zoe was driving. Where was Malcolm? What did they do to Malcolm? Clare stands again and props herself up along the glass window to reach the dressing table. She leans into her reflection. Her hair is matted with blood. Her pupils are dilated. The wooziness is not just from the blow to the head. They must have given her something. Sedated her.

Get a grip, Clare mouths to her own reflection. You find a way out of this, or else you die.

When a surge of energy finally comes, Clare moves to the door and finds it locked. How can it be locked from the outside? She tries the large windows, locked too.

"Fuck," Clare says, fist to the window's glass. A sob rises in her throat. Where is Malcolm?

"Hi," says a voice behind her.

Clare spins. Zoe. She has closed the bedroom door behind her. She points the gun at Clare. The same blood-spattered gun that Jason just held. They may only have one gun between them.

"You can't keep me here," Clare says.

"Sit," Zoe says, pointing to the bed. "You're a little unsteady."

Clare obeys, retaking her spot on the edge of the bed. Zoe plops into the armchair by the door.

"Where did Jason go?"

Zoe waves a dismissive hand. "Oh, God. Who knows? He hasn't been the most reliable partner. But you'd know all about that, wouldn't you? He's not the sharpest tool in the shed either. Kind of disappointing, actually."

Partner? In broad daylight, Clare sees Zoe truly for the first time. Malcolm's wife: Zoe Westman. Her hair has been cut to a bob, curly and dark just like Clare's. For two months this woman has been at the heart of the mystery behind Malcolm. His missing wife. And now she is here, and her smile is cold. The handgun rests in the triangle formed by her legs crossed on the armchair.

"I've been waiting a long time to meet you," Zoe says.

"You can't keep me here," Clare repeats, standing.

"Relax." Zoe lifts the gun and motions to the bed. "And sit the fuck down."

Clare does as she's told. Her brain is scrambled, slow. She knows this feeling too well. She must work against it. Clare faces Zoe dead-on, her posture straight, her hands spread on her legs.

"What do you want?" Clare asks.

"Malcolm likes you," Zoe says.

"No," Clare says. "He hired me. He was looking for you."

Zoe throws her head back in laughter. Her neck is thin, pale, her fingers long and curled around the gun. Clare notices that Zoe still wears a simple wedding band on her left hand. Zoe must catch Clare's gaze, because she lifts her hand and wiggles her ring finger.

"I couldn't bring myself to take it off," she says, pointing to Clare's hand. "Feels like a bit of a shield. I noticed you don't wear yours anymore."

Clare says nothing.

"It's kind of wild, isn't it?" Zoe continues. "We could be twins. We share the same taste in men, clearly. And we're both definitely Malcolm's type."

"Charlotte," Clare says. "Where is she?"

"My sister?" Zoe says. "That's not really your business, is it? You don't know anything about Charlotte. But she's been helpful to me. It's always been easy to get her to do my bidding. I always knew what buttons to press."

"She was hurt. You hurt her."

"*I* didn't do anything. Your trigger-happy husband, on the other hand . . ."

"You. You're the one who sent me the video," Clare says.

"See?" Zoe taps a finger to her temple. "You *are* smart.

But also kind of naive. I figured you'd take it to the police and tell them all about Grayson's friendship with Malcolm. I knew you'd figure it all out. But you *didn't* tell them about Malcolm. You left that part out. You really would do anything to protect him."

"Where is he?" Clare asks finally. "Where is Malcolm?"

"Still here. Of course he is." Zoe twists a finger through her hair. "Jason has this notion of revenge. You know, tie the guy to a chair. Toy with him. You stole my wife, so now I get to have my way with you. Eye for an eye. That kind of thing. I think your Jason's watched too many bad action movies."

Clare is statue still, listening. She knows Zoe could be bluffing. All she can think to do is keep Zoe talking, to engage in a way she knows Zoe will be unable to resist.

"You had your father killed. You wanted to pin that on Malcolm."

"Give me a break." Zoe rolls her eyes. "Dad wanted to die. I was the only one with the guts to get it done for him."

The perfect crime, Malcolm called it last night. Zoe smiles strangely, as though Clare were her studio audience. She's taking pleasure in this.

"What do you want from me?" Clare asks.

"Me? Nothing. Jason's the only reason you're still breathing."

"You can kill me. Kill us. But it will all catch up to you, Zoe. It was already catching up to you."

"That's where you're wrong," Zoe says. "Nothing was catching up. You don't understand anything about money. It keeps you free. The world has opened up to me since my dad died. The real money wasn't in buying and selling stupid plots of land. That part of the business was bullshit. Small coin, especially in Lune Bay. After my dad died, I figured it out: the real power was with us women. I'm sure you know that, Clare. The power that women have over men. The way we can control things. You can build a whole empire on that alone. And I did."

"Young women," Clare says, her voice gruff. "You mean like Kendall Bentley? Stacey Norton? You traffic women. And then a lot of those women disappear."

"I hate that word," Zoe says. "Traffic. It implies force. I never forced anyone to do anything. I incentivized them. Fair and square. And they didn't disappear. They just moved on."

"You lured them in with money, with drugs, and then you used them. I'm guessing you even used your own sister."

"Fuck you, Clare. Like I said, you don't know anything about Charlotte."

"Malcolm was onto you," Clare says. "He figured out what you were doing a long time ago."

Zoe laughs again. "Oh my God. It's actually kind of amazing. You want so badly for him to be the hero."

Clare's head aches. Zoe loves the attention. She can't help herself. Clare has to keep her talking. Buy some time.

"So you did it, then?" Clare prompts. "You built an empire."

"I did," Zoe says. "It was easy to find people to do the work for me once I left Lune Bay. People in other places. Depressed little towns. Lost young women. Angry men. They're everywhere. The work is really about oversight. Just being the wizard behind the curtain. But you? You knew. You were starting to catch on. To figure it all out. You knew. And I can't have that. I would have killed you this morning if it was up to me. But Jason is such a lightweight. He wanted time. He wants the last word with you. I think he's just crazy enough to draw this out."

Clare's head throbs now. She presses her fingers to her temples, dizzy. *You knew.* There is a knock on the door.

"Here he is, right on cue," Zoe says. "Speak of the devil."

Y*ou knew.*
Zoe has left, taking the gun with her. They've switched places. Jason is in the chair now. The bedroom door is ajar. Clare remains frozen in place on the corner of the bed, sitting as motionless as she can, her body buzzing with terror. How many scenes just like this one have played out in Clare's life? Jason's hands are bloodied from the small cuts zigzagged along his knuckles. Jason studies her, his head cocked to one side. He wears a slight and crooked smile. In their marriage Clare endured many variations of Jason's temper, but this is unfamiliar. This rage feels too quiet, too cold. More threatening. Inhuman.

Take the upper hand, Clare thinks. Find a way. Find a way out, or you die. Clare breathes, steeling herself.

"Jason," she says quietly.

"I've missed you, Clare."

"I know you have."

"Everyone thought you were dead. Your dad and your brother. Even Grace. I think they wanted you to be dead, Clare. Maybe I did too."

Clare feels a stab in her chest. He smiles at her.

"You said I owe you the truth, Jason," Clare says. "I'll tell you anything you want to know."

"Do you love him?"

"Malcolm?" Clare asks. "Malcolm is a stranger to me, Jason."

It used to be one of her tricks, repeating his name. *Jason*. Quietly, gently, repeat his name.

"Jason? Just now Zoe said something to me. She said I knew. I don't know what she meant by that."

"Oh, come on. You knew. That's why you left, isn't it?"

It takes all of Clare's might not to lift her hand to her forehead. She cannot let him see that she is dizzy.

"Jason," Clare says. "Were you working for Zoe?"

"I don't like it when she puts it that way," Jason says. "Working *for* her? Fuck that."

Zoe's words swirl in Clare's mind. Depressed towns. The oversight. In the months before Clare left she had been so absorbed by her own plans, by plotting her escape, that she'd kept as much distance from Jason as he'd allow. And the death of their baby had granted her more space than he'd normally give. *You knew.* No, Clare thinks. I didn't.

"How did Zoe find you, Jason? I don't understand."

"You know the way things were at home," Jason says. "Everyone losing their jobs. The place was turning into a shithole. It never felt like enough for me. For us. You know about that, Clare. There was a market for it. Our hometown girls were popular, especially in the city. I was dabbling in it. Helping these girls find their clientele. Then Zoe found me, offered me a template to work from. She made everything so easy. Finding girls, finding clients for the girls. She had it down to a science. My job was just execution."

Clare is nauseated. She cannot look at Jason. She bites her lower lip until the metallic taste of blood fills her mouth. The pain focuses her. She straightens.

"Why did you hire Malcolm?" she asks.

"You left me, Clare. You fucking left me."

His words are monotone, his fists opening and closing. This rage is too quiet.

"Jason," Clare says.

"When I told Zoe you'd taken off, she seemed almost giddy about it. Like your disappearance was some stroke of luck. She gave me Malcolm's name. 'Hire this guy to go after her,' she said."

The room spins. Clare closes her eyes. The pieces falling together. "You were already working for Zoe when you hired Malcolm." This is not a question. Clare understands now. She is certain.

"Yeah. And I was doing pretty well for myself too. Zoe said I couldn't afford to leave town and look for you myself. I had a business to run." Jason laughs bitterly. "Little did I know, she was fucking with me. Malcolm was her ex-husband, for chrissake. She wanted him to find you. She was playing a game with us, Clare. That's Zoe for you. Puppeteering us all."

"Jason," Clare says. "What have you done?"

"We were going to have a baby, Clare. I wanted to take care of you."

A baby. At that word, a shock of wrath surges through Clare. No. This has to end.

She stands. Jason stands too.

"Sit down," he yells.

But his hands are at his sides in fists. He has no weapon.

"Where is Zoe?"

"Sit down!"

And then he lunges. But Clare evades him and he loses his footing as he charges at her. Clare stumbles through the bedroom door and slams it closed behind her. She descends the stairs two at a time. At the bottom she turns a corner into the living room. Malcolm sits in a chair, his wrists tied behind his back. His face is bloodied. He looks up at her, blank, half-conscious. Where is Zoe? Clare rushes to Malcolm and fumbles to untie his wrists. She hears the door open upstairs, footsteps descending.

Zoe appears from the kitchen. She holds the gun two-handed, walking towards Clare. But the gun's safety is on. That gives Clare an instant enough. Clare bolts past Malcolm and lunges at Zoe. They tumble together to the ground, rolling, Clare working to wrest Zoe's grip from the gun. It fires.

No. This is not where I die, Clare thinks. I am not still here, still alive, only to die now.

The gun is in Clare's hands. She scrambles to her feet and backs away, the weapon pointed at Zoe. Malcolm is gasping in the chair, conscious now, his shirt soaked with blood. Hit by the bullet fired in her struggle with Zoe. Jason is in the doorway. Clare swings the gun back and forth from Zoe to Jason as she backs herself into the corner. Jason comes at her. Everything slows, quiets. Clare takes aim and fires.

At impact Jason spins, wide-eyed. He drops to his knees, then forward to all fours. Clare watches as he lowers himself to the floor, to his back, one hand gripped to his chest. A dark circle of blood radiates out from under his shirt.

"Get down," Clare yells to Zoe, the gun aimed at her.

Zoe obeys, crouching to the floor. And then Clare goes to Malcolm. She unties his wrists with one hand, the other hand still pointing the gun at Zoe. She can see that Zoe is saying something, but Clare's ears ring. She hears nothing.

On the floor, Jason's eyes are open but vacant. A drop of blood appears in the corner of his mouth. His breath slows. Jason's blood pools on the floor. He opens his mouth as if to speak, but he can't. He smiles instead.

Jason. Clare doesn't say his name aloud. She lowers to him and puts a hand on his chest. His heartbeat is dull under her fingers. He takes three short breaths before his heart stops.

The corner room in the Lune Bay hospital is warm and bright, the late-day sun casting its beam along the foot of Malcolm's bed. Clare stands unnoticed in the doorway. Malcolm's eyes are closed, his shoulder bandaged, his arm in a sling. He looks peaceful despite his swollen eye, the stitched cut on his lip. Clare feels a flip in her chest at the sight of him. She steps into the room.

"Hi," she says, hesitant.

Malcolm opens his eyes and smiles at her, groggy.

"Hey," he says, opening a hand to her. "Come here."

Clare chooses the chair next to the bed. She sets her hand in his.

"Look." He pats his bandaged shoulder. "My gunshot wound matches yours."

"Funny that," Clare says.

"I guess that makes us even."

"I'm not so sure it does."

"Well, technically *you* pulled the trigger," Malcolm says. "That has to count for something."

"No," Clare says. "I was trying to save us. I had to get the gun from Zoe. You just got caught in the crossfire."

"I got lucky," he says. "I was lucky you were there."

Clare lowers her eyes. It's been nearly eight hours since she called the police to Malcolm and Zoe's house, Jason on the floor in a pool of blood, the life drained out of him. Clare held the gun to Zoe as the sirens drew closer. Malcolm was shot, but alive, breathing, talking to her. Clare has a vague memory of Zoe pleading for her release. *Just let me go.*

"No," Clare said. "This is over."

When the police and paramedics arrived, Clare set the weapon down at their command and allowed herself to be ushered out of the house. She watched from the back of a police cruiser as Malcolm was taken away by ambulance. A while later, Somers arrived and found Clare, and finally the tears came. Clare buried her face into Somers's shoulder and wept until her chest ached.

On their way to the hospital, Somers received word that Charlotte had been found at the motel, alive but barely, a gunshot wound to her abdomen. And now, in this hospital room, Malcolm searches Clare's face with such intensity that Clare can't look at him.

"How's your head?" he asks.

"Fine. Five staples. A mild concussion. I'll recover. I'm guessing you spoke to Germain?"

"I did. He was here a while ago. I told him everything I know. About Zoe, the Westmans. It was a start. There's still a lot of ground to cover."

"They let me interview with Somers." Clare gestures to the

door. "She took my statement. She's in the hall, actually. I think she'd like to meet you."

"I'd like that," Malcolm says.

Clare goes to the hallway to wave Somers in. Somers drops her bag inside the door and circles the foot of the bed, surveying Malcolm's injuries with a frowning nod.

"You took a few knocks," she says.

"Could have been worse," he says. "If Clare hadn't been there."

Somers sits on the edge of the bed. Clare is amazed by her ease, the assured way she sets the tone. Somers and Malcolm exchange a long look, some kind of understanding passing between them that Clare can hardly bear to witness. A bond, she knows, rooted in a mutual concern for her. Everything is different now. They are safe.

"What happens now?" Malcolm asks.

"Well, we unravel it," Somers says. "All of it. Lots of rot to dig out here in Lune Bay. Lots of criminal tentacles that seem to stretch far and wide. Looks like we'll have to open up Donovan Hughes's case again too. So much for his chances of an appeal. That Austin guy, the journalist? He's already downstairs in the waiting room with his goddamn notepad." Somers shakes her head. "Kavita Spence is willing to talk. I can see pretty clearly that my efforts on the Stacey Norton case were thwarted by some pretty crafty cover-ups here in Lune Bay. People in high places were only too happy to bury all leads for the right price. The fact that I didn't smell the rot earlier on is something I'll have to live with."

"I can relate to that," Malcolm says. "A lot of people were in on it."

"Seems so," Somers replies. "It looks like you were the only person actually looking for these young women."

"And Douglas Bentley," Clare says. "He's been searching for his daughter for a long time."

"He deserves the truth," Malcolm says.

The truth. In the year Malcolm spent looking for missing women, he'd discovered that Stacey Norton vanished without a trace, Malcolm's only leads pointed to her death. He never found Kendall Bentley either. He only found her boyfriend in a rooming house a thousand miles from Lune Bay, ravaged by addiction and refusing to tell him anything about what happened to Kendall.

"I wish I had a better answer for him," Malcolm says. "What about Clare? She won't face any charges, will she?"

"No," Somers says. "The case for self-defence is pretty clear-cut. Zoe isn't going to cooperate, but that's no surprise."

"And Charlotte?" Clare asks.

Somers grimaces. "She just got out of surgery. They did what they could. Hard to say. She lost a lot of blood. Fingers crossed she'll pull through."

Pull through. Again Clare sees it in a flash, Jason's body on the floor, his fists still clenching open and closed as the color faded from his skin. At some point this morning, a uniformed officer interrupted Clare and Somers's interview to tell them that Jason had been officially declared dead. His body was transported to the coroner's office for an autopsy. And when the officer looked at Clare and asked her if she was Jason's next of kin, Somers had scolded him with a livid calm that had him skulking out the door.

"Hey." Somers points upward, as if an idea has just come to her. She returns to her bag by the door and withdraws some papers, handing them to Clare. "I printed this up for you when I stopped in at the detachment this afternoon."

Clare scans the papers. "An application form?"

"To the police academy back home," Somers says. "Program's only ten weeks. They need women."

"You're giving me an application form to be a cop?"

"I need a partner," Somers says. "Would you pass a security clearance?"

"Depends," Clare says.

The three of them laugh.

"Well, then," Somers says. "Partners? Somers and . . . O'Kearney?"

"I'm going back to my maiden name. Driscoll."

"Seriously? Somers and Driscoll? That has TV written all over it."

Clare's laughter shifts. She suddenly chokes back tears. "I don't think I'm cut out to be a cop. Like you said, Somers. I work better without all the rules."

"Well, then we'll get you a license to work as a private investigator."

Finally, something releases in Clare. She rests her head into folded arms on the bed and cries. Her shoulders heave, the tears flowing until her palms are wet. She feels a hand rest on her arm, but she doesn't look up to see whether it's Malcolm or Somers touching her. What they don't know, what Clare will not tell them now, is that it was one year ago today that she lay in a hospital bed after the stillbirth of her baby. It was on that day, one year ago, that Clare resolved to leave, to run. She's endured so many days and nights since, alone and struggling, and then Malcolm, and this strange work, and today, this morning, Jason dead. Malcolm alive, here.

"You've been through a lot," Somers says.

Clare shakes her head and looks at them.

"You've survived a lot," Malcolm says.

Survived.

"I made stupid choices," Clare says. "I've been reckless. I was always reckless."

"Okay, sure," Somers says. "Some people make stupid choices and nothing happens. And others make the same choices and spend their lives paying for it. It's about luck and chance as much as anything else. It's not just about you. And you have to trust people, Clare. Within reason. Most people are good. Your life story so far might lead you to believe otherwise, but really? Most of us are good."

Silence hangs among them as her tears abate. Clare's head aches, the staples stretched taut. She rubs her eyes into her sleeve and looks at Malcolm, holding his gaze for the first time since landing in his room. Somers detects whatever passes between them and stands.

"Listen," she says. "I'm going to head back downstairs and make sure that Lune Bay's finest are marching in line. Okay?"

"Okay," Clare says.

"You know where to find me."

Somers extends her hand to Malcolm. Then she collects her bag and exits down the hallway. Alone again, Clare withdraws from Malcolm's bed and hugs her knees to her chest on the chair. She can see it in his face, the things he wants to say. But Clare can't bear to hear them right now. He must sense as much, because his expression shifts to a gentle smile.

"You'll be okay," Malcolm says.

"I hope so."

"No. That wasn't a question. You'll be okay. I know you will."

"Thank you," Clare says.

"You know," Malcolm says, "if you take the south door out of here it's only about a two-minute walk to the ocean. You could use some fresh air. Some time."

Time. Clare stands and hovers for a moment.

"Go," Malcolm says. "I'm not going anywhere."

And so Clare does. She follows the hallway to the south end of the hospital, down four flights of stairs and through the exit door to outside. The sky is pink again, this time with dusk. Beyond the hospital parking lot is a pathway. Clare follows it. She can hear the roaring hum of the ocean before she sees it. She passes through a grove of trees until the blue line of the ocean's horizon comes into view.

And as soon as her feet hit the sand, she feels it. The letting go. Her chest opens. She can finally breathe. She walks to the water's edge and removes her shoes. There are things to do, Clare knows. Decisions to make. But for right now, she will stand here by the ocean and let this sensation take hold, this welcome reprieve from what haunts her.

This almost feels like freedom, Clare thinks, her feet planted in the sand. Like a beginning. Like hope.

ACKNOWLEDGMENTS

ONE OF the most remarkable things I've learned in my time as a published author is just how many hands it takes to bring a novel from a writer's desk into readers' hands. I have been so buoyed by the passionate and hardworking people I've met in the publishing, bookselling, and arts industries in Canada and beyond. Our love of books is alive and well thanks to them. I am grateful to have been given the opportunity to meet so many of you as the Still books took flight.

First, to my most incredible editor, Nita Pronovost, whose name could easily appear on the cover of this novel alongside mine. I feel so privileged to work with an editor as skilled and committed as Nita. She always finds a way to yank me out of the depths of writing and editing despair and to push me when I'm lagging. I'm so grateful for you, Nita. Always!

And with Nita comes the outstanding team at Simon & Schuster Canada, including Kevin Hanson, Adria Iwasutiak, Felicia Quon, David Millar, Sarah St. Pierre, Jillian Levick, Mackenzie Croft, Rita Silva, Jessica Scott, and Catherine Whiteside. A big shout out to S&S alums Brendan May, Amy Prentice, Siobhan Doody, and Lauren Morocco for the fun times we had along the way. Thank you as well to the team at Gallery

Books who took on the Still books with gusto, especially Sara Quantara, who has been a pleasure to work with from afar.

To my agent, Samantha Haywood, and her team at Transatlantic Agency—especially Stephanie Sinclair and Rob Firing—for their belief in the Still books and in me. You have all my faith and my deepest gratitude.

To the team at Lark Productions for all their amazing efforts to bring Clare and her story to life, especially Erin Haskett and Samantha Morris Mastai.

As the Still series draws to a close, I want to offer my sincere thanks to those who championed my books and helped launch them into the world, in particular Martha Sharpe of Flying Books, Tara Parsons and Shida Carr of the former Touchstone Books, and Chris Bucci, Martha Webb, and the team at Cooke McDermid.

To my fellow educators and my students at WEA and Contact and beyond, with all my thanks. To the friends in my life who prop me up when the going is tough and who humor my long-winded texts or calls when I've got a brain twist to work out, especially Mariska Gatha, Natasha Hughes, Kendall Anderson, Hollis Hopkins, Doug Stewart, Elisa Schwarz, Jenna King, Tara Samuel, Aviva Armour-Ostroff, Tamara Nedd Roderique, Claire Tacon, Allison Devereaux, Lee Sheppard, Sarah Faber, and Tom Ryan. To generous early readers, especially Sam Bailey and Jennifer Peshko. To our Duff neighbors for keeping us in your fold even when we decamped west. To the luminous and magical Teva Harrison, who made such an indelible impression on me before her death in April 2019. Forming a friendship with you, Teva, was one of the best things to come of this life as a writer.

To the amazing hockey families from the Sharks, the Eagles, and the Titans, whom we spend more time with in the winter months than with anyone else; we're so grateful for the fun you

ACKNOWLEDGMENTS

bring to early morning and late evening jaunts to the rink. In particular to my Eagles benchmates: Riyaz Deshmukh, Caroline Godfrey, Julian Binavince, and Patrick Dunphy. Our epic email threads have kept me sane and laughing even when the writing life was a slog. To my kids' coaches and teachers for stepping in as caring adults in their lives and supporting them as they look to find their place in the world.

To my parents, Dick and Marilyn Flynn; my sisters, Bridget and Katie Flynn; my brothers-in-law, Chris Van Dyke and Mark McQuillan; and my in-laws, Beth and Jamie Boyden; with all my love and thanks. To my extended family in Ontario, Quebec, PEI, Nova Scotia, and beyond: the Flynns, the Keefes, the Carraghers, the Wilsons, the Bradleys, the Manuels, and so many more. A special thank you to my nieces and nephews Jack Boyden, Charlotte Boyden, Stuart Boyden, Luke Boyden, Jed Van Dyke, Margot Van Dyke, Peter McQuillan, Sean McQuillan, and Owen McQuillan. To my aunt Mary Flynn for all her support and love. And in memory of Tim and Sue Stuart, who were forever champions of my writing. We miss you every day.

To Ian, simply put, with all my heart, for everything. To Flynn, Joey, and Leo, with all my love and all my thanks, for your cheerleading and for your patience when I was deep in a writing groove.

To Millie, my canine editor and best dog friend. You've made the writing life a lot less lonely.

Ten years ago, when Clare first formed in my writing mind, I never would have imagined where the next decade would take us. I am so thankful for the readers who've allowed Clare to flourish in your own imaginations, and especially to the booksellers who worked so hard to put my novels in readers' hands. Without you to bring my stories to life, these are just words on a page.

ABOUT THE AUTHOR

AMY STUART is the #1 bestselling author of two novels, *Still Mine* and *Still Water*. Shortlisted for the Arthur Ellis Best First Novel Award and winner of the 2011 Writers' Union of Canada Short Fiction Competition, Amy's writing has previously appeared in newspapers and magazines across Canada. In 2012, Amy completed her MFA in creative writing through the University of British Columbia. She lives in Toronto with her husband and their three sons. Connect with her on her website AmyStuart.ca and on Twitter @AmyFStuart.